PLANNING ON MURDER

David Williams is a Welshman, educated at Hereford Cathedral School and St John's College, Oxford, where he took a history degree. After service as a naval officer, he ran a large London advertising agency before becoming a full-time writer in 1978. *Planning on Murder* is his seventeenth Mark Treasure mystery: two of them have been shortlisted for the Crime Writers' Association Gold Dagger Awards. He lives with his wife at Wentworth in Surrey.

Acclaim for David Williams:

BANKING ON MURDER

'A nice wily Williams whodunit'   *Sunday Times*

'Elegant and literate'   F.E. PARDOE, *Birmingham Post*

'A beguiling, read full of the sly wit and neat observations one can invariably count on from this accomplished writer'
JAMES MELVILLE, *Ham & High*

TREASURE BY POST

'Deft as ever'   *Observer*

'Yet another fine Mark Treasure novel. As always, Williams's characters are top-notch . . . the humour plentiful and unforced, and the crimes marvellously complex'
Million Magazine

DAVID WILLIAMS

Planning on Murder

HarperCollins*Publishers*

HarperCollins*Publishers*
77–85 Fulham Palace Road,
Hammersmith, London W6 8JB

This paperback edition 1994
1 3 5 7 9 8 6 4 2

First published in Great Britain by
HarperCollins*Publishers* 1992

ISBN 0 00 647 882 4

Set in Baskerville

Printed in Great Britain by
HarperCollinsManufacturing Glasgow

This one for
Nicholas Campbell Williams

CHAPTER 1

'Stopping people from using land is like . . . like cutting off a man's hand,' said Lord Delgard gruffly. His visible right eye blinked twice—though it might have been winking. With the left eye concealed beneath a black patch it was difficult ever to be certain. 'Cutting it off at the wrist,' he embellished, in an increasingly crusty tone. On the whole, this seemed to qualify blinks not winks.

'Except this isn't common land, Tug. It's ours,' his wife replied softly. Petite and gentle, she had neither winced at the simile, nor shifted her attention from her tapestry frame. It was quite a large frame, and the design was nearly complete. It showed yellow roses in a cream and pink vase on a deckled mauve background. Artistically it was fairly inert—although perhaps a credit to the weaver's industry.

'Part of our heritage, yes,' the eleventh Viscount agreed, but absently, because he was already thinking of something else.

Since Lord Delgard had been christened Timothy Urquhart Grantly, it followed that he would come to be called Tug, a sobriquet that happened to match his appearance as well as his initials. He was a short, square, thickset figure. His bald, bullet head rested tightly on a hardly discernible neck above a chest that butted forward like an eminently seaworthy prow. He shifted his feet, widening the gap between legs clad in tweed knickerbockers and thick woollen stockings, and tightened the grip of his fists that were clasped behind his belted Norfolk jacket. 'Oliphant should be here by now,' he complained, nodding at the mullioned bay window in front of him as if holding it responsible for Oliphant's non-appearance. 'I need a full report on what he did in London yesterday. And this morning.'

'It's two golf courses and an hotel they'll be building, of course,' said Lady Delgard as if she were disseminating these facts for the first time. It was her way of moving things on from severed hands, a practised way, learned through forty-seven years of marriage to a one-eyed, battle-scarred, ex-regular soldier with a penchant for sanguine allusions.

'Cutting off hands is what the Muslims do to thieves,' offered the Honourable Bea Delgard, the Viscount's spinster sister, who lacked Lady Delgard's sensitivity. She was seventy-seven years of age, and two years junior to her brother. Except for his lordship's total absence of hair the two might have been twins. Bea (short for Beatrice) temporarily abandoned the racing section of *The Times*, scratched one elbow vigorously, and searched the large pockets of her openknit cardigan for her cigarettes. She was only half expecting her brother to respond to her comment.

'You could call what's planned here theft,' he said, brushing his moustache with the end of a straight forefinger. He turned from staring out southward across the windswept open courtyard, and the park beyond, flexed his gammy left leg, and limped across the corner of the room. Then he stared eastward through the window that gave on to the just as windswept upper terrace. It was mid-October and unseasonably bleak, even for East Anglia.

Gunner, Lord Delgard's bulldog, remained seated, slumped in the side-saddle, full frontal manner of his breed, and next to where his master had been standing earlier. His long tongue wiped the whole of his nose for the third time since he had started following Delgard's movements with sad inquisitive eyes.

'Major Oliphant will he here directly,' said Lady Delgard. 'He was asked for four and he's always punctual. Of course the London train could be late. Why don't you sit down, dear?' she suggested from her upright chair.

The three were in the ground floor small parlour in the west wing of Vormer House, a stately edifice—towering, symmetrical, deservedly conspicuous, and justifiably haughty. It was built of honey-coloured Ancaster limestone, and modelled in the shape of a squashed letter H. The house's architect is unknown, but the huge areas of glittering glass to all aspects, the touches of Renaissance detail, the elegant columned chimneys, and the curving Flemish gables testify that the originator was a man of education, taste and fashion, with strong artistic inclinations.

Vormer is opened to the public on two days a week, from April to September, but the west wing, which includes the family's private apartments, is not part of the tour. Lord Delgard regarded it nearly as an obligation to share his ancestral home with the populace at large (in return, of course, for a reasonable price of admission), but he was not moved to do this more often than on Tuesday and Thursday afternoons, and he drew the line at letting the peasantry tramp through his living quarters—particularly his bathroom (something regularly requested), whatever the extra sense of intimacy such an experience might be expected to provide.

The rooms in the off-limits west wing are no less elegant than those in the rest of the house, but on the whole their fitments are more reflective of modern living. For instance, the small parlour contains some handsome furniture and paintings—but also a television receiver and a CD player, items that visitors to an Elizabethan house might in any case find incongruous, or even disillusioning.

'It can't be theft. You're getting money for the land,' Bea insisted, with discomforting frankness. She was seated on the sofa facing the big stone fireplace where burning logs were spitting and crackling. She inhaled deeply on a Capstan Full Strength cigarette, making it do much the same as the logs.

'There'll be crumpets,' said Lady Delgard with apparent inconsequence, but the satisfied air of a benefactress whose bounty knew no end.

'That's beside the point,' her husband said, pausing in

his stride, looking at his wife, but replying to his sister. He was referring to the irrelevancy of money, not crumpets.

These three elderly co-habitants let subjects float like balloons whose buoyancy was perilously maintained by occasional and, sometimes, seemingly inapposite verbal taps.

'I've already said, it's stealing from the local people who use the park,' Delgard continued, and who hadn't said exactly that, but no matter. He settled himself into a winged armchair to one side of the fireplace. Unlike the house, the nine-hundred-acre park was open to the public daily throughout the year, and there was no charge. 'That's the point the MP chap, what's his name again—?'

'Charles Finton, dear.'

'Yes, the point he was making the other night. Said his bush telegraph reports were strong on depriving the locals.'

'Major Oliphant was catching the one-forty from King's Cross,' supplied Lady Delgard, looking up reflectively while rearranging a curl of soft hair over her right ear, a shell-like feature: she had been a great beauty in her day. 'He told me as much yesterday. Or was it the day before? I suppose it must have been the day before. Yes. Today's Tuesday,' she went on, pausing briefly it seemed from the effort of accurate recall. 'There's no buffet on that train. He'll not have had a proper lunch. A sandwich, I expect. The crumpets will be welcome.'

'But they'll be able to play golf instead of whatever else they've been doing in the park.' Bea was responding to her brother.

'Balls,' he said, half under his breath.

'And bowls perhaps?' Lady Delgard's sense of hearing was still particularly acute. 'Ah!' She cocked her head slightly. 'That'll be the Major now. I've told Alice to bring the tea in with him.' Neither of the last intelligences seemed to register with her husband.

'You'll have to join the club to play golf. Or stay in the hotel. Whole thing's thoroughly elitist, of course,' Delgard observed with the confidence of an enlightened aristocrat: even so, he and his elite forebears had enjoyed exclusive privileges in the area since shortly after the Norman Conquest. ''Afternoon, Oliphant,' he went on, eyeing the middle height, slightly stooped and stocky individual who was now marching through the impressive double doorway, arms swinging with unnecessary energy for one who wasn't engaged on a parade ground. 'Brought the tea with you, have you?' Delgard completed, showing that one of his wife's comments had registered at least.

Oliphant stopped dead, glancing rapidly from side to side as if some kind of an attack on his person was imminent. 'I can get it, if you want, General,' he volunteered uncertainly. His left cheek gave a violent and sinister twitch. He had continued to address his employer as General since their army days.

'Come and sit down, Major. Alice is bringing the tea in directly,' said Lady Delgard, moving her tapestry frame to one side.

Small, ample Alice Sting was housekeeper and cook-general at Vormer. She appeared now on cue behind the Major and pushing a large trolley with outsize wheels and laden with tea-things. 'There's enough mushrooms for dinner after all, mi'lady,' she confided, while arranging the trolley in front of Lady Delgard. 'Want me to hand round, do you?' She was wearing a light blue woollen dress with a cotton pinafore over the front.

'No. We'll help ourselves, thank you,' said Lady Delgard, lifting the top from a silver dish. She nodded approvingly at the hot crumpets revealed beneath the cover. Gunner the bulldog did the same from his new position close to the trolley.

'Who did you see after you left Henfold's yesterday, Oliphant? Since we spoke on the phone? Did you see Gradson then?' Delgard demanded before the other man had quite finished greeting the ladies. Henfold Developments was a property company. Gradson was the Delgard's London lawyer.

'No one. There was no time left. Not yesterday, I'm afraid,' Oliphant replied. 'I saw Gradson first thing this morning. Gave him your instructions. He'd heard again from the Tudor Heritage Trust. The Trust is definitely supporting the planning application to the Thatchford District Council.' He rose again from where he had just seated himself, on the sofa next to the Hon. Bea, and moved to fetch tea for both of them. Alice Sting had already left the room.

'I should think they would support us, too,' said Delgard forcefully, also standing to help himself to a buttery crumpet which he started to consume while waiting for his wife to pour his tea. 'Since they're getting the house, the park, the pictures, and everything except our immortal souls. And three million pounds on top of that.' He wiped some butter from his chin and fed a bit of crumpet to the dog. 'I've been having second thoughts, Oliphant, I can tell you. Strong misgivings. Am I really doing the right thing allowing the park to be carved up?'

The Major's square and flattish face took on a solemn expression. His dark, very sunken eyes under bushy eyebrows darted sidelong looks at the two ladies as he tried to gauge the seriousness of Delgard's statement.

Right or wrong, Oliphant had been praying fervently that there would be no turning back now. As manager of an estate that had precious little left in it to be managed, his future depended on his becoming secretary of the golf club planned to occupy three hundred acres of the park. More to the point, it was the only way he was going to raise the money to pay off his debts, which were pressing. At fifty-two his prospects of other sorts of gainful employment were virtually non-existent if his present job ended—as he feared it was bound to do soon, whatever happened. Dan Sting (Alice's husband), the estate foreman under Oliphant, was already well able to manage Vormer park and gardens with a permanent work force of only two, and extra seasonal labour when needed.

Oliphant was really superfluous, and he knew it. It had been different when there had been tenant farms and village houses to supervise. Except for his debts, his own future requirements were quite modest. His wife had left him five years before this. Since then he had lived alone but comfortably enough in one of the remaining estate cottages, an arrangement he hoped could continue if things worked out as planned. He had put out strong feelers about the golf club job to the Henfold executives in charge of the development. They had been encouraging, though there had been no specific promise as there had been about the discreet payment they were making him for encouraging Lord Delgard to accept the plan. The payment was to be made on completion of the deal, but by the sound of it, even that could now be in jeopardy.

'People are free to walk on a golf course if they wish, General,' he said, his cheek twitching uncontrollably. 'So long as they don't interrupt play. And the courses will only take up a third of the park in any case. I'm quite sure more people will use the park for walking and so on than do at the moment. Especially when the hotel is built.'

'Hotel visitors will use it, you mean? Not locals?' asked Bea.

'Both, I should think.'

'What d'you mean by "for walking and so on"?' Delgard inquired sharply as he moved back towards his chair, balancing his teacup and a piece of chocolate cake in the saucer.

'Well, the Tudor Heritage Trust will keep the Easter horse show going. And the gymkhana in the summer.'

'Of course they will. Those things are institutions. But no nonsense like motorbike rallies, or pop music festivals, eh? No tomfoolery of that kind?'

'Certainly not, General. Apart from anything else, the

Trust accepts that events like that wouldn't suit the members of the golf club.'

'Oh wouldn't they?' countered Delgard, fixing the other man with the steeliest of one-eyed stares. 'Well, they wouldn't suit me either, though I suppose we'll be taking a back seat in future.' He sighed noisily. 'And I still wonder if it wouldn't be better to keep the place for my lifetime. Both our lifetimes.' He looked across at his wife. 'Hand it over when we're dead and gone. When we can't be driven mad by other people's behaviour. Insensitive behaviour.'

Oliphant shifted in his seat. 'Henfold and the Trust would both prefer you to make the gift now, as originally intended.'

'Why? Because if we live too long the Trust will want more than three million for an endowment on the house, and Henfold won't want to pay more for the three hundred acres?'

'That's part of it, yes. I mean, not in those precise terms, but—'

'But near enough,' Delgard interrupted.

'It's also because this way there can't be misunderstandings about intentions. Complications over the entail. Not while you're ... you're ...'

'Not while we're still around to sort them out?'

'Also in the matter of the planning permission for the golf club and the hotel, General. From Thatchford Council. Henfold believe it's more likely to be given if you're here to support it.'

'Hmm. Except I'm not sure I want to support it any more.'

'Yes you are, Tug,' put in Lady Delgard indulgently. 'There's really no alternative. Not if you want Vormer to stay as it is.'

'And if everything's left till after your death, there's the risk that Henfold may not be interested in honouring the same plan. Or any plan at all,' Oliphant cautioned.

'Isn't it less complicated too? To do it all now?' asked
Bea. 'Over inheritance tax, I mean.'

'There needn't be any inheritance tax. Not either way,'
said her brother, wiping chocolate icing from his saucer
with an extended forefinger. 'Not if Gradson gets the legal
part right. We'd just have to be sure the endowment money
was guaranteed. If it wasn't, the Trust wouldn't take on
the house.'

'And, of course, we mustn't forget the Trust is arranging
that we can go on living here for as long as we choose. All
three of us,' Lady Delgard added. 'Isn't that so, Major?'

'Well, not all three of you. Not exactly. Not in this house,'
said Oliphant, embarrassed by the question because it
meant confirming something negative. He bent over his
cup, vigorously stirring his tea, like a witch with an under-
sized cauldron.

'But we've settled all that,' said Bea, pulling down the
front of her cardigan. 'We can stay here so long as one of
you two is still kicking. But if I'm the last survivor they'll
move me into a horse-box.'

'Actually, into the Dower House,' Oliphant supplied,
and looking up gratefully under protruding eyebrows. 'The
Dower House will be repaired so that you all have the
option of going there if you choose. That's been confirmed
again by Gradson. It was one of the things he talked to the
Trust about on the telephone while I was with him.'

'I shan't be moving to the Dower House, but you and
Bea might after I'm gone,' said Delgard to his wife, then
after sucking some of the chocolate from his finger he went
on, 'Well, I might, I suppose. If I get tired of the invading
hordes here. Did Gradson get anywhere with the Trust on
that one, Oliphant?'

The other man shook his head. 'He says they still intend
to open the house all day for six days a week, through the
season.'

Delgard absently allowed Gunner to lick the rest of the
chocolate from his hand. 'Well, they'll have to get extra

staff to do that,' he said, while patting the animal's head. Gunner responded with an appreciative belch as his master continued, 'I suppose they'll want to have a tea-room and gift shop too?'

'I gather so, General.'

'And larger lavatories?'

'Probably.'

Lord Delgard stared threateningly at the fire while meta-phorically consigning tea-rooms, gift shops and larger lava-tories to the flames. 'So where do Henfold stand now on the whole shooting match?' he demanded gruffly.

'They're all ready to buy the three hundred acres from you for the sum agreed, General. That's as soon as outline planning permission for the hotel, the golf club, and the courses is approved by the Council.'

'And when's that likely to be, do we know?'

'The proposal goes before the full Planning Committee at the meeting tonight, General.'

A heavy silence followed Oliphant's announcement. It was broken by Lady Delgard, who remarked despondently: 'I wonder if they're really as downright yellow as I've made them?'

'Just about,' Bea observed.

It was as well that Oliphant hesitated to protest at this apparent impugning of the Planning Committee's courage.

Lady Delgard and her sister-in-law were ballooning again—about the roses in the tapestry.

CHAPTER 2

Around four hours later, most people in the audience of London's Olivier Theatre had left their seats for the twenty-minute interval. The Olivier is one of three audi-toria in the Royal National Theatre complex on the South Bank of the Thames.

'So who played the lead in the original production?' Julius Kuril, Chairman of Henfold Developments, asked loudly of his male companion who was standing ahead of him at the crowded bar.

'Mrs Patrick Campbell. They say it's what made her a legend in her own time,' answered Mark Treasure, Chief Executive of Grenwood, Phipps, merchant bankers. He pocketed his change and picked up the two glasses, turning to pass one back to Kuril. 'That was in 1893,' he added, as the two men elbowed themselves away from the crush.

'Well, she couldn't have done it better than Molly's doing tonight,' Kuril insisted firmly.

'You must tell Molly later. Except she'll say you weren't around in 1893, so you can't make a true comparison. My wife is nothing if not objective.'

Molly Forbes, Treasure's celebrated actress wife, was performing the name rôle in the play they were seeing—a revival of *The Second Mrs Tanqueray* by Sir Arthur Pinero.

'Well, I'm so grateful you asked me,' said Kuril. 'It's a marvellous production. Sheila will be disappointed not to be here, but we just don't know how long she'll be away.'

Treasure had invited the other man to the play on the spur of the moment, and to have supper with Molly and himself at the Savoy Grill afterwards. This had been at the end of a meeting at Grenwood, Phipps that morning. The property developer had mentioned that his American wife had been called to New York at short notice to visit her ailing mother, and that this had meant cancelling their previous arrangements for the evening.

Henfold Developments were newish customers of the bank's. Treasure hardly knew Kuril and had been glad of an opportunity to improve on their personal acquaintance. It happened that he had been abroad himself when the play opened the week before, and he was seeing Molly's much acclaimed performance for the first time too.

Both men were tall and lean, and in their early forties, but Treasure was as fair in colouring as Kuril was dark.

Kuril's nearly olive complexion he owed to Russo-Jewish grandparents, émigrés at the turn of the century, while Treasure's family had its roots in the Welsh borders. The two men's educational backgrounds differed too. The banker had graduated from Oxford and later from the Harvard Business School: Kuril had left school in Nottingham at sixteen to work for a local estate agent. It was said that he had made his first million from property by the time he was twenty-one.

'Shall we try the terrace outside?' Treasure suggested. 'Better air than in here. I think it's warm enough still.' He led the way across the concourse. 'Heard any more on the Vormer House business you mentioned this morning?' he asked as he held back the glass door to the terrace. There were very few people in the area outside.

'Yes. I meant to tell you. Lord Delgard's estate manager—'

'With a name like elephant, you said?'

'Oliphant actually. He was in the office most of yesterday afternoon. Lord Delgard is close to agreeing the plan at last.'

'To sell you enough of the Vormer home park for you to build two golf courses and a clubhouse?'

'Incorporating an eighty-room hotel. That's assuming we get planning permission, of course,' but Kuril sounded confident on the last point.

'Well, I'm still surprised,' said Treasure as they moved across to lean on the wide parapet. 'Delgard can't be on the breadline surely? Why, the pictures alone at Vormer—'

'It's not the present that bothers him,' Kuril interrupted. 'It's the long-term future for the house. He's got enough money to see himself out comfortably. But when he and his wife are gone, inheritance tax could wipe out the place. And the noble and gallant Viscount is seventy-nine years old.'

'Yes, I suppose he'd have to be all of that.' Treasure put his whisky glass down on the concrete ledge. 'Wasn't he a colonel at the Battle of El Alamein?'

'Yes. And a brigadier by D-Day. Got a DSO and an MC. Didn't leave the army till he was fifty. They say he could have been one of the really top soldiers if he'd stayed on.' Kuril had offered all this in a tone more amused than impressed.

'But not such a hot shot at running his family estate?' the banker questioned.

'Nor their local industrial interests. He rather fancied himself at that, too.' Kuril sniffed, then pinched the end of his prominent nose. 'D'you know the Delgards owned the lace factory where my father worked? As a clerk? That's until the banks foreclosed on it, which incidentally put my father on the street. I was ten at the time.' The eyebrows lifted reflectively.

'And now you're about to save Lord Delgard's bacon for him?'

'That may be overstating it. And he's been blowing hot and cold up to this point. Which is why I'd not mentioned the project at the bank till today.' He looked about him to be sure they weren't being overheard before continuing. 'Delgard certainly isn't on the breadline, but he's in a tricky situation. He's got no children. No direct heir. Even the indirect ones have been dropping like flies recently. When the old man snuffs it the title goes to a remote Australian relative called Legion. He went on record last year saying he'd let the house fall down before he'd spend money on maintenance. Also said he'd sell the park to developers.'

'That can't have endeared him to Delgard,' said Treasure while staring at Somerset House, floodlit on the opposite side of the Thames. It was a building he never thought did justice to its site. 'Letting Vormer House fall down is easier said than done, of course,' he went on. 'It's Elizabethan isn't it? Protected?'

'To the hilt. Listed Grade 1.'

'What about the home park?'

'Ah, that was redone by Capability Brown in the seventeen-sixties. As a deer park.'

Treasure marked the rising optimism in the tone. 'And I suppose it's not as well protected as the house? In conservation terms. Are you hoping to develop your bit of it for housing as well as golf? I'm not sure I'd approve, mark you. I was there once. It's very beautiful. I don't remember any deer. Only sheep.' He swallowed some whisky.

Kuril did the same, then rested his glass with one hand in the crook of the opposite arm. 'I admit I got interested after the press reports of what Legion said. I had Maggie Halliwell go to see him when she went to Sydney.' The dark eyes had a calculating glint in them. 'I agree it'd be sacrilegious to turn the park into a building estate. But then, I might be persuaded to drop my er . . . religious scruples in the face of such a profitable cause.' He was grinning now. 'Don't worry, Mark, it's not going to happen.'

Treasure assumed that this was more because of official restriction than any forbearance on Kuril's part. 'Vormer's only a mile from Thatchford, of course,' he said reflectively.

'An expanding town and an official industrial development area,' Kuril completed, again in an amused sort of voice.

'And with the whole of the A1 scheduled to become a Motorway, a lot more people are going to live and work there.'

'Yes. But Delgard is determined nobody should ever interfere with Vormer House,' Kuril put in seriously. 'He also wants to keep the pictures and furniture intact as a collection, in perpetuity. Wants the house to go on being opened to the public too.'

'So he's planning to hand everything over to the Tudor Heritage Trust, you said? On those conditions they'll want a hell of a lot of money to go with it. To endow it. Have they named a figure?'

'Yes. Three million.' Kuril turned about, leaning his back against the parapet. 'With the estate farms and all the agricultural land already sold off, the only way the old boy could raise that kind of wind was to sell pictures, and he wouldn't do that.'

'Which is where you and the golf courses come in?' Treasure finished his Scotch, and checked the time with the illuminated face of Big Ben, half a mile away to the left, across the river. 'Want another?'

Kuril studied his empty glass as keenly as if he'd lost something in it. 'Mm . . . better not,' he answered in a determined voice.

'So Henfold Developments will be paying three million for three hundred acres of the park. Expensive?'

'Not relative to the potential.'

'So everybody's happy? Except possibly Mr Legion in Australia. He'd have done better to have kept quiet. He might have inherited the lot.'

'Not possible.' Kuril smoothed a hand over the prematurely balding area above his forehead to the thick black hair at the back. 'Delgard would have seen to it he inherited nothing. There's no family entail, except possibly a few disputed fields. No, our proposal is the only runner. But we're still not quite home and dry yet.'

'The golf courses were your idea?'

'For starters, yes. It was a tentative suggestion, floated in to his lordship six months ago. Golf courses, and a sort of Tudor clubhouse.' He gave a cynical grimace. 'Good sporting attraction and plenty of tourist appeal. At first, Delgard pretended to have apoplexy. Then he had second thoughts and checked me out. It wasn't difficult. Or for me to know he was doing it.'

'You'd never met him?'

'Not then. We've met since. He even accepts a regular day's shooting from me now, but you couldn't call us mates. Remember, I'm still a local back street lad.' He smoothed the front of his silk tie between the lapels of the impeccably cut Savile Row jacket.

'Except you now own a weekend house nearby as big as Vormer?'

'It's three miles away actually, and not nearly as big. Really not. It's just a manor house. And we don't have a home park either. Just a few dozen acres.'

'Otherwise you'd have built a golf course there by now?' Treasure chuckled.

'Mmm? Probably not. We like our privacy.' A mischievous grin followed the comment. 'Anyway, his lordship eventually sent his Major Oliphant to talk seriously to the Tudor Heritage and then to see us. Incidentally, the Major's all for the scheme, notably for reasons of his own, and we've er . . . encouraged him in that direction.' Kuril pinched the end of his nose again. 'Anyhow, when he told us the price was going to be three million, we explained that a couple of golf courses with a reach-me-down clubhouse would hardly justify that sort of money. Even a clubhouse with tastefully exposed timbers.'

'Which is when you added the hotel?'

'And an up-market leisure centre, the whole complex still discreetly sited in relation to the house. There's a Victorian gazebo on the spot at the moment.'

'Must be a bloody big gazebo.'

Kuril chuckled. 'Not really. But it's there to establish there's been building on the site before. And it's of no historic or æsthetic importance.' He nodded as if to reassure himself on the last point.

'Meaning you can knock it down with impunity?'

'Yes. Of course, we intended doing the whole package from the start. And a bit more if we could. Question of softly, softly.'

'Total cost?'

Kuril shrugged. 'With all the trimmings? Fifty million plus. We've done the market projections. It's a goer all right. On a four-year pay-back.'

'And the bit more you mentioned? Would that be a few choice houses along the fairways, also discreetly sited?'

'That's just a pipe dream, I'm afraid.' It was difficult to gauge whether the tone was speculative or resigned.

Treasure decided not to press the point. Instead he asked: 'How much of the fifty million will you want the bank to pick up?'

'I was hoping you'd ask. Quite a lot of it. Obviously we're a bit strapped at the moment.'

Treasure found the comment almost comical. The project the two had been talking about that morning involved a big funding operation by Grenwood, Phipps. The bank had been putting together a syndicate of financial institutions to back a major Henfold industrial and housing develop- ment in Czechoslovakia. The monies required had exceeded a billion pounds, spread over two years. In the circum- stances, fifty million for a golf hotel in middle England looked like small change and a very low risk. 'I think we can probably cover that for you,' said the banker. 'When we've seen the plans.'

'But there'll be some local money too,' Kuril added, his eyes now intently following the movements of two noisily attractive blonde young women who had just come out on to the terrace.

'And all assuming the basic planning permission will be given by Thatchford Council?' Treasure questioned.

Kuril nodded sharply. 'We're fairly confident there. It was the main reason for letting in local money. Naturally there's a certain amount of opposition to the project. Always is with this kind of thing. We build the negative drag into the feasibility studies these days. In this case the drag isn't massive.'

'From environmentalists, I suppose?'

'Yes. Which covers everyone with a public or personal axe to grind. The greens and the reds on the Thatchford Council. Plus a few local landowners who wish they'd come up with the idea themselves.' He paused. 'Oh, and the usual Johnnie-come-lately commuters. People living in villages to the south of Vormer who've moved there from the larger towns in the area. They're the worst sort of objectors usu- ally. Always deploring plans to alter what they call the traditional community. That's exactly what they altered themselves, of course, gentrifying cottages and degutting old schoolhouses. But they still feel entitled to behave as if they'd been born and weaned in a place. As if they were the usurped instead of the usurpers.' He shifted his stance. 'I hate hypocrisy, don't you?'

The words had come with great feeling even though they might take some justifying from a successful and by all accounts often ruthless property developer. But, Treasure reasoned, it was evidently cant that Kuril was deploring and nothing else.

'Humbug is certainly one of the least tolerable of human frailties,' he commented lightly, 'but one of the most transparent too.'

'Those girls should have more clothes on,' said Kuril unexpectedly, his tone and facial expression implying the very opposite of his words. 'It's not that warm out here.' His eyes had scarcely left the two parading blondes since they had first appeared.

Treasure felt the girls rated a glance, but not the rapt attention they were aware they were getting from his companion. Both were the short, cuddly type and a touch overweight, but with breasts that one would have to describe as prodigious. The clothes they had on were sexy but lacking in style—including tight, very short skirts that would have better suited figures with less ample calves. Their highly audible conversation had been punctuated by raucous laughter and much friendly pulling and pushing of each other. 'They seem well enough covered in some respects,' the banker remarked amiably, then returned to the previous subject with: 'I suppose it's the hotel that produces the objections to the Vormer scheme?'

'Not necessarily just that. People think a golf club greatly increases traffic. Wears out the roads, clogs the drains, and destroys the flora and fauna. Lot of nonsense,' Kuril said while continuing to watch the girls. 'We've got the local MP on our side, by the way. Charles Finton. Know him?'

'No. Only of him. Isn't he in the Ministry for the Environment?'

'Only just. Parliamentary Private Secretary to the Minister. Ambitious type. Politically, I mean. Failed barrister. Wouldn't light any fires in vulgar commerce, I can tell you. There's damn-all competition in politics these days, of course.'

'Isn't Finton quite well off in his own right?'

'No, but his wife is. Enough for both of them.'

'I suppose he's your MP in the country too?'

'Yes. We see quite a bit of them. Sheila gets on with Mrs Finton. Felicity, her name is. Now there's an unusual woman.'

Whatever it was that made Mrs Finton singular was something Treasure was denied discovering at that point, since the conversation was ended by the insistent echoing of the final interval gong, a sound well amplified on to the terrace. It sent the two men moving back to their seats. In Kuril's case, this began with a spirited, almost indecent spurt so that he was in time to pull the terrace door open for the simpering, and coyly grateful young women with whom he also chose to exchange some words. It was the last enterprise that sent them on their way doubled up with mirth.

Meantime Treasure found himself idly speculating about whether Sheila Kuril might also be noisy, short and cuddly. On the whole he decided she was probably not, and that this was a female specification that more likely attracted his companion extra-murally, as it were, rather than maritally—a shamelessly unsupported conclusion, he admitted to himself, but one that even so had begged a further question.

CHAPTER 3

'Order, ladies and gentlemen. Order, please.' Councillor Arthur Motwell, the fleshy, Yorkshire-born owner of A. P. Motwell and Sons, building contractors, and Chairman of the Thatchford District Council's Planning Committee, banged his gavel again with unnecessary force. Then he leaned back expansively in the leather upholstery of the Mayor's seat. This was raised on a dais facing two rows of similar fixed but not quite such opulent places, the rows arranged in the shape of a horseshoe on two tiers—making the principal feature of the permanent furnishings of the well lit, modern Council chamber.

The present Thatchford Council offices, still regarded by many as new, had been erected in the previous decade. They were a legacy from the last period when the Labour Party had held a majority on the Council and had elected then to invest ratepayers' money in what Labour's political opponents had regarded as unnecessary new accommodations. This decision was still used as convenient evidence of Labour Party profligacy (the building had cost much more than was first estimated), though few councillors of any political persuasion would have chosen to go back to the old Victorian town hall. This last was in any case an academic consideration since the other building had been knocked down.

Besides the seats for the Mayor and councillors, there were tables and chairs in the central well of the Council chamber for Council executives and secretaries, and tip-up seats for the press and public in raked rows behind the councillors and facing the Mayor. Although there were committee rooms in addition to the Council chamber, the full Planning Committee had met here since Councillor Motwell had been made its Chairman. Motwell was some

years off becoming Mayor (an office allotted through senior-
ity not merit), but he enjoyed behaving as if he had risen
to that status already.

'Order, please,' he repeated, not so much because the
previous injunction had failed to provide quite enough of
it, but because he enjoyed exercising his authority. He
loosened the knot of his tie a fraction under his several
chins, while aiming a look of still tolerant admonition at a
few individuals among the sixteen ususally fractious male
and female councillors seated before him. They were
arranged in party groups—Conservative, Labour and
Liberal Democrat—clumped irregularly along both rows
of seats like surviving teeth in a cankered jaw.

'Order yourself, Chairman. It's you who's out of order,
not us,' Madelaine Task protested to calls of 'hear, hear'
from those around her. She was seated directly opposite the
Chairman on the upper row, and her words were easily
distinguishable above the continuing hubbub. Short and
plump, Mrs Task, thirty-three, a Labour councillor, a
bohemian dresser and a schoolteacher, was well used to
getting herself heard over the clamourings of the unruly.
She brushed her long and lacklustre hair away from her
quite pretty face, and straightened the heavily framed spec-
tacles which also did nothing to enhance her appearance.
'Vested interests have to be declared,' she shouted in a
high-pitched but unbreathy, strained soprano, leaning forward in her seat, and stabbing a pointed index finger at
Motwell. 'You've not declared any interest yet. You and
your like are a disgrace.' She looked about her for support,
and got it in good measure.

'I'll thank you to keep a civil tongue in your head, Councillor Task,' Motwell responded, unruffled. He prided himself on coolheadedness in the Chair, especially when it came
to controlling looney Trots. 'Time's getting on. We've
nearly covered a long agenda. Some of us could do with
liquid refreshment. That applies to members of all parties,
I'm sure, not forgetting the press,' he continued amiably,

bestowing a smile first at a right of centre Labour crony
who looked mildly discomforted at being singled out as
potentially both a traitor and a drunk, and then at George
Pike, the chief reporter from the *Thatchford Advertiser*. Pike
had no qualms about nodding back his agreement since he
was thirsty and worked for an acknowledged Tory paper.
'So can we press on without people dragging in irrelevances,
and wasting the time of overworked officials.' Motwell
beamed at Harold Jepton, Chief Executive of the Council,
seated at the centre table just below him, and currently also
filling the office of Director of Planning on a temporary
basis.

The Thatchford Council had several vacancies on its permanent staff at management grade: Director of Planning
was one of them. The previous incumbent had left recently
to take up a better paid post with a property company which
had funded several lucrative projects in the area in recent
years. It had been an appointment that for obvious reasons
had caused a lot of local gossip as well as criticism.

'What Councillor Task said wasn't irrelevant, Mr Chairman,' offered Councillor Barry Winkler in a considered and
painfully slow delivery. He had been standing to speak
when the noise had subsided. Much older than Motwell,
who was fifty-seven, he had been a councillor for longer
than anyone else present. A gaunt, retired widower, he
was a Liberal Democrat, the minority party that held the
balance of power on the full Council which had been hung
at the last election. 'It needs to be disclosed . . . if councillors have shares . . . in this proposed golf club,' he added
soberly, drawing in long breaths between phrases. 'That's
what she meant,' he added, paused undecidedly, then sat
down again.

'Councillor Bender?' the Chairman called immediately,
nodding at a lanky, effete-looking young man sitting with
the Conservatives and who, like a number of others, had
signalled an urgent desire to speak next.

'But that's the whole point, Mr Chairman,' said Bender,

beaming triumphantly as he stood, leaning forward from
the waist, elbows bent, fists holding back his open jacket
and resting behind his hip bone. This was the pose his
mother said made him look very like a tall Winston Chur-
chill, although the resemblance had never struck anyone
else. 'That's the whole point,' he repeated. 'Nobody has
shares in any golf club because there isn't any golf club.
Not yet. There can't be unless and until this Committee
gives planning permission for it. But I believe we should do
that without delay. It'll bring jobs and trade to the town.
Tourists and sportsmen—and sportswomen of course,' he
added quickly. 'To see one of the finest Elizabethan houses
in the country and to play what'll be two of the greatest
golf courses in Europe.'

'Will Councillor Bender categorically deny rumours that
he's been given shares in the golf club? Like other Tory
Councillors?' interrupted Mrs Task from her seat, and fixing the Chairman with an accusing stare.

'We're not here to bandy rumours, Mr Chairman,'
Bender responded, still on his feet and waving one hand
dismissively before returning it carefully to a position
behind his waistcoat.

'Or deny them either?' questioned a male voice from near
Mrs Task.

Bender ignored the comment. 'Outline planning permission for the golf courses and necessary supporting buildings in Vormer park has been applied for by General the
Viscount Delgard,' he continued. 'Lord Delgard is a local
hero, dignatory and benefactor whom we all respect.'

'Speak for yourself,' called the same male interloper.

'Irrelevant,' called Mrs Task at the same time.

'Whom all responsible and patriotic members respect,'
Bender corrected in a crushing tone. 'The plans have been
approved in sub-committee. If we approve them tonight,
they can be passed in full Council next week. Then Lord
Delgard can sell the land to Henfold Developments. The
money he gets will be given with the house and the rest of

the park to the Tudor Heritage Trust. They'll maintain
both for the benefit of the whole nation, but the people who
live in this area will gain much more than anyone else.'

'Especially the ones with free shares in the golf club?'
called the persistent Mrs Task.

'Order,' cautioned the Chairman banging his gavel so
hard that the reverberation hurt his shoulder. 'Councillor
Bender still has the floor.'

'Thank you, Mr Chairman. Henfold have announced it'll
form a separate company to build and manage the development—'

'Handing out shares to Tories who're in on the deal,'
Mrs Task protested again loudly from her seat.

'Offering a chance to anyone in the area to participate
by buying shares,' Bender continued, obliquely responding
to the interruption. 'There's nothing secret about any of
this. The press has been given total disclosure of all the
plans and the thinking behind them. We all have the same
chance to support the creation of a fine local amenity.'

'Local eyesore,' shouted another male voice from the
Labour group. 'Local elitist amenity for the bloody rich,' it
continued, warming to the subject as Bender took his seat
again.

'Councillor Mrs Task?' said the Chairman, submitting
to the inevitable, and looking at the time.

'If Delgard is giving his house and two-thirds of his park
to a trust, he's doing it to escape tax,' Mrs Task affirmed
in her sharp interventionist tone even though she now had
the floor officially. 'So the least he can do is give the rest of
the park to this community, not close it off for ever as a
golfing playground for the rich. And another thing.' She
jerked her head up as if it had been tugged from behind.
'What's been called the necessary supporting buildings for
the golf courses includes a huge hotel. The hotel isn't
needed.' She punched the air with her hand. 'And it isn't
supporting anything but the greed of its owners.' She
punched the air again. 'This so-called complete disclosure

is a load of codswallop. Let Delgard start again, we say.
Let him give his house to this Council—'

'Point of information, Mr Chairman,' exclaimed Bender,
rising to his feet and continuing after a nod from Motwell.
'We're not a charity. If Lord Delgard gave us Vormer we'd
have to pay inheritance tax on it when he and his wife are
dead. And on everything in it.'

'The tax could be paid by trading some of the pictures
to the Revenue in lieu. There's plenty of precedence,' countered Mrs Task—a claim that evinced groans of dis-
approval from the Tory group. 'Then Vormer House could
become a local cultural centre, and the park a local recreation area.' This produced more groans. 'Of course, the
Tories resent the idea. That's totally in character for them.
They did damn-all to improve cultural amenities in the
district for the twelve years they were in control of this
Council. Well, this year's election changed that. They can't
block benefits for the people any more. Or feather their
own nests, or their friends' nests, approving every fancy
development rich speculators put up to a biased planning
department.' There was a loud irruption of support from
her own party members at this, and outraged noises from
the people she was smearing with the blatant reference to
the recently departed Director of Planning. 'From now on,'
she continued, 'the Tories won't be getting away with anything. Not now there's a strong majority in the other com-
bined parties to stop them.' She nodded pointedly in the
direction of the Liberal Democrats, although her words had
implied a degree of cooperation between them and her own
party which had yet to be demonstrated on any important
issue. 'They won't be getting away with anything,' she
repeated. 'Especially not something that reduces leisure
amenities. That's why, Mr Chairman, I move for the rejection of this planning application.'

Only the Labour members seemed to respond favourably
to this, and not all of them, nor was there an immediate
seconder for the proposal.

'Councillor Winkler,' called the Chairman, anxious to give a hearing to the Liberal Democrats, though he was less sure than he had been at the start whose side Winkler would take. Certainly the Liberal Democrats had voted with the Tories on the matter when it had been before the planning sub-committee the week before.

Winkler rose unsteadily. 'Mr Chairman, I believe it's impossible to regard this issue as a straight planning proposal any more.' There were calls of 'hear, hear,' from his own party members as well as Mrs Task's. 'We're supposed to judge all planning applications on the same criteria. That's broadly on whether it's beneficial or detrimental to our environment.' He paused, sucking in breath, pressing the backs of his legs against his seat and lightly touching the desktop in front of him with his long, skinny fingertips. His worn, wrinkled face was grave, his frail shoulders stooped as he went on. 'But it seems to me, Mr Chairman, this application goes a lot deeper than that. You could say it goes back into history.' The speaker this time made a sighing noise, in witness that he could nearly claim to do the same. 'We're discussing the future, perhaps the ultimate survival of a truly stately home . . . the place that's been the centre of affairs in this community for more than four hundred years. For most of that time its aristocratic owners have determined the . . . the destiny of generations of ordinary local folk.'

There were cries from Labour of 'shame' at this last comment though Winkler affected not to hear them.

'Until very recent times, the Delgard family had more influence in this area than the elected representatives who sit in this building.' He scanned the chamber slowly and without appearing to enjoy the experience, or perhaps the concomitant need to exercise an evidently arthritic neck. 'This building,' he repeated, 'and before that, the much nicer Town Hall that was here before the modern excrescence we're in replaced it,' he added gratuitously.

The additional shouts of 'shame' from Labour which had

punctuated the reference to the Delgards were balanced by the same call from the Tories confirming his view of the building.

'Whether you find the Delgard family's past influence shaming or not doesn't really matter,' the speaker went on. 'It was there, and its effect mapped the historic and social development of the area as nothing else did. For centuries. That's why I find it inappropriate, to say the least, the very least, that Vormer House, the enduring symbol of that influence and that development should have its fate, perhaps . . . perhaps its very survival, decided once and for all by the . . . the incidental acceptance or rejection of a mere planning consent by . . . by this Committee.'

Winkler looked about him again, this time, it seemed, to assess the calibre of his fellow councillors rather than the æsthetic shortcomings of the room. Then, frowning, he continued breathily, 'The whole community should be directly involved in so . . . so far-reaching a decision, not just a few elected and inimical Councillors.' He took out a handkerchief and blew his nose, not loudly, but slowly, before adding: 'Unlike Councillor Task, I don't believe the Council should want to own Vormer even if it was offered to us. The maintenance costs would be too great. But I admit it's a point of view . . . one that should be put to the people. To the community. And there are other points of view too.' He began a lengthy pause, either to gather plenty of breath, or because he'd lost his own drift, or because he was finished, it wasn't clear whether he knew which himself. He remained standing, though that could have meant he had forgotten to sit down.

Jeremy Bender rose to break the silence. 'On a point of information, Mr Chairman, can we know whether Councillor Winkler is suggesting we ask the Ministry of the Environment to set up an official public inquiry on this matter, because if he is—'

'That's not what you've got in mind is it, Barry?' asked

Motwell in a tone that managed to be all at once friendly, threatening and cajoling.

'Not yet, Mr Chairman,' Winkler replied, still standing and coming back to life suddenly. 'I'm formally proposing that a single public meeting should be called to air the issue . . . with everyone represented who should be. And that further consideration of this planning application be postponed till after that meeting has taken place.'

'Seconded, Mr Chairman. And I withdraw my own motion,' cried Mrs Task quickly from her seat, partly because her motion had been greeted with something less than enthusiasm, but more because she was confident that Winkler's proposal would achieve the same result if by a more circuitous route.

There were affirming shouts from enough Labour and Liberal Democrats to make the outcome of the ensuing vote a foregone conclusion.

CHAPTER 4

'So what's this meeting tonight supposed to resolve?' asked Molly Treasure as the Rolls-Royce sped northwards. Her husband was at the wheel.

'To absolve and resolve,' he said.

'People's consciences you mean?'

'That's right.'

It was four-thirty on Friday, November 9th, and three weeks since the Thatchford Council Planning Committee meeting. The public meeting agreed on then was due to take place in the Thatchford Community Centre at seven. Julius Kuril had coaxed the Treasures into attending, to add, he said, credibility and glamour to the Henfold case. His plea had been gilded with an invitation to the couple to spend the weekend at his country home, Stigham Manor, with a pheasant shoot on Saturday morning as an added attraction. They had been able to accept because both the plays Molly was in at the National Theatre were out of the repertory for ten days. Treasure had also welcomed the visit as a chance to talk through problems that had arisen on the Henfold Czechoslovakian project.

'I still don't understand why there's such a fuss about building a golf course in a corner of a huge home park,' said Molly. 'There's plenty of room up here for everything, for heaven's sake. Much more than they need for the sheep and cows. Unlike Surrey.' She peered to left and right at the rolling, unspoiled East Anglian countryside that flanked the Great North Road as far she could see in the gathering dusk. And there wasn't a sheep or a cow in sight, which seemed to confirm her premise.

Treasure frowned. 'Two golf courses. And there's more to it than that. Local sentiment.'

'But if the whole deal means Vormer House is protected for ever, local sentiment ought to be in favour.'

'I should have said local political opinion. That's hotly divided. On ideological grounds. And there's opposition from environmentalists but not as vocal as it was. From their viewpoint the plan's really quite civilized.'

'Because it's mostly about keeping the land green, not building over it?'

'Yes. What's left of the green protest seems to have been reduced to a left-wing front. Some Labour members on the Council are opposed on principle, claiming the plan's elitist.'

Molly shrugged her shoulders, at the same time rearranging the line of her seat-belt across the jacket of the cashmere suit she had on. 'National politics should never have been allowed into local government. Daddy used to say it meant the end of objective decision-making on local issues.'

'He was probably right too, but that battle was lost a long time ago. The Tories have ruled Thatchford for twelve years, but now they've lost their overall majority it seems every issue is heavily contested. Some of the Council meetings are pretty hairy, I gather.'

'Fisticuffs?'

'Verbal, certainly.'

'So who's actually in control politically?'

'Effectively the Liberal Democrats. The LDP. They have fewer seats than either of the two other main parties, but the balance of power's with them. Conservatives and Labour have exactly the same number of seats each.'

'Wasn't Lord Delgard's father a Liberal?'

'Yes. He was a minister in a Liberal cabinet before the First World War. The family's always been Liberal, and they were Whigs before that. Julius Kuril told me it's the deputy leader of the LDP on the Council who brought about tonight's meeting. Chap called Winkler. Solicitor and local historian. He's on the Planning Committee.'

'He's against the golf course plan?'

'Not necessarily. According to Julius, he believes the future of the Delgard family seat should be decided by the populace at large.'

'Why? The place isn't theirs. It's the Delgards'.'

Treasure chuckled. 'A trenchant sentiment which would have made your father proud of you, but it's not the way Winkler sees things. He feels Vormer is emotionally and historically part of everyone's local inheritance.'

'What's that mean in practical terms?'

'Nothing much, really. It'll be interesting to see how many turn up for the meeting.'

'To claim their emotional inheritance?' Molly pulled a long face.

'Except Julius feels that Winkler's insistence on the public meeting saved the whole plan from being turned down altogether. The local tradespeople are all for the Henfold scheme, and so are the local industrialists. Neither of their views seem to have been properly aired at Council level. I should think they'll he voiced tonight, though.'

'Because Julius has seen to it? And they'll be well

reported later too, because Julius will have fixed the local press?'

'I think his public relations machine is pretty efficient,' Treasure agreed carefully.

'Julius must be an incorrigible fixer. But dishy with it. I imagine he's charmed all the local females on to his side.'

'I've no idea. His wife's back now, of course. I gather she'd been campaigning pretty formidably before she left.'

'God, the energy Sheila Kuril must have.'

'You mean her charity work?'

'Yes. Everyone says she's a positive dynamo.'

'Mm. The most effective charity fund-raiser in London. Maggie Halliwell, Julius's indispensible assistant, she told me—'

'Who'll be staying the weekend too?' Molly interrupted.

'Yes.'

'I'll be interested to meet Mrs Halliwell. Didn't you say she really runs Henfold?'

'If I did I was exaggerating. But yes, she's the engine-room. Julius put her on the board last year.'

'Attractive, is she?'

'I'd say so. Julius doesn't.'

'He's told you that?'

'In a way. And they both affect amusement if people imply they're emotionally involved.'

'And you think that proves they're not?' the actress questioned.

'That's too deep for me,' her husband answered. 'I know Maggie's been running the Henfold Australian interests on her own recently. And very efficiently. It's quite a substantial operation by itself.'

'And does Julius leave it to her because he's so involved in Eastern Europe?'

Because of that and, for the moment, this Vormer side-show.' He sniffed to show he didn't approve.

'Property development companies don't have big boards of directors?'

'This one doesn't, certainly. And, yes, they do tend to be all chiefs and no Indians. Julius is the genius behind Henfold, but once a project sparks he likes to move on to the next brainchild. Maggie is the perfect partner in that respect.'

'A consolidator of sparkling projects?'

'I suppose so.' He shifted a little in his seat. 'Anyway, it was she who told me yesterday that in the week Sheila's been home she's sold out a whole Festival Hall concert for that handicap charity of hers. Mostly on the telephone. She doesn't just sell tickets. She sells tiers of seats at a time.'

'Well, bully for Sheila,' said Molly, fairly sure that the estimable Sheila exerted commercial blackmail on Julius Kuril's business associates to make them buy. 'Sold a few rows to Grenwood, Phipps, did she?' she asked aloud.

Treasure cleared his throat. 'Probably. She did ring me,' he added, as though the point hardly rated a mention. 'I put her on to the head of our charity committee.'

'With instructions to buy ten rows in the middle tier?'

'Hardly that, but . . . but yes, I expect I said something encouraging. Henfold is a pretty substantial customer,' he ended defensively.

'Of course, and it's all good for performing artistes as well as the charities,' said the actress, smoothing her skirt, and sounding a touch like an archbishop making the case for a just war.

Her husband nodded agreement. 'I hope Julius does get shot of this Vormer thing tonight,' he said, changing the subject. 'It's taking up a lot of everyone's time.'

'Because it's really just an ego trip on his part?'

'Oh, it's much more than that. There's serious money involved, and a glittering prospect, but . . .' Treasure paused, scratching his forehead before continuing. 'Yes, I suppose you could say Julius has become fixated by it. That's partly because, in the end, it'll be a boost to his ego. One has to remember he was raised in this area in pretty reduced circumstances.'

'And if the plan goes through he'll end up more important locally than Lord Delgard?'

'Different sort of quality to the importance, of course, but that could be broadly true.' He straightened his shoulders and moved back even further into the seat. 'Julius told me that Delgard was once instrumental in putting his father out of work. That's the kind of thing you never forget.'

'Or forgive?'

Treasure hesitated. 'I don't believe that came into it. At the time he mentioned it, Julius was simply rubbishing Delgard's capacities as an industrialist. The job was lost because a factory had to be closed through mismanagement. The mismanagement not the sacking would have been the unforgivable sin in Julius's eyes.'

'So if what he really wants to do is take the place of the local lord, why doesn't he do the thing properly? He should buy Vormer House himself, not let the Delgards give it to the Tudor Heritage. Then he and Sheila could live there and please themselves about golf courses and anything else.'

Treasure shook his head. 'Not Julius's style. Don't ever mention this to anyone else, but what he's got in mind for himself is a life peerage. In the present circumstances, buying Vormer would be a pretty insensitive way of advertising the fact.' He chuckled. 'Apart from that, the place is too big, and there'd be no financial benefit for Julius in the deal.'

'And that's the only thing that motivates him?'

'It's the principle that's made him seriously rich, whether you approve of that or not.'

'I didn't say I disapproved.'

'Not quite.' He reached for her hand and squeezed it. 'Anyway, Lord Delgard is insisting that whoever takes on the house now must guarantee its maintenance for ever. Julius wouldn't want a personal obligation of that size in this area. Not at this stage. He told me they're already finding Stigham Manor a bit too far from London for weekending, so he won't be looking for more substantial property roots up here. Much better for a well-established charitable trust to take on Vormer.'

'But Julius is putting up the money? The three million that goes with the house when the Trust gets it?'

'Henfold's putting it up, yes. As the purchase price of the land. It's Delgard who's choosing to give the money away with the house. Henfold should get it back in the small change when they float the golf club as a public company.'

'You said it's going to cost fifty million?'

'To do everything properly, yes. And it'll take two years to get everything built and running. By then Thatchford should be a much more important commercial centre.'

'What if it isn't?'

'Julius will have burnt his fingers. So will I. That is, Grenwood, Phipps. We're staking Henfold. But there's every reason for optimism on that one. The Henfold feasibility study for the project suggests the risks are very small. Even if Thatchford doesn't prosper as much as we expect, we'll still end up with one of the best golf and leisure complexes in the country. Idyllic setting. Close to plenty of other important commercial centres. Good communications by road, rail and air. Long term it really can't miss.'

'So why are you pushing it like a frantic radio commercial?'

'Am I?' He frowned. 'Probably because the whole thing now depends not on the merits of the scheme but on whether these Toy Town councillors give it planning approval.'

'Their decision being deeply affected by the meeting tonight?'

'Democratically one hopes so,' he said seriously. 'I mean, it'd be nice if we do hear some really objective opinions. Freedom of speech is important—'

'But prejudiced because it favours the articulate,' Molly interrupted.

'That's very profound, darling.'

'Well, don't sound so surprised. Except Tom Stoppard

said it first,' the actress responded reluctantly. 'Aren't three hundred acres more than one needs for two golf courses?'

'Yes, and that'll be part of the attraction. It allows for sensitive development. Without destroying the character of the parkland. Some of the newer golf clubs have fairways crammed in like tramlines. There'll be lots of space along both courses too.'

'For putting houses on? Like Wentworth and Sunningdale?'

Treasure affected a shudder. 'Don't even whisper that to anyone else up here. Housing development is exactly what the opposition is predicting Henfold has in mind long term.'

'Well, hasn't it? Pretty houses overlooking pretty fairways?'

'Would mean that a third of Vormer park had really been sacrificed for housing, not recreation. Public access reduced even further. Wild life habitats destroyed. The basic character of the environment changed. It's exactly what would kill the whole planning application.'

'But isn't housing really what Julius wants in the end? I mean, wouldn't the profit on say a hundred classy houses—'

'Quite alter the financial picture? You bet it would,' Treasure cut in with a chuckle. 'It'd practically cover the whole up front cost of the basic project.'

'So Julius would get it for nothing?'

'Yes. But it's not going to happen.'

'I see,' but she sounded unconvinced. 'So why should Julius expect to get a life peerage?'

Treasure pouted. 'For political services.'

'But he's not a Member of Parliament? Wouldn't he at least have to be an MP first?'

'No. Again not his style. Being an MP anyway. Or to have to be elected to anything. No, I . . . I believe it's quite likely he'll become Treasurer to the Tory Party in the New Year.'

'Meaning you know he will?'

Treasure hesitated. 'They've sounded him out about accepting. But that really is between us,' he said. 'And he'd be good at it. Very good.'

'Raising money?'

'Yes.'

'Like his wife?'

'Who again would be a great help.'

'And it'd mean a life peerage?'

'Not necessarily, but it usually puts you on the inside track.'

'Whether or not the Tories are in government?'

'Sure. But if they did put him in the Lords, he'd expect a Cabinet job when they are in office.'

'But for any of this to come about, you need to be seriously rich to start with? And generous?'

'And clean as the driven snow.'

'Morally, you mean? Would that present a problem for Julius?'

'I'm sure not.' He slowed the car before the turn-off for Stigham Manor, the road that also ran close to Vormer House.

'So why mention it? Are there secrets in his life? Come on, I promise not to tell,' she encouraged, folding her arms tightly and leaning closer to him in earnest anticipation.

'Honestly, there aren't any secrets that I know of. I was generalizing, that's all. If you intend going into public life these days it's important there isn't any dirt to dig out of your background.'

'Hasn't that always been so?'

'In a way, yes. But not nearly so much as now. Not since we caught the American investigative habit. And things can be slightly different too for a chap who starts life in private commerce and decides later to switch to the public sector.'

'Because he may not have been as careful as he should have been at the start? As circumspect?' Molly sounded indignant. 'Are there really two sorts of morality applying?'

'There shouldn't be, but I suppose there are.'

'And that applies to aspiring life peers as well as MPs?'

'Aspiring life peers as young and bright as Julius who can easily end up in the Cabinet. There's plenty of recent precedent.'

Molly mused for a moment as the car moved on to the secondary road, gathering speed again. 'Does this political ambition account for Julius's friendship with the local MP here?'

'Charles Finton? I don't believe it's that much of a friendship. Julius thinks Finton's a bit . . . a bit lightweight, but not as lightweight as a lot of other politicians. I think he uses him as a sounding board. As for Finton, he values Julius's patronage.' He glanced at Molly. 'But of course you know Finton, don't you? I'd forgotten that. I expect he'll be at the meeting.'

'No, it's his wife I know. Felicity. We were at school together. She's two years younger than me, except I honestly don't believe anyone would credit it. I'm not being cocky either. She used to be quite a looker. As a deb. But she's let herself go.' Molly paused, leaning forward and pulling down the sun visor so that she could examine her face in the mirror—for a more practical reason than simply to affirm her last comparative judgement on her appearance. She took out her lipstick. 'I think it's because her husband neglects her. They say he's a womanizer. They could be wrong, of course,' she added, but in a tone that suggested she didn't believe they were.

CHAPTER 5

'Would we like this hard skin off, Miss Delgard? From underneath? Won't take a sec. Better off, I always think.'

'I expect so, Mrs Weggly.' The Hon. Bea watched with

less than total confidence as the sixty-year-old chiropodist searched for a different scalpel in her instrument box, straining her eyes through thick lenses while making the selection.

The new scalpel was longer than the one that had just been used on what was left of the corn on Bea's right little toe.

'Must have missed it last time. Been doing more walking, have we?' questioned the white-coated Mrs Rose Weggly, with a professional air, and before making several delicate adjustments to the elbowed examination lamp. She was small and stout, with fat, stumpy legs now widely parted. Her large bottom was balanced on the cushion of a low, steel stool set on efficient castors so that the user could move it around her patients in a scootering movement. Her lap was covered with a white linen towel, the dip in its centre serving as a catchment for the instruments she was using.

'Up here, then. So I can get at it properly,' Mrs Weggly continued before the patient had answered the question about the walking. She lifted Bea's foot from the lower footrest of the treatment chair to the higher heelrest. In contrast to the stool, the chair was old, wooden, and, because it was elevated on a plinth, somewhat thronelike: Bea always thought of it as a high profile commode.

'Oh yes.' There was a sharp indrawing of breath after Mrs Weggly had more closely examined the calloused skin deposits on the underside of Bea's big toe. 'Oh yes,' the chiropodist repeated with the measured solemnity of a cardiologist confronted by several blocked arteries and a dangerously enlarged aorta.

What Mrs Weggly referred to as her surgery was the back room of her son-in-law's shoe-shop in Coin Row, a narrow street off Thatchford's Market Square, and—appropriately in the circumstances—open to pedestrians only. The place served its purpose well enough, particularly as Kevin Task let Mrs Weggly have it rent free, and more particularly since Mrs Weggly was the only local chiropodist in private practice—people either came to her for treatment or had to make a special journey to one of the larger towns: in the main they came to her.

'Going to the meeting tonight, are we?' inquired Mrs Weggly, who invariably addressed patients in the plural, as some people do children, and with an equal lack of reason.

'I'm thinking of going, yes,' replied Bea guardedly, drawing her skirt more decorously over her unstockinged knees.

Bea's gaze returned determinedly to the badly framed print of a Renoir portrait depicting a melancholic and almost certainly goitrous female. She found this lone wall decoration more compulsive than the sight of her own feet and what was being done to them. A normally bold and garrulous woman, she became the opposite when her body was being subjected to treatment of any kind. This had extended even to visits to the hairdresser until she had given up having her hair done professionally. Nowadays she relied on Mrs Sting who obliged in the Vormer House kitchen with a quarterly scissoring of hair-ends.

'That's it, then. And me finished for the day as well,' said Mrs Weggly, leaning back with pride. She flicked off the lamp and gathered up the instruments from her lap.

'Oh good,' replied the patient with undisguised relief.

'So as I was starting to say just now, it's awkward for me. All this fuss about what's to happen to Vormer park,' Mrs Weggly continued, her talkativeness stoked by the other's near silence. 'Not so much as for you and their Lord and Ladyship, of course,' she added, and palpably with more justification than she was consciously feeling. 'But with my girls taking different sides . . . Well, you see the problem, don't you?' Absently, she removed some cotton-wool swabs from between the patient's toes. 'Not that I've got any time for my Madelaine being Labour. Well, we know that well enough, don't we, Miss Delgard?'

'I hear she's been fairly outspoken at the Council meetings,' Bea commented, her normal confidence beginning to return. She searched for her elastic-topped stockings in the large handbag where she had put them earlier. She normally wore pantyhose, but not to the chiropodist's.

'That's right.' Mrs Weggly made a tutting noise. 'Kevin, that's her husband, he's not that way inclined at all, you know? No politics about him. Not interested. More musical, he is. Plays records all the time.' She lowered her voice, although the walls of the old building were too thick for her words to penetrate through to the shop. 'You'd wonder if her being a Labour Councillor wouldn't be bad for his business too. In a town like this. Him having such an upper class clientele. Same as me.' She nodded meaningfully at her high-born patient, then rose from the stool, pushing it to one side as she carried the used instruments to the washbasin in the corner: the practice didn't run to a sterilizer. 'You'd think Madelaine would have enough on her plate any road, what with her teaching full time, and a husband to look after,' she continued, while rinsing the instruments. 'They've no children, of course. Accounts for a lot, that does, I always think. Whoever it is.' Her lips had shut tight between each phrase. 'It's not that there'd be any difficulty in that department either. None at all. Well, not so far as I know, and I live in the same house.'

Bea wondered if mere propinquity could provide proof of a couple's fecundity, but didn't trouble saying so. There were probably other grounds for the claim. 'And your . . . your younger daughter?' Since the inquiry had been intended as a dutiful one she was annoyed with herself for not remembering the girl's name.

'Janice?' Mrs Weggly provided. 'Oh, she's still got her typing and duplicating agency, but she works for Mr Finton the MP as well. That's separate from the other. Personal.'

'I didn't know.'

'A lot don't, Miss Delgard. And Madelaine for one does her best to make sure they don't. Janice working for Mr Finton causes no end of trouble between Madelaine and her. Him being Tory, you see?'

'Does Janice go to London for that, then?' Bea was straightening one of her stockings.

'Oh no. She's his constituency secretary. When he's here, like. That's mostly at weekends. Longer in the summer.'

'So it's a part-time post?'

'More than that really. And he wants her to go to London. Well, of course he would. Smart worker like Janice, and a good-looker as well. Hard to find down there, I've no doubt. But she's not having it.' Mrs Weggly began wiping a scissors with the clean cloth she had taken from a stack on the shelf above the basin. 'Strictly between you and me, I don't believe she likes him that much. As a person, I mean. As a man.' She paused, for appearance's sake, openly weighing whether she should go on in the same vein, before deciding, with evident relish, that she should. 'There's rumours about his being a one for the ladies, you know?' The tone became more conspiratorial. 'Janice hasn't said anything, but I wouldn't be surprised if he's made advances to her that haven't been well received. Well, they wouldn't be. Him being a married man with children. Janice is very strict about that kind of thing. That's her upbringing, of course.'

'But she hasn't given up working for him?'

The perplexed expression that the question had first evoked gave way to a canny one. 'She'd not do that. Not provided he didn't make a real nuisance of himself. And mark you, it's only my intuition. About him making advances. Janice hasn't said a thing. And the money's good. She did tell me that, though she has to work for it. He's always bringing her extra stuff. Nearly every weekend. Confidential, a lot of it is. Not the kind of thing she could give to one her employees in the agency.' The word employees had been emphasized through careful articulation. She began putting the dry instruments back into the box. 'Mr Finton says his London secretary's not as fast as Janice. Not as efficient either. Philippa Boyden something-or-other her name is. Boyden-Pent. With a hyphen. That tells you what sort she'll be.' The speaker sniffed. 'Debutante, no brains, and learned her shorthand in one of those finishing schools, as like as not. She'll be the kind that's up all night dancing, and that.' The last two words were accompanied by a screwing up of the eyes and a slow nod that signified worse depravities had remained unspecified.

Although the rugged Miss Delgard had been a debutante in her day, she overlooked the last affront to the aristocratic or perhaps the merely hyphenated classes, and inquired: 'And Janice's typing agency is still in Plum Street?'

'That's right. And fancy you remembering that. But of course, you gave her some work, didn't you? Just after she started.'

'Yes. She typed and duplicated an appeal letter for me. For my riding charity. Very nicely done it was, too. Janice was always efficient, I remember. Even as a young Girl Guide.' Bea had once been a luminary in the movement.

'She wouldn't give up the business now.' Mrs Weggly patted the top button of the white coat. 'Doing ever so well it is. And that's another reason for putting up with Mr Finton. Contacts, see? Fair's fair. He's put a lot of work her way. Through introductions. Through his important friends. She even gets work from what's it called, er . . . Chicken something? The people buying the park?'

'Henfold Developments?'

'That's it. They're London, of course. But they have people working up here.'

'Mr Kuril, the Chairman, owns Stigham Manor.'

'That's who I meant. He's one who's used her. In an emergency I think that was. Anyway, Janice has got the flat over the shop as well, now. Gives her extra office space, but it's meant to be for living in. That's what the lease says. No room for her widowed mother there, though. There wasn't in her last place either. Three bedrooms this one has too. Needed for business expansion, Janice said. That means more machines, I suppose, or bigger tanks for her tropical fish. Crazy about those fish she is.' Mrs Weggly sighed noisily. 'No, for all her politics, I'm afraid Madelaine's the better daughter to me. My hubby didn't leave a pension, and our house was only rented. It's lucky I've got my qualification. But the chiropody doesn't pay that much, not with the cost of living these days.' The speaker moved stiffly across to a small table and chair. There was a metal cash box and a large, open appointments book on the table top. 'Of course, they've never really got on, the two girls. Especially since they grew up.'

'Politics divided them?' Bea re-arranged her skirt, then brushed it roughly before stepping down from the chair.

'That and Janice's boyfriends. Madelaine's always watched over her little sister when it comes to that. Ever since my hubby died. Protective, she is. But Janice can't see it. She's a good girl, like I said, but she can't stand Madelaine interfering in her life.'

'I suppose you can hardly blame her. Not at her age. Twenty-six, isn't she?'

'Twenty-eight last July. That's what I say, but Madelaine won't leave off.'

'Is there any particular beau at the moment?' Bea was as interested in town gossip as the next person, and quite relaxed now the foot treatment was over and she was fully dressed.

'Oh, I'd be the last to know that. Very cagey she is. And Madelaine wouldn't know either. Very cagey,' Mrs Weggly repeated as she opened the lid of the cashbox. 'That'll be just the ten pounds this time then, Miss Delgard. Would we like to make the next appointment now?'

'You said that last Friday. You promised faithfully to tell her last weekend.'

'But you know I couldn't, lovey. Not in the end. We've been into that. It was the wrong time. Half term. I'd forgotten the boys would be home. You said you understood.' Charles Finton, Member of Parliament for Thatchford, Parliamentary Private Secretary to the Secretary of State for the Environment, husband to Felicity and father of her two children, had emerged naked from the bathroom of his secretary's flat in Hornsey, North London. The third floor flat was in a purpose-built block near the High Street.

Finton's muscular frame was not quite dry from the shower, and he had still been towelling his short wiry hair as he moved from the corridor back into the bedroom. 'My God, is it four-thirty already?' he exclaimed after picking up his watch from the bedside table. 'I was supposed to be in Thatchford by half six. I'll need to drive like hell.' He dropped the towel, and snatched up his jockey shorts from the chair where he'd put the rest of his things. He was a big man, square-jawed, with a rugged, open countenance that betokened strength of purpose. It was a face that endeared him to voters, especially women voters.

'Never mind the time. Are you going to tell her this weekend or not? I have to know, Charles. I have to know one way or the other.'

Philippa Boyden-Pent was twenty-five years old, a natural red-head with a Junoesque figure, long straight hair worn loose, and large greenish-blue eyes. Her features were a little too coarse for her to qualify as a beauty—her nose in particular was too wide, her lips, though inviting, were a little too thick: sensuous was a better summary of her considerable physical attractions. Contrary to Mrs Weggly's guess, she had never been a debutante. She had been educated at a London Comprehensive, and her father, Alfie Pent, was an engine driver with British Rail. Boyden had been her mother's maiden name that she'd adopted along with the hyphen after leaving secretarial college. She had been ambitious then: she was more so now—with her aims better defined. She was kneeling upright in the centre of the bed, the turned back double-duvet billowing under her. She pushed the hair from her face, the movement accentuating the firmness of her breasts which were naked like the rest of her well-made body.

'I really can't tell her this weekend, lovey. I mean, of all weekends it can't be this one, can it? I'm coping with a tricky town meeting, and whatever happens after. And that could be even trickier. You realize the whole deal could end up as a shambles? I mean, I'll have to be absolutely on top of things the whole time. And God knows how many visiting VIPs Julius is bringing. And there'll be the media. In droves. If Felicity threw a tantrum in the middle of all that—'

'She's not going to. Tantrums are not Felicity's style.'

'You don't know her like I do. She could do anything. Commit suicide, even.'

'No she couldn't.'

'She could, I'm telling you. Try to anyway. She might not go through with it, but it'd get out that she'd tried. She'd see to that.'

'Is this another way of saying you're never going to tell her? You've changed your mind? About the divorce? About marrying me?'

'Of course not, lovey. I adore you. I can't go on living without you. You know that. Just now was heaven. Pure heaven. It always is, pet. Telling Felicity's only a matter of timing. Honestly.'

Her eyes hardened at his last word because it was precisely his honesty that she was doubting. He had been doing up his tie as he spoke, stooping in front of her dressing-table mirror. While he had been making his protestations he had been looking at himself, not at her. She had noticed that and it grated. He might be in a hurry, but his words could have come with some endearing action to support them, or a glance at least in her direction. 'How much more time?' she asked.

He let out a sharp breath, mouth wide open, brow furrowed, indicating heavy thought. 'Well.' He paused briefly. 'Obviously between now and Christmas is going to be difficult.' This time he looked across at her and saw her face drop. 'Lovey, you know that as well as I do.'

'Because the boys will be home for the holidays, I suppose?'

'No. Because if the PM does decide on a government reshuffle at the start of the recess, and what he said on Tuesday as good as confirms he will, the last thing I want is negative publicity. My name on the front page of every newspaper between now and the end of the session.'

He did up the zip of his trousers with a firmness she found uncomfortably symbolic.

'Divorce hasn't hurt other members of the government,' she said, smoothing her hand across her remarkably flat stomach.

'It isn't just divorce. It's . . . it's the circumstances. You and me. The two of us.'

'Well, there couldn't very well be less than two of us,' she responded acidly.

'Sorry, I'm not putting it properly. God, you're lovely,' he uttered next with extreme fervour. He moved to the bed, sank down beside her and pulled her to him, kissing her on the lips, gently at first, then more ardently, caressing her with both hands.

'Who's going to know the circumstances?' she asked when his lips moved further down her body; her tone was less tart than before. 'We're not going to advertise you've been sleeping with me for over a year. Felicity's not going to sell her story to the newspapers.'

He looked up. 'They'll find out. The bastards always do. They'll invent what they don't know. All at the worst possible time. It'd kill my chance of promotion.' He released her gently but firmly, stood up, paused to stroke her cheek with his hand, then reached for his jacket, needing to get away. 'The PM's quite prudish, you know? And his wife. About people having affairs.'

'We're not just having an affair,' she protested.

'About divorce, then.'

'But the PM's not going to make you Chancellor of the

Exchequer or Foreign Secretary, for God's sake.' The irritation was back in her voice.

'But there's every chance he'll give me a junior ministry. You know that. You'd like that, wouldn't you?'

'Of course I'd like it. But not if it's a reason to keep us apart.' She slumped forwards on to her elbows, one hand going to knead the edge of the duvet. 'And that's all it is, isn't it? A reason. Whether anything happens or not? Be honest, like you say. Because there'll always be another reason when this one gives out. It'll be half term again, or the school holidays again, or something happening in the constituency again, or . . . or bloody Felicity's having a depression again.'

'No, it won't be. None of those things. Not any more. Not when the right time comes. Just leave it to me for a bit longer. I'll do it. I promise.' He was almost believing himself.

She got up suddenly, pulling on a short, half-sleeved silk gown. 'You've been promising since the summer,' she said, standing a step away from him, searching his eyes with hers, her arms folded in front of her, the strong bare legs set apart, their tops just covered by the hem of the gown. 'You've got to tell her soon, Charles. Really soon. I can't go on like this. Not any longer. I mean it. OK, tonight's no good. Nor tomorrow, if you say so. But why not Sunday? You could tell her then. No, listen.' She had moved quickly against him, letting the gown drop open, putting her hand over his mouth to stem his protest. 'Why don't I come up with you now? You could call her. Say we're still working at the House. That you'll need me in Thatchford this weekend. I can bring enough work to prove it too. You've done it before. Then on Sunday we could tell her together. In a civilized way.' She smoothed the lapels of his jacket. 'It'll help if I'm there. I promise. Better to talk it through all together.'

He shook his head gravely, taking her hands firmly in his, looking straight into her eyes—and steeling himself not

to give away how appalled he was at her crazy suggestions,
and their horrible consequences. 'It won't work, lovey. It'd
upset her if you came up tonight. I'd be on edge. I have to
tell her myself. Alone. In my own way. When the time
comes. If you were there . . .' He hesitated while thinking
up a fresh angle. 'Look, I thinks she suspects what's happening already. Or suspects something—'

'No she doesn't. God, we're so bloody careful, she
couldn't possibly suspect anything.'

'But you haven't been up at the weekend for months. Not
since I hired Janice. That's what Janice is supposed to be
for, after all. Weekend work. Felicity knows I've already
laid her on for this evening. For the meeting.' The delivery
had accelerated, the urgency in the tone had deepened,
matching his need to escape. 'And . . . and for tomorrow's
surgery, and anything else that comes up. I mean . . .
Janice is laid on.'

Philippa stepped away from him. 'What you mean is,
Janice is for laying in Thatchford, and I'm for laying in
London? Thank you for making it all so clear,' she finished
slowly, and then, without warning, slapped him hard across
the face.

CHAPTER 6

'My Mr H. could always go to Lord Delgard of course,
Major. Talking about that only yesterday, he was.'

'No, please . . . he doesn't need to do that. I'll find the
money. I promise. I . . . I just need a little more time, that's
all. You tell him that.' Claude Oliphant's hand struggled
below the desk to pull out his handkerchief from his trouser
pocket. Then he wiped his mouth, and, he hoped less obtru-
sively, blotted the beads of sweat at the side of his face. He
tried to stop his hand shaking as it moved—to prevent

Larkhole, on the other side of the desk, from knowing how
nervous he was. But that was a forlorn hope.

The two were alone in the room the divorced Oliphant
used as an office in the estate cottage he occupied rent free.
There was a bigger, official estate manager's office in the
stable wing at Vormer House half a mile away. Oliphant
used that for regular business with callers. But he wouldn't
have chosen to see this caller there, and the business they
were engaged in was anything but regular. Not that he had
been given any option about where or when to see Larkhole
who had presented himself on the doorstep ten minutes
before this: at the time, Oliphant had been about to change
for the meeting in Thatchford.

Larkhole was a Cockney—a seedy, pale-faced runt of a
man in a worn black overcoat. His greasy flat hair was
parted in the middle, divided like the pencil thin black
moustache that ran along the very edge of his upper lip.
He knew very well just how frightened he'd made his punter
so far, and how much more frightened he'd make him before
they parted. Applying the frighteners was the point of the
visit, that's if he couldn't actually collect the money owed,
and he'd figured at the start there wasn't much chance of
that. It was how Larkhole made his living, putting the fear
of God into people who owed his employer money. Larkhole
knew all about the fear of God. He'd been brought up strict
Calvinist.

'I'll tell Mr H. what you say, Major O., but will he
believe you?' Larkhole shook his head, squeezed his eyes
half closed and looked altogether deeply troubled. 'That's
what we got to ask ourselves, innit?' He sat further forward
in the upright chair, crossing his legs, and pulling the sides
of the coat together over his knees like a self-conscious vir-
gin applying to join a nunnery. 'I mean, that's why Mr H.
sent me to see you. Special journey,' he went on giving
a loud sniff and clearing his throat after it in a very
unpleasant way. 'To know if you was serious. You've been
telling Mr H. the tale for a good while now. And the inter-

est's been mounting. Well, you know that. I've given you them figures.'

Oliphant's eyes dropped to give the impression he was examining the short typed sheet Larkhole had brought. Except he was familiar enough with what was on it. All except the last entry which was an update on the interest since the previous weekend.

'I paid an instalment last month, you know? When I was in London. I came in myself with it. Only the office was shut. I put it through the door,' Oliphant insisted, the twitching in his left cheek now entirely out of control.

'I know that, Major O. And it was entered. In the ledger. But it wasn't enough, see? Not enough to cover the interest you was owing then. You'd have been told that if you'd seen Mr H.'s clerk. He rang you about it last week, didn't he? And I'd have been here before this myself. If I'd been up this way. It's why I had to come special today, like I said.' This wasn't true. There had been other calls to make in the area, other backsliders to chivvy or discipline: he'd be staying the next two nights in Nottingham. Oliphant was small fry and didn't rate a special trip. But he still needed bringing into line. And it had fitted well enough to call this evening, after Larkhole had done a collection job up the road in Warkborough. He wiped a watering eye with a not very clean finger. 'See, you've got to cover the interest, Major O. That was the agreement.'

'There was no agreement. Not in writing.'

Larkhole looked pained. There was only one answer when they tried that one. Slowly he said: 'Nor nothing to say Mr H. won't have both your legs broke, Major. It can happen all the same. And worse.'

Oliphant drew back, his left hand lifting to hold the side of his face. 'And that's a barefaced threat. It's ... it's deplorable. I'll report it. To the police.' But his colour had turned ashen.

The caller looked even more pained than before. 'No you won't, Major O. Mr H. figured the money you lost gambling wasn't yours. What you lost before you came to him, like. Mr H. is clever that way. It was Delgard estate money, wasn't it? That you had the disposing of?' Open-mouthed, the speaker drew a breath in sharply between his clenched teeth. 'Very dangerous thing to do, that was.' He shook his head from side to side. 'Means all kinds of trouble if you're found out.'

'It's not true.'

'In that case there's no problem. Mr H. can go to his lordship. Get him to bail you out of the mess you're in.'

'No, no. He mustn't do that. It could cost me my job. My future.'

Larkhole displayed a perplexity as profound as it was steely. 'But it'd get Mr H. his money, wouldn't it?' he said. 'You being a trusted employee with nothing to hide?'

Oliphant's hands went to finger his temple. 'I wouldn't want Lord Delgard involved,' he uttered lamely, knowing that this as good as confirmed that he'd stolen estate money—he could see that from the resolution in Larkhole's eyes. He cursed himself for saying more than he need have done when he had taken on the loan in the first place. 'Lord Delgard isn't . . . isn't that sort,' he added. 'He's hard. Going to him could ruin me and . . . and my chances with everything else.'

The caller moved back in the chair. 'Hard is he, Lord Delgard? Mr H. was wondering about that. I expect he'll take your word for it. Pity in a way.' The words were heavy, weighed down by grave consequences.

Oliphant's mouth opened and shut again without his actually saying anything. Then he leaned forward, dropping his arms heavily on to the desk, fingers grasping at nothing. 'I just need time, don't you understand? I've got a new job starting here any day.'

'You mean if they get the OK for the golf courses?'

'You know about that?'

'Mr H. keeps abreast of things, Major O.' The local newspaper had been full of the story.

'Well, I'm certain of a top job there. With the developers. With the golf club. I'll be able to pay off—'

'The interest, Major O.,' the other interrupted. 'That's all Mr H. is looking for. For the moment. It's the house rule, see? Never deviates from the rules, Mr H. doesn't. Well, you can see his point of view. Go easy with one client, word gets round, everybody wants you to go easy, and then where are you? Bankrupt. No use to anyone.' He made a pained face. 'So that's your only problem, as I see it. Get up to date on the interest by next Wednesday and you're laughing. Otherwise . . .' he paused to sigh. 'Well, I told you what can happen. Don't risk it, Major. And I'm speaking as a friend. Someone what's got your best interests at heart, believe me. Myself, I hate violence. Really Mr H. does too. But the people he uses for that?' He sucked air through his bared teeth again, even more abruptly this time, as if the thought was too painful even to entertain. 'Animals, Major O. That's the only way to describe that lot. Animals, they are. No warning there won't be, neither. Not when they come for you.'

Oliphant wiped his whole face with his handkerchief. 'But hurting me won't get you your money. It's senseless, for God's sake? Can't you see that?' The tone had become frenzied, not just desperate as before.

Larkhole's only response was a lift of the thin black eyebrows.

Oliphant swallowed. 'All right. I'll try. I'll do my best. I swear. I think I can do it. But by Friday, not Wednesday. Friday, please?'

Larkhole's face was now a study in contentment—in the joy of peace after a storm averted. 'That's more like it, Major O. More like the regimental spirit, eh?' He tapped the end of his nose with thumb and forefinger, leaving the finger in the air pointing at the Major. 'Tell you what. I'll speak to Mr H. for you. Ask him to stretch it the two extra days. Leave it to me. No promises, mind, but if I do this for you, you won't go letting me down? Not after, will you?'

He watched the wretched, grovelling Oliphant nod eagerly. 'Of course you won't,' Larkhole added, the indulgent smile deepening. 'I'll be off, then. No need seeing me out.' He got up briskly, knowing he'd succeeded—he'd lay anything on it. The interest would be paid by Friday. People like Oliphant always had a last resort—even if it was only another loan shark. But it took the threat of violence to make them act. They always accepted what he said about that. He should have been an actor—or better still a preacher, like his mother had wanted.

Oliphant waited for the front door to slam, then he broke down and sobbed, burying his face in his shaking hands. It had been too much. This on top of everything. The tension of the last two weeks. He was so ashamed of himself for running scared before that despicable creature—almost more than he was about landing himself in this mess in the first place. He simply hadn't realized he'd become a heavy gambler—not till the debts had grown from hundreds into thousands. And they had seemed to do that almost overnight. That had been in the previous year. The stupidity had been to borrow from the estate funds, then from an unscrupulous money-lender. But the bank had refused him any more help, just when the estate audit had been due. He had known the rates of interest were extortionate. But at the time it had been his only recourse. It meant nothing that he'd actually stopped gambling by then either. Taken a grip of himself, as he was trying to do again now.

He cupped his hands before his mouth. What he needed was a drink, but there wasn't any in the house. He began taking deep breaths instead.

He only had to hold things together for another week, he told himself. The Henfold people had as good as promised him the job, and they'd been absolutely definite about the consultancy fee—so long as the plan went through. There was nothing in writing, but there couldn't be, of course. But he'd done his bit, as he promised he would—used the influence he'd told them he had with Lord Delgard. He'd exaggerated the extent of that, but they'd believed him, enough at least to volunteer that fee. And after the meeting tonight he was sure Henfold would advance some of it, perhaps all of it. That would cover his debts. Wipe the slate. He was sure the meeting would be a success—not least because for him failure and its consequences didn't even rate thinking about.

Maybe Henfold would need to wait to pay him till the Council met on Wednesday, to have everything confirmed, but there'd still be time then.

The ringing of the telephone next to his elbow made him jump. He picked it up. 'Yes?' he asked breathily.

'Major Oliphant? *Gazette* here, sir,' said a brisk male voice. 'We've had a report we think you'd want to comment on. It seems . . .'

'Sure you won't change your mind, Bea? Come with us?' asked Lady Delgard regarding herself in a conveniently placed mirror. She dabbed at a recalcitrant lock of hair sprouting from under the fur hat she was wearing.

'Of course she's sure. She'd say so otherwise. Wouldn't you, Bea? Come if you want?' Lord Delgard nodded at his sister but without expecting answers. He turned to his wife. 'Are you ready, then? Sting's had the Bentley at the door for ages. We'll be late.' It was just after six-thirty.

'No, Tug, there's plenty of time. I still think you should ring and tell them we're coming.'

'Well, I don't,' he replied impatiently. 'Come on, it's going to rain any minute. Sting drives very slowly these days. Especially if the weather's bad. He's getting on.'

'Like the rest of us. And that includes the Bentley,' completed the Hon. Bea from where she was standing in the north entrance hall of Vormer House. She was there seeing the others off. 'I'm sure you're doing the right thing, Tug.'

'Then I think you should come with us and hear him do it,' said Lady Delgard.

Her husband gave a dismissive grunt and did up the top

button of his British warm. 'Sit, Gunner,' he ordered the dog, which promptly sank back on to its rear, making a noise like a heavy sandbag being dropped.

'No. There are times when you can fix a third wheel to a chariot, but tonight isn't one of them,' Bea stated firmly, both hands thrust into the pockets of her unbuttoned cardigan, spoiling its shape, the newspaper stuck under one arm. 'You don't want me wrecking the show.'

'Show? Don't know what you think's going to happen,' remarked her brother, pulling on his gloves. 'It's a meeting for local people to express their opinion, that's all,' he completed the disclaimer.

'And after all the cogitating there's been, I just hope they express the right one,' said Lady Delgard.

'With what Tug's doing for the community, they should fête you both. That's if they've got any sense. So off with you. And have a good time at Stigham Manor afterwards.'

A moment later Bea watched them go down the steps arm in arm. Daniel Sting was holding the back door of the car open ready for them. He had his chauffeur's peaked cap on and saluted Mary Delgard before helping her in.

It was just like old times, Bea thought. She was disappointed not to be going too. It was not any lack of a sense of occasion that had stopped her, far from it—only a stronger sense of propriety, a feeling that it wasn't her place to be there.

They were good to her, those two. Gave her a home, and the tacit assurance that she was loved and wanted which was even more important. Not that any of the three went in for mawkish demonstrations of sentiment. Mary showed tender feelings from time to time—quite frequently, come to think of it—but not in a soppy way. There was no need to make others uncomfortable to prove you cared for them: even when you cared for them quite a lot. An involuntary shrug of Bea's shoulders manifested just how much genuine heartfeeling was bedded in that last thought.

She closed the front door and made her way through the

wide, panelled corridor, and round the corner, along to the small parlour. There was some cold supper arranged on a tray there for later, for when she planned to be watching a tape on the television set. Gunner knew about the tray and was plodding earnestly in her wake.

Bea put another log on the fire, and lit one of her Capstan Full Strengths while she watched the wood catch. Then she settled into her favourite place on the end of the big sofa. Although she took the newspaper in her hands, she let it lie on her lap, her eyes fixed thoughtfully above its edge, staring at nothing in particular.

Alice Sting had gone to her married daughter's in Vormer village just after tea. Bea wondered if they'd be going to the meeting in Thatchford too. She hoped so. She was sure that there would be strong support for the golf course plan, and afterwards a moving response to Tug's generosity. And if there were scenes of universal gratitude and affection, Tug and Mary deserved to have the stage to themselves without an aged relative hanging about spoiling the effect.

It was hard to imagine when there could be another opportunity for a public tribute to Tug. At his funeral, probably, except he'd only be able to enjoy that in spirit. She picked up what was left of the malt whisky Tug had poured for her, and finished it. He had poured one for himself too, when they had been waiting for Mary to come down.

Their father had been a malt whisky drinker. Bea's very first and indelible memory had been of Papa in the Victory Parade in 1919, marching through Thatchford at the head of a company of the county regiment. She and Tug had sat with Mama at the back of the saluting base. Both children had been dressed in sailor suits. The flag-draped base had been set up in the square, where the war memorial was now. And Grandfather, the 9th Viscount, had taken the salute as Colonel of the Regiment. Mama had declared proudly that all the soldiers in Papa's company had been workers from the Vormer estate.

Of course, aristocracy meant something in those days, and for quite a long time after those days in this part of the country, despite what people said. The tenant farmers, the farmworkers, the servants in the house and on the estate, they all had a proper respect for the owners of Vormer. People said there had been too much curtsying and pulling of forelocks then, but Bea seriously disputed it. What those same people forgot, in some cases conveniently forgot, was the stern sense of obligation that the family had always felt towards its workers and dependants. State aid was no substitute for *noblesse oblige*. It wasn't the State that was now making a present of Vormer to the people. On the contrary, it was the State that would otherwise effectively be confiscating it through taxes and death duties, and more than likely leaving it to fall down afterwards.

If Tug had featured less as the local figurehead than previous viscounts, at least he should now be remembered better than any of them for his generosity. Giving away everything simply had to be the greatest single benevolent gesture the family had ever made. There was nothing that could possibly stop it. And it more than made up for the errors Tug might have made in running the estate and the family industrial enterprises. Bea's shoulders gave another involuntary twitch. In any case, he had been a soldier, with no love for vulgar commerce—and a damned brave and honest soldier he had been too.

Bea just wished she could make everyone appreciate that Tug could have made life a lot easier for himself and Mary, in their declining years. He could so easily have let things stay exactly as they were and made no provision for posterity . . .

The urgent ringing of the telephone on the other side of the room abruptly broke into Bea's thoughts. She stabbed out the cigarette, got up from the sofa, and, still clutching the newspaper, walked over to the instrument. Gunner,

who had been half asleep, used both front paws strenuously
to push himself into a sitting position while he watched her
movements.

'Thatchford 8263,' she said into the instrument.

'Ah, good evening. *Gazette* here. Can I speak to Lord
Delgard, please?' the caller inquired.

'No, I fear you may not,' Bea replied pedantically, wishing people would pay more attention to their grammar.
'He's out.'

'Is that Lady Delgard by any chance?'

'No, it isn't. It's Lord Delgard's sister.'

'Ah, perhaps you could help us. We've had a report . . .'

CHAPTER 7

The Thatchford Community Centre is a weather-streaked,
concrete monolith erected in the 1960s—a stark witness to
that worst of all periods of British architecture. Its principal
auditorium is large and bare, but equipped with internal
movable walls, making it divisible, as required, into inde-
pendent sections—less large but just as bare.

Friday is the regular night for four of the most popular
of the organized activities followed at the Centre. In conse-
quence, having the undivided auditorium taken over for a
public meeting at seven o'clock on that particular evening
of the week was considered by some as highly unreason-
able—specifically by members of the karate club, the glee
society, the furniture renovation class, and the dog-training
group.

Even though there had been a week's notice of the usurp-
ing event, and other arrangements had been made to house
three of the disaccommodated groups (in church halls,
members protested, at inconvenient locations), Council
officials had suffered a good deal of whingeing from angry

community tax payers thus provided with a new and valid cause for community outrage.

The wrath of the complainers would have deepened if they had known in advance that far from filling the auditorium, attendance at the meeting was destined to be hardly better than that at the normal Wednesday afternoon Darby and Joan Club bingo sessions. Nor was the audience composition much different from the other one—the only marked dissimilarity being in the presence of a number of bewildered dog-owners with their equally bewildered pets. Although changed venues had been fixed for the karate, glee, and furniture renovating enthusiasts, nothing had been done about the dog-training group which met fortnightly, those in authority mistakenly assuming that the next session was not until the following Friday. It was these uninformed animal lovers who, arriving after the public meeting had started, settled in the back row to wait, in the wildly optimistic hope that their class, normally scheduled for seven-thirty, would follow whatever it was that was happening already.

If the body of the hall was underpopulated, the diminutive platform had the opposite appearance. In the absence of the Mayor, who had succumbed to shingles earlier in the week, it had naturally fallen to Arthur Motwell, as Chairman of the Planning Committee, to take charge of the meeting—naturally, that is, in the judgement of Arthur Motwell. A formal challenge from the Labour Party about his assumption had been made and just as formally rejected at the previous night's Council meeting: the Liberal Democrats had abstained from voting, and with the Mayor away—he was a Labour Councillor—the Tories had a bare majority.

There had been no dissension about who should sit on the platform with Motwell. Julius Kuril and Mark Treasure were to represent the promoters of the Vormer House golf club plan, present in full view for challenging by all who opposed it. Harold Jepton, the Chief Executive of the Council, was to answer for the local government secretariat, and as MP for the borough, Charles Finton was necessarily included, although he arrived only seconds before the meeting started.

Unfortunately, this official group of five was equipped with chairs, a table, and a single microphone intended to accommodate only three, set up on the Centre's smallest portable dais. All this had been provided on a wrong briefing to the maintenance staff, a fact discovered when it was too late to lay on a larger platform and an extra microphone: the maintenance staff went home at five and the caretaker didn't possess a key to the relative storeroom. The error was compounded when Lord Delgard made his unexpected appearance, having earlier refused an invitation to be present. On arrival, he had mounted the platform and taken a seat at the table ahead of anyone else. Extra chairs had later been provided without difficulty, but this didn't prevent the group looking like six well-turned-out survivors clinging to a half-submerged raft.

That there were less than a hundred and fifty people in the audience was not in the main due to the heavy rain now falling outside, nor even to simple apathy. Nottingham Forest, the First Division football team most supported in Thatchford, was engaged that evening in a televised second replay match against League rivals Sheffield United. This event had radically reduced attendance at the Community Centre, and, like the rain, it had culled more Labour voters than it had Conservatives. Added to this, there was a marked absence of adherents to what had earlier been dubbed 'the green alliance opposed to the plan', since most 'greens' had now decided tacitly to support it—which meant simply that they wouldn't be turning up to oppose it.

The proceedings had been opened with a bland and unnecessary explanation by Arthur Motwell about its purpose, followed by his lengthy and complimentary introductions to the others on the platform. The Yorkshireman had then pushed the microphone past Kuril and Treasure towards Harold Jepton, knocking it over in the process.

Jepton, a thin, sandy-haired man with large ears, sunken eyes and a heavy cold, had followed with a tedious description of the golf course plan, also superfluous since he had largely repeated what Motwell had said already.

By this point even the dog-owners at the back were over-informed as to the purpose of the gathering.

Jepton was seated as close to the end of the platform as it was possible for him to be without his chair falling off the edge, a fact that severely restricted his movements, and made even taking out his handkerchief a fairly perilous activity. His words had been orchestrated by occasional piercing whines from the microphone—a result of its having been moved or damaged, or both—and punctuated by occasional affirming nods from some of the speaker's platform companions, though not from Lord Delgard. So far his lordship had sat rigidly upright in his chair, squashed between the chairman to his right, and Finton on his other side. His arms were folded tightly in front of him, while he examined the audience with a one-eyed, malevolent scowl.

Ordinary attendants at the meeting had tended to scatter themselves in the back half of the hall in ones or twos, though mostly ones, like stars in early twilight. A heavily built middle-aged man, with tanned skin and dressed in a city suit, was the sole and conspicuous occupant of a seat in the front row to the right of the centre aisle. Behind him, George Pike from the *Advertiser* and the paper's photographer were the only media representatives present, sitting with the four LDP Councillors, present en masse out of respect for Barry Winkler who had instigated the meeting. Councillor Mrs Madelaine Task and five male companions, all Labour Councillors, were in the same row, on the other side of the aisle, with several members of the town's Chamber of Commerce with their wives two rows behind them.

The only significantly large group—of about twenty people—was concentrated in rows six and seven. Treasure had lightly dubbed this the carriage trade. His wife was near its centre, flanked by Lady Delgard in her ancient mink coat and hat, occupying an aisle seat. Sheila Kuril and Felicity Finton, who arrived late, were on Molly's other side. Jeremy Bender, who Treasure had been introduced to with others before the meeting started, was behind Molly, keeping a place, he said, for Claude Oliphant who hadn't yet appeared.

When Motwell had at last invited comments from the audience, it was Mrs Task who almost predictably put the first question.

'Does the Chairman of Henfold Developments deny there's a secret agreement between his company and Tory members of the Planning Committee?' she demanded after getting to her feet. She was swathed dramatically in a red wool serape.

'I certainly deny we have secret agreements with Tory Councillors or anyone else,' Kuril answered without emotion, leaning forward between Motwell and Treasure. He had switched off the temperamental microphone before speaking, but his assumption that his voice would carry without amplification had been a mistaken one: his words produced calls of 'speak up' and 'can't hear' from the rear of the hall.

'Why don't folk at back move forward? There's plenty of room,' boomed Motwell searching for the switch on the microphone.

Needless to say, nobody moved.

'You mean you haven't agreed that once consent is given for the golf, you're going for permission to build two hundred big houses along the courses?' Mrs Task demanded further, sorting through the papers in her hand. 'And that Councillors have been promised free shares in the golf club company as payment for getting you these consents?' she completed, her best open-air meeting voice requiring no extra amplification.

'I've agreed no such—'

The rest of Kuril's reply was drowned by a prolonged and devastating squeal from a microphone suddenly reactivated by Motwell. Almost everyone clapped hands to ears till the piercing noise abated—except it was replaced by the furious barking of a dozen terrified dogs who had been brought for training, not aural harassment.

It was some time before things returned to normal, with the dogs calmed or led out, and the microphone tamed by an electrical engineer from the audience. The man had volunteered his services, which were effective but also tediously protracted, his machinations on the platform effectively stopping anything else happening.

When Kuril had at last been able to refute Mrs Task's double accusation, she promptly turned her fire on an unprepared Charles Finton.

'So will our Tory Member of Parliament explain what his secretary has told a London newspaper this evening?' she asked, shuffling the papers again. 'She's said there are secret agreements, and that if the Council is daft enough to approve the golf plan, she'll produce letters to prove the agreements exist.'

This intelligence generated a distinct stir in all parts of the room.

'That's a preposterous allegation, and I don't believe a word of it,' said Finton, but suddenly very red in the face.

'If there were agreements, even secret ones, I'd know about them. I'd have to, wouldn't I?' added Kuril, which seemed plausible but not entirely conclusive as a denial. His manner had remained that of a disinterested if slightly amused observer.

The normally self-possessed Motwell seemed momentarily lost for words.

Lord Delgard's look of ill-will aimed at the audience in

general altered to one of pained distaste directed at Mrs
Task in particular.

Jepton blew his nose—with difficulty.

'Could we have the name of the newspaper, please?'
asked Treasure, surprised at Motwell's failure to put the
same question—or any question.

'I'm not divulging that. I have to protect my sources,'
Mrs Task replied darkly, as if suggesting that exposure
could well bring Tory hit gangs into action against her
informant. 'And I'm still waiting for Mr Finton's denial, if
he dares make one.'

'Of course I deny that any secretary of mine could have
letters proving there are secret agreements. There aren't
any such agreements. Mr Kuril's just said so. So how could
there be letters about them?' said Finton, a touch more
convincing than before. 'Clearly the accusations we've just
heard are inventions, politically motivated. Clearly they
are.'

Treasure winced inwardly at the word clearly which
when used by a politician he had long since come to believe
meant dimly, or debatably, or even doubtfully. Finton had
used it twice.

A brief whispered exchange had meantime been going on
between Motwell and Kuril. Motwell now leaned behind
the still stonily silent Delgard to speak to Finton on his
other side. Then Motwell quickly pulled the microphone
towards him. 'Ladies and gentlemen,' he began, his
avuncular manner back in place, his tone confident and
businesslike. 'You've heard the denials from the platform.
Right firm denials they were, and all. As Conservative Party
leader on the Council I can also deny that there are any
secret agreements between us and Henfold Developments.
Categorically so. What Madelaine Task is alleging is a load
of tripe, and I believe she knows it.'

Mrs Task leaped to her feet. 'I insist—'

'In a moment, Mrs Task,' Motwell interrupted, drown-
ing her words with his, nodding tolerantly enough at her,

but indicating with a firm hand that she sit down again. 'You see, ladies and gentlemen, there are no letters. And if there was a call to some newspaper, it was a put-up job. I mean it wasn't a call from any secretary of Charles Finton's.'

The speaker glanced to left and right, nodding at Kuril and Finton who each nodded back as he went on, 'Well, as you saw just now, I've had a word with the two gentlemen whose good characters have been indirectly impugned by these accusations and . . . and these daft hearsay reports. They've magnanimously agreed to overlook Councillor Mrs Task's preposterous and unsupportable statements. That's if she withdraws them straight off. If she doesn't, we'll need to close the meeting. For legal reasons.' He made a brief, ominous pause. 'Perhaps a delaying tactic may be what Mrs Task was after. Perhaps she wants to hold up the good folk of this town from voicing their democratic view on an important issue. That could well be the case after she calculated that most in the audience tonight are in favour of the plan. I'm not saying that tabling information she thought was true wasn't a fair political ploy. But now Mrs Task knows her facts were wrong, like as not she'll want to withdraw what she said. Especially as she'll have actions for damages pending against her if she doesn't.'

All members of the platform party had their eyes fixed on Mrs Task at the end of Motwell's homily. Although she had earlier resumed her seat with reluctance, she hadn't risen again immediately he finished speaking. This was because she had been drawn into an animated consultation with her companions. It was at this point that the big, weatherbeaten man seated in the front row stood up. While he looked to be in his fifties, he had moved with the alacrity of a somewhat younger man.

'Mr Chairman, while Mrs Task is making up her mind, could I say a word, please? It'll be a brief one, I promise you, and relevant to the proceedings.' He smoothed the thick greying hair at the back of his head with one hand, while his lowered eyes searched the floor as if for inspiration. 'I'm Australian, as you've probably detected from the accent, and Australians tend to be doers, not talkers.' He looked up to beam at the platform party, then turned to do the same at the audience. 'The name is Edmund Legion, Ted to my friends. They tell me I'm next in line to inherit the Delgard title.' He gave a little bow towards Lord Delgard who, to make a change, was regarding him with neither indifference nor distaste but rather with curiosity. 'Well, let's all hope it'll be a long time before I do inherit the title. His present lordship and I have yet to be introduced, but I wish him a long life. I've been in this country a few weeks but I haven't made myself known to many people before tonight. Been doing some necessary fact-finding, as you might say. And to some purpose.'

There was a serious expression on his bronzed face as the speaker went on. 'A while back in Sydney, I made a statement to a newspaper. A damn fool statement that I now regret. Especially I regret it got picked up by some of the papers here in England. I said then I didn't care about the title, or what happened to Vormer House. That I'd be happy to see the park turned into a housing estate. Well, that was all a load of nonsense. Now that I've seen the place, I'm just as keen as Lord Delgard to have it kept the way it is for all time. That's why I support its being given to this charitable trust. It's the perfect solution. And if and when my turn comes, I'll try to be as worthy a holder of the title as the present generous and public-spirited incumbent, even though by then there'll be no house to go with the honour.' His gaze had gone to studying the area around his feet again. 'That's all I have to say, Mr Chairman.' Then he looked up again quickly. 'Oh, except a point about any part of the Delgard estate that's entailed, legally entailed, that is. I mean anything that says I might be entitled to inherit property along with the title. If there is anything like that, I'm formally and publicly disavowing the benefit, actual or potential. And I'll he happy to confirm that in writing to anyone who wants me to. Thank you.' He sat down solemnly.

'Thank you, Mr Legion,' said Motwell. 'I'm sure all of us here will be pleased to hear what you said. Especially those of us in favour of the plan before us. Very gratifying. And public-spirited.' He glanced at Mrs Task who was in renewed, animated conversation with her worried-looking colleagues. 'Perhaps Lord Delgard would like to comment?' he completed, hoping both to build on success and to give more time for the impetuous Mrs Task to be counselled on the seriousness of her situation.

Lord Delgard's florid face brightened for the first time. Moving his chair backwards, he stood up, at the same time waving aside the microphone that Motwell was tentatively pushing towards him. 'Thank you, Chairman,' he began, thrusting his hands behind him. The head was steady, the chest well forward, the feet anchored apart in the character-istic at ease position. The stance altogether advertised a military background—as well as the cut of the double-breasted, grey flannel suit he had on which had been expensively tailored, if not very recently.

No one else in the platform party had so far stood up before speaking. Delgard doing so had obliged the others around him to give him more space in an already cramped area, but his stance still seemed appropriate, even expected by people in the audience, many of whom sat up straighter involuntarily through his example.

'Ladies and gentlemen,' he went on. 'I've come here this evening to speak my piece. And that's all. It seems now'll be a good time to do it.'

The words were clipped, the voice powerful, the tone assured. General the Lord Delgard was no less used than Mrs Task to making words carry without artificial aids—in his case across parade grounds, several hunting fields and countless battlefields. 'The last speaker confessed to chang-ing his mind about the future of Vormer,' he went on, then gave a sniff. 'I've always been of one mind on the subject.

Only had to decide how that future could be achieved. Best achieved. The house and contents preserved, I mean. Wouldn't matter to most people what happens to their houses. Not after they've gone. Why should it?' His eye came to rest on Mrs Task, who glared back at him. 'Only bricks and mortar, after all. Or stone and mortar in the present case,' he corrected, thrusting his hands into the side pockets of his jacket. 'Stored up riches on earth are no use to a man when he's dead, of course. Bible's right about that.' He added a paranthetic and seemingly grudging endorsement to Holy Scripture. 'But I've never regarded Vormer House as mine. It's been in my family for centuries. Part of the landscape here. The heritage. I'm just the present tenant. We've tried to look after it. To date. Even improve it. Previous houses on the site went back to the Conquest. Like the family. Not fashionable to speak of that kind of thing any more. Of course, all your families go back a long way too. Stands to reason.' He looked momentarily disarmed by his own profundity, then countered it with: 'But in our case we've had to keep careful records. That's the difference, probably.' He nodded in extra affirmation. 'Our name comes from the words *de la garde*. That's French. Means of the guard. Another way of saying we defend things. Yes.' He paused and nodded again.

'Belt up or get on with it, grandad,' called an impatient, uncultivated male voice from the back.

'Belt up yourself,' countered an equally uncultivated, female voice from nearer the front. 'Listen and you might learn something.'

The last robust instruction was followed by calls of 'hear, hear', and an outburst of clapping from various parts of the room.

Lord Delgard had missed the verbal exchange but was gratified if slightly bewildered at the applause.

'Afraid I'm not finished yet,' he continued, misinterpreting the reason for the clapping. 'Not quite.' He cleared his throat, then smoothed both ends of his moustache.

'There'd be little chance of anyone inheriting Vormer being able to keep it up by himself. Death duties would see to that. And there'd be no chance at all for the generation after that. That's why giving everything to the Tudor Heritage Trust is the right thing to do. And to do now.' He watched his wife smile and nod her approval. 'But we can't do it without endowing the Trust. They need money to keep the place up in the future. That's fair. We can get the money by selling a piece of the park. To build golf courses and a hotel. It's a wrench. Far bigger wrench for my wife and me than for anyone else. But there it is. Case of the end justifying the means. Golf courses won't destroy the landscape. The opposite with any luck. Wasn't so sure about the hotel. Had a long argy-bargy about that. They can't do it without, you see? What they now intend to build looks acceptable. We'll just have to see they keep to the plan.'

He stopped to contemplate for a moment. No one broke the ensuing silence.

'The alternative to all this is to sell pictures and furniture now, so there'll be money to pay the taxes later,' he went on, the tone dubious. 'That'll leave an empty house, and nothing for death duties after the next tenant dies. No assurance of anything that way. Not on, is it? Not in my view.' He was staring at Mrs Task. 'But if there's no consent for the golf, I suppose that's what we'll have to do. Pity. Won't please visitors. More to the point, seems to me it'll deprive local people of a share in a local amenity.' He paused and searched the whole room with his single eye before ending: 'Well, you and the Council will have to make your minds up. I wish you luck. My wife and I will be leaving now. Leave you to it. That's best. Thank you, God bless you, and good night to you all.'

Without resuming his seat, Lord Delgard carefully stepped down from the rear of the platform and limped, straight-backed, in the direction of the front row. His wife had already left her seat and joined him there. The clapping had started as soon as he had stopped speaking. As the couple left the auditorium arm in arm, almost the whole audience was standing, following the example of the platform party. Shouts of 'bravo' and 'well done', were raised over the sound of the applause.

As Molly Treasure was later to remark, 'There was hardly a dry eye in the house.'

CHAPTER 8

'Molly, your glass is empty. April, give Mrs Treasure some champagne. No, on second thoughts, just give me the bottle, then go see if that hot food's ready yet,' Sheila Kuril commanded in a sharp, penetrating New Jersey accent.

April, large, matronly, and with a hardly obliging expression, wordlessly surrendered the napkin-wrapped bottle of Dom Perignon from which she had been dispensing with less than practised accuracy. She then made off with bent shoulders towards a door close to the bottom of the elaborately carved wooden staircase.

The servant's raven-haired, pencil-slim employer gave an exasperated sigh. 'She's one of my dailies brought in for the evening,' she said. 'We have a live-in couple, but hiring temporary staff around here for a weekend party gets more of a problem by the month. Especially at short notice. I swear to God it's easier in America.'

'But pricier, of course?' said Molly, tipping her glass to make the pouring easier.

Her hostess shrugged her delicate shoulders, bare except for the two thin straps supporting the sleeveless, V-necked black velvet dress. 'My mother can always get off-duty servants from her country club in Chatham, that's where she lives. They may be expensive, but they sure as hell know about serving food and wine.'

The galleried main hall of Stigham Manor was large,

square, and rose through two storeys. Logs were burning fiercely in the open marble fireplace. There was an ornate coat-of-arms carved into the overmantel—though this had no genuine armorial connection with the present owners of the house, nor with anyone else who had ever owned it either. Good German tapestries on the walls, chessboard Dutch tiling on the floor, heavy chandeliers, and a massive, uneven Tudor refectory table set in the centre served eclectically to promote a venerable sort of ambiance. In truth, the dressed stone building had been put up in 1864 by a successful local manufacturer of patent medicines. The place had latterly fallen into decay before it was rescued by Julius Kuril and then 'done over' by his wife six years before this. The hall made an impressive setting for a party. Nor was it so crowded now as to make conversation difficult—only Sheila Kuril tended to talk at a pitch more suited to the kind of public meeting she and the others had just attended.

'Let me take charge of that bottle for you, Mrs Kuril,' offered Arthur Motwell on joining the two ladies. 'It's a grand party,' he continued looking about him expansively as if it was his party. 'And it was a grand meeting, if I say so myself that shouldn't. We fairly saw off the Roundheads, didn't you think? It was a rout, was that. Mostly thanks to Lord Delgard, of course.'

The more influential supporters of the golf course project had been invited back to Stigham Manor for drinks and a buffet. Because they had left the meeting early, Lord and Lady Delgard had arrived at the manor predictably ahead of everyone else, including the host and hostess. This hadn't bothered them at all: April had invited Lord Delgard to help himself from the bottle of malt whisky on the bar, and Lady Delgard had used the opportunity to study the tapestries unhindered. The couple were now talking to Mark Treasure and Ted Legion close to where Molly was standing. A remarkable, elegantly dressed brunette in her early forties with dark alert eyes, a slim, imperious nose, and hair pulled back dramatically to an oval bun had just come down the staircase and joined the Delgard group. The actress watched her husband greet the woman with some warmth and correctly guessed that this was the famous Maggie Halliwell.

'I think you controlled the whole affair with great aplomb, Mr Motwell,' said Molly. 'Especially the skirmishes with Mrs Task. At the start, I expected a lot more trouble from the floor. Tribute to your experience in public life, I expect.'

'Happen folk were on their best behaviour with a celebrity like yourself present, Mrs Treasure.' Motwell returned the compliment, one hand resting his glass above the fourth button of his tight-fitting ample waistcoat. His other hand was holding up the champagne bottle as if it were a prize he had just won.

'You and your husband were a wholly civilizing influence, Mrs Treasure,' Charles Finton volunteered, fixing Molly with his disarming, honest smile. He had come across from near the fireplace at that moment, his wife at his side.

'Oh, absolutely, Molly,' Felicity Finton agreed with feeling. Abruptly she leaned her trunk sideways towards her husband, then away again in the opposite direction, feet well anchored throughout, the whole movement resembling the heave-ho section in a sailor's hornpipe.

Tall and plumpish, with pink cheeks, lank hair, and prominent front teeth, Felicity Finton was given to exaggerated body actions—angular ones, completed with gusto and much neck-stretching as though she were attempting to see over or round the heads of people in front of her, even when there wasn't anyone in front of her.

'Mrs Task wasn't inhibited by anyone's presence at the start,' Molly commented flatly.

'Absolutely,' said the energetic Mrs Finton again, arching her back and inadvertently accentuating the already pronounced thrust of bosoms beneath the red wool dress.

'Isn't that the truth?' Mrs Kuril agreed hotly, her eyes

on her husband. He was engaged some distance away sharing a joke with a flaxen-haired young woman in, or more accurately, mostly out of a dress with a very short, tight skirt.

'Then you should hear the way Madelaine Task goes on at Council meetings,' said Motwell, pouring himself more champagne. 'She was on her best behaviour tonight, all right. More so after she'd been put down the first time.'

'Were you surprised when she withdrew what she'd said?' asked Molly. 'I mean, even after your spirited denial and your legal threat. There must be grounds of some kind for what the newspaper told her?'

'None at all, Mrs Treasure. It was a hoax all right. Pulled on the *Daily Gazette*,' Motwell responded with confidence. 'Yes, we've found out the name of the paper. As like as not they were simply trying to get corroboration for the story when they called Madelaine Task. Of course she figured it made a grand opportunity to try something on. To put doubts in people's minds. I mean, can you credit secret agreements? What a load of codswallop. Discontented secretaries? Same thing.' He swallowed some champagne, afterwards smacking his lips appreciatively. 'Yes, George Pike from the local *Advertiser*, good friend of mine, he was at the meeting. Did some fast checking for us straight away. As for Mrs Task protecting her sources, George thinks the *Gazette* will certainly have rung other people.'

'Which others?' asked Molly.

'We don't know yet. It's odd they didn't get on to Charles or Julius. Odd or significant. They'd be the best people to give them the information they needed, of course.' Motwell filled his glass again, then emptied what little there was left in the bottle into Finton's empty glass. 'Any road, you've no doubts about the loyalty of your secretary have you, Charles?' he asked, while giving the upturned bottle a final purposeless shake.

'None at all,' Finton replied with almost too much spirit. Sheila Kuril cleared her throat. 'If you ask me, I'd say the Task woman could have cooked up the whole thing on her own.'

'Including the hoax call?' questioned Molly.

'It's possible,' said Finton speculatively, in a lowered voice, and looking about him as if fearing he might be accused of condoning slander. 'In any case, as Arthur here said, it was a piece of barefaced political opportunism,' he ended on a safer premise.

'But not damaging enough for you to feel you ought to sue Mrs Task anyway?' Molly pressed. 'I wondered about that. I mean, it was pretty irresponsible of her. In view of your position in the government. And magnanimous of you to let her off the hook.' She smiled. 'Or did you make up your mind too quickly?'

Finton looked wise and indulgent. 'One wouldn't have been so magnanimous if she'd persisted. If she hadn't withdrawn. But the alternative is messy. Injunctions. Court hearings. It's usually best to kill that kind of thing on the spot if you can.'

'Because if you go for legal action, before it comes to a court, there'll be plenty of gossips who'll say there's no smoke without fire,' said Mrs Kuril. 'They even say it after you've gotten the damages. You did the right thing, Charles. All of you. I know Julius thinks so. But you were the most vulnerable.' She was watching her husband again with what could have been taken for a benign and approving gaze. He was still with the young blonde. 'Excuse me. I don't know what's happening to the food.' She moved away in the direction of the kitchen—which surprised Molly, who more than half expected her to join Kuril first.

'My husband thinks you were right, too,' Molly said next, turning to Finton. 'Anyway, after Mr Legion and Lord Delgard had spoken, Mrs Task's sideshow seemed irrelevant.'

'Absolutely, Molly,' said Felicity Finton, who seemed never to say anything else.

'It was the better part of valour for her to withdraw

completely at that stage, of course,' said Motwell. 'His lordship and Ted Legion had the whole room on our side. Then
when Barry Winkler got up to endorse their sentiments, she
knew the case was hopeless.'

'He was the nice elderly man? Deputy leader of the Liberal Democrats?' asked Molly.

'That's right. With their support spoken for, the golf
course scheme will go through on the nod at the Planning
Committee next Wednesday. Has to.'

'So you didn't really need the man from the Chamber of
Commerce to say his piece as well?'

'No, but it all helped, didn't you think? Confirmed to the
opposition they were on a loser. Certainly not worth an
expensive pasting in the law courts as well as certain defeat
in Council. The town's solid behind us. The vote at the end
showed that all right. It'll lose Labour a lot of support,
will this. At the next election.' Motwell was looking as
immoderately pleased as he was sounding. The show of
hands vote he had called for at the end of the meeting had
been overwhelmingly in favour of the Henfold plan.

'Mrs Task's retraction was a bit short, of course,' Molly
mused.

'But complete, even so. Stuck in her gullet to have to say
it. No mistake about that,' replied Motwell.

'And you've been in touch with your secretary?' Molly
asked the MP.

'With Philippa Boyden-Pent? Yes. I just called her in
London. She absolutely couldn't credit what Mrs Task had
said. Can't understand why I'm not suing the wretched
woman.' Despite the easy delivery of this very incomplete
and inaccurate report, the speaker was wincing inwardly at
his true memory of the exchange. 'She's eh . . . she's coming
up here tonight. Staying the rest of the weekend.'

'Is she?' said his wife in a surprised voice.

'Yes, darling. Sorry, thought I'd mentioned it. There's a
lot on at the moment. One way and another. Philippa very
kindly volunteered to help out.'

'Didn't someone tell me you have a local secretary as well?' said Molly. 'I suppose it couldn't be that it was she—?'

'Oh, she's only part-time,' Finton interrupted dismissively. 'She's useful to have as an extra hand here at election time, that's all, really.'

'And Charles is letting her go soon, anyway. Aren't you Charles?' Felicity Finton had found a subject at last on which to expound on her own account.

Finton coughed. 'Probably.'

'She has far too much other work to do,' Mrs Finton went on. 'For instance, she should have been at the meeting tonight. Never showed up, though. Charles rang her before and after the meeting. Engaged first time. Didn't answer the second.'

'That's why Philippa's coming up,' the MP put in quickly, pleased with himself for thinking of something that certainly supported the earlier, vaguer reasons.

'Trouble is, the local woman runs a typing agency in Thatchford,' Felicity Finton provided in a deprecating tone.

'Not to mention she's Madelaine Task's younger sister,' Motwell expanded. 'Except in fairness the two don't see eye to eye over politics or anything else. Frankly, I'm surprised you're dropping Janice Weggly, Charles. Good little worker, we've always found. Claude Oliphant says the same. We both use the agency for overspill work. Very obliging, the whole staff. One of the ladies will always fit in a rush job. Come to think of it, it was you recommended Janice to me in the first place.'

It was at this point that Treasure and the two people with him joined the group. 'Molly, I gather you haven't met Maggie Halliwell or Ted Legion yet?' he said, taking advantage of the lull in the conversation created by Finton's failure to respond to Motwell's comments.

'I caught sight of you briefly at the meeting,' said Molly to Mrs Halliwell as they shook hands. 'You weren't there at the start?'

'And I was in and out several times later, I'm afraid. Things to see to,' the other replied in a pleasing Scottish accent. 'I sat at the back for a while too. With those dogs,' she completed with a grin.

'As the legendary power behind Henfold you're expected to be busy,' Molly said, noting that the woman's darting eyes were the same deep brown as the expensive silk jersey suit she was wearing.

'Not as powerful tonight as Mr Motwell's local reporter friend, I'm afraid. He got to the source of the problem before we did.'

'Even so, Julius says you're quite indispensable to the organization,' Molly insisted. As she was speaking, she noticed Kuril leave the girl and head in the direction of the front door, probably to greet a late arrival.

'Do I have permission to quote that? When my contract's next up for renewal?' Maggie Halliwell smiled. 'Felicity, we haven't said hello yet tonight.' She moved across to embrace Mrs Finton.

'How do you do, Mr Legion,' said Molly turning to the big Australian.

'Great honour to make your acquaintance, Mrs Treasure. Please call me Ted. Everybody else does.'

'Ted is an old fan of yours,' said Treasure.

The man swallowed. 'That's right enough. I saw you when you played *The Importance of Being Earnest* in Sydney.'

'Goodness, that was more than fifteen years ago.'

'I made it fourteen. Anyway you don't look a day older.'

'Well, thank you. Isn't that gallant?' Molly countered with a genuinely appreciative grin. 'Have you been explaining why you've made your visit to Britain so clandestine?'

'It hasn't been that exactly. Well, not quite.' He was looking across at Mrs Halliwell as he spoke. 'It's just that I've been kind of kept in reserve. Wouldn't you say that, Maggie?'

Mrs Halliwell smoothed her long neck. 'He was our ace in the hole if required for tonight.'

'You don't say?' questioned Motwell, making it plain that this was news to him.

'And well played in that case,' Molly commented, and wondering if her husband had also been unaware that Legion's presence had been stage-managed, presumably by Kuril and Mrs Halliwell.

'But my bit was hardly necessary. Not with Lord Delgard taking the whole meeting along with him like that,' said the Australian.

'No, I thought you added a lot of colour. And conviction,' Molly commented. 'Tell me, does some part of the Delgard estate really pass with the title? As you suggested it might?'

'Well, maybe I overdid that. Some real estate was legally entailed in time past. But not any more,' said Legion.

'You mean the claim you said you'd renounce doesn't exist?'

'In essence that's right.' Legion looked embarrassed. 'Except the opponents of the golf development have been pretending it did exist.' Again he looked towards Mrs Halliwell.

'As a delaying tactic,' she volunteered. 'It's a wee bit complicated. But nothing holds up a planning application so much as even the hint of a dispute over ownership of the land involved. Two generations ago, three farms that used to be entailed with the Delgard title were sold off. The legal conveyancing was sloppy. Neither of the succeeding Viscounts have tried to benefit from the fact.'

'But we did know the green opposition originally wanted the next one to try,' Motwell said.

'Ted was contacted in Australia and asked if he would. And at first he half agreed. Then I spoke to him and he changed his mind. Sensibly and selflessly,' Mrs Halliwell completed, smiling warmly at the subject of her compliment.

'It would have been dishonest to do anything else,' said

Legion, returning the smile, his gaze continuing to hold Mrs Halliwell's afterwards. 'As I understood it, there was no real case. Only the chance of a delay, as Maggie said.'

Molly sensed that the rapport between these two went a lot deeper than one that rested simply on a business relationship. 'But your early indifference to inheriting the title and to what might happen to Vormer House, that was all exaggerated, Ted?' she asked.

'It was from the time I realized the error of my ways,' he admitted somewhat sheepishly.

'Ted's been telling us about his conversion to being part of the British aristocracy,' put in Treasure lightly, and would have continued in the same vein if a perplexed-looking Kuril hadn't suddenly appeared at his side.

'I'm so sorry to interrupt,' said the host who was looking more ruffled than penitent.

'D'you need me for something, Julius?' Mrs Halliwell asked promptly.

'No . . . no. Not you Maggie, thanks.' Kuril made an evident effort to collect himself. 'It's Charles. Could you spare a minute? You too perhaps, Mark? There's someone in my study who wants a word.'

'If you say so,' the MP replied. 'Sounds ominous. Hope it's not a policeman.' He gave a confident smile as he looked around at the others.

'As a matter of fact it is a policeman. He seems to know Mark already. I'm afraid there's been an accident.'

'Someone hurt?' asked Felicity Finton.

'Janice Weggly. Lady who runs a typing agency in the town,' Kuril answered.

'Why, we've just been talking about her,' said Motwell. 'Is she badly hurt?'

'I'm afraid so,' Kuril breathed out sharply, clenching and unclenching his hands in front of him in an uncharacteristically agitated manner. 'I mean, it's rather worse than that. It seems she's dead.'

CHAPTER 9

'This is Detective Chief Inspector Furlong,' said Kuril.

Despite his rank, the short, wiry policeman looked to be scarcely into his late thirties. He had been standing before the fireplace in the close-carpeted, booklined study, admiring the Robert Bevan painting hanging above the mantel. When the others came in he swung round quickly like an athlete, fists clasped, arms loose but springy at the elbows. 'Good evening, Mr Finton,' he said, coming forward fast to shake hands with the politician. Then he turned to the banker. There was a broad grin on the deceptively boyish, freckled face as he continued: 'And Mr Treasure. It's good to see you again, sir.'

'And you. You're working up here now?'

'For more than a year, sir, yes.'

'And you've been promoted?'

'All part of getting married. To a local lady.'

'In that case she must be the Chief Constable's daughter,' Treasure chuckled.

'Not quite, sir. As a matter of fact, he doesn't have one.' The grin broadened briefly before it was switched off suddenly and replied by a studiously sombre expression. 'Mr Kuril's probably told you, I've brought bad news, I'm afraid.'

'How did Miss Weggly die? An accident, was it?' asked Finton.

'No. She was pretty certainly murdered, sir.'

'Good God! When? How?'

'This evening. We believe between ten to and twenty past seven.' Furlong clasped his hands behind his back, while his body began making short but rapid forward and backward movements as he spoke. 'I'd be grateful if you could help us work out what she might have intended to do this evening, sir. I gather she was supposed to meet you at the Community Centre?' He had ignored the MP's question about how the woman had died.

'Yes. Before the meeting there. I arrived later than expected. Direct from Town. There was terrible traffic on the A1. When Miss Weggly—Janice—wasn't there ahead of me, I'm afraid I was very irritated.' He sighed and shook his head.

'She was your secretary, sir?' The policeman's impatient rocking movements continued—as though he was trying to egg on the man he was questioning. Treasure remembered being mildly irritated by this pendulum action from previous encounters.

'Up here she was my secretary. Part-time. I have a full-time p.a. in London. Naturally, that's in addition to the calls I put on the secretarial assistance available to me at the Department of the Environment. As PPS to the Minister, you understand?' The last less than pertinent information had been vouchsafed evidently to remind the Chief Inspector that the speaker's status was a good deal more uplifted than that of an ordinary Member of Parliament.

'Quite so, sir,' Furlong acknowledged dutifully. 'But Miss Weggly was meeting you at the Centre tonight on a working basis?'

Finton's eyebrows lifted. 'She was being paid for it, if that's what you mean. It certainly wasn't a social engagement. That's why I was annoyed.' Bending his elbows, he slipped both his index fingers into the lower pockets of his waistcoat. This was meant to be a commanding gesture, and also gave a better view of an impressive gold watch-chain. The chain was a prop that the owner had acquired only recently. 'I rang her from the Centre, but the line was engaged.'

'What time would that have been, sir?'

'I don't remember.' He shrugged. 'I suppose—'

'I can tell you exactly. It was four minutes to seven,' Kuril put in, leaning his arms over the back of a leather-

bound chair that he had swivelled about to face the policeman. The chair was one of twelve set around an oblong
table in the middle of the room. 'It was just before the
meeting was due to start,' the speaker continued. 'We were
standing in the hall at the Centre.'

'And you used the payphone there, sir?'

'No. I had my mobile with me.'

'Did you ring Miss Weggly again, sir?'

'Not then, no. I assumed she'd turn up eventually.'

'But when she didn't?'

'I rang again at the end of the meeting. From the car.
My wife was with me.' The fingers of one hand now went
to brush away some imaginary blemish from the lapel of
his jacket.

'Why did you ring then?'

Finton looked up sharply. 'Well, to find out what had
happened to her, of course.'

'Were you or your wife worried that she might have had
an accident, say?'

'Between her place and the Centre? It's scarcely five hundred yards from the middle of Plum Street.' Finton hesitated. 'Well, my wife might have been worried. I just
thought Janice had probably forgotten. Why are our feelings so important?'

'They aren't, sir. I was just interested, that's all.' A smile
followed the comment. 'Did your wife travel up with you
this evening?'

'No, she's been at our house here all week.'

'So Mrs Finton arrived at the Centre independently? Did
she use her own car, do you know?'

'No, she'd have walked. Unless she got a lift from someone, because of the rain. You can ask her. She's here.'

Treasure was surprised that the politician hadn't sensed
that Furlong's bland request for help had already got
uncomfortably close to being an interrogation—or if he had
sensed it, why he hadn't become more circumspect with his
replies.

'Thank you, sir,' the policeman replied. 'Would you say Miss Weggly is usually forgetful?'

'Not usually, no.' Finton pouted, then decided to amend what he had said. 'Her memory wasn't infallible, of course. And recently she hasn't been the fastest worker around. As a matter of fact, that's why my London p.a. will be here tonight. We're going to see if we can catch up with the backlog of work over the weekend.'

'And that was arranged before you knew about Miss Weggly's death, sir?'

'Yes.'

'I see. Does that mean you were actually dissatisfied with Miss Weggly's work?'

'You could say that, yes. Seems an unkind thing to mention now. Now that she's dead.'

'Were you about to fire her, perhaps?' Furlong was evidently less concerned than the other man with the social niceties.

'That was a possibility. But she didn't know it. And I'd prefer it wasn't mentioned to anyone else.'

'I understand, sir. And was she supposed to be bringing anything to the meeting tonight? Letters for signing, for instance? Papers she'd typed? Anything like that?'

'Some letters, yes. To constituents. And part of a speech. Nothing vitally urgent, I suppose. It was stuff left over from last weekend that I wanted to be shot of tonight. Before starting the next weekend round tomorrow. I was here till lunch-time last Monday. We did dictation in the morning before I went to London. Oh, and there were a few things for typing I'd put on tape Sunday night. That's fairly typical of the pattern, I'm afraid. There's no let-up in this job.' The speaker had seemed to be more anxious to impress with the extent of his labours than simply to answer the question.

'Your house is in St Wilfred's Close, sir? Did Miss Weggly usually come there for work? Or did you go to her agency?'

Finton shook his head. 'Either place. There was no strict rule. We sometimes worked from the office in the Conservative Club in Carter Street. That's where I hold my Saturday morning surgeries, you understand? Janice was often involved with those, of course.'

'Yes, sir. And was that where you were on Monday morning?'

Finton paused. 'No. That happened to be one of the times I went to her office.'

'In Plum Street?'

'That's right.'

'Would that have been on the lower or the upper floor?'

'It was in her office on the ground floor.'

'Had you ever been to the upper floor?'

'I don't remember. I don't believe so. Tell me, why are you interested—'

Treasure believed that Finton was going to challenge the line of questioning—and not before time—except that Furlong chose that moment to interrupt with: 'And you didn't go to the agency on your way to the Community Centre this evening, by any chance?'

Finton's expression went blank. 'Certainly not. Surely I told you how late—'

'Sorry, sir, you did, yes,' the policeman interrupted again. 'Actually, I was wondering whether you might have been there at roughly seven o'clock last Friday evening? On your way home, perhaps?'

The MP thought for a moment. 'Er . . . I looked in, yes. Very briefly. To sign some things. But it was later than seven. About half past.'

'Was there anyone else there? Besides Miss Weggly, I mean?'

'Not that I saw. There might have been. I only popped into the front office. Why d'you ask?'

'In case you noticed an employee or another caller who might have been there tonight at that time. It'd help if we could establish if any regulars were about on a Friday evening.'

'I see. Well, I can't help, I'm afraid.' He had glanced at Kuril before he replied.

'Never mind, sir. Perhaps you can tell me whether any of the letters Miss Weggly would have been bringing tonight were to do with Henfold Developments? With proposals for building on the new golf courses, sir?'

It was Julius Kuril who answered this. 'Mr Furlong, there aren't any proposals for building on the golf courses.'

Furlong was still looking at the MP and waiting for his reply. He affected not to have heard what Kuril had said.

'None of the letters was about building proposals of any kind,' said Finton. 'And as for proposals for building on the courses, Mr Kuril's quite right, there aren't any. Not that he or I know of anyway.'

'Thank you, sir.' The policeman nodded at the speaker, then at Kuril.

'Are your questions to do with the allegations made my a Mrs Task at the meeting tonight, Mr Furlong?' asked Treasure. 'And I think we might sit down, don't you?' he added, pulling out one of the chairs from the table.

'My question was to do with what Mrs Task said, sir, yes,' replied the policeman. 'I expect you know she's also Miss Weggly's sister.'

'I believe we all knew that,' said Kuril, turning back the chair he had been leaning on so that it faced the table. 'Are you aware that Mrs Task withdrew her allegations unreservedly before the end of the meeting?'

'Yes I am, sir.'

'It seems that the misleading call to the newspaper was a hoax,' Kuril continued. 'We know for certain that Mr Finton's London secretary didn't make any such call, and it seems wildly unlikely that Miss Weggly did.'

'Apart from anything else, they'd neither of them have had any grounds for claiming they had letters to expose,' said Finton. 'The whole thing was really too bizarre.'

'I'm sure that's right, sir.'

'Good. And please do sit down, everyone,' Kuril encouraged, contriving to sound relaxed but not yet wholly succeeding. 'Drink for anybody? Mark, you're the only one who brought a glass in, except it's empty. If it was whisky, there's plenty over there on the trolley. And everything else. Including champagne. Mr Furlong, can I get you something?'

'Nothing, thank you, sir. I'm sorry to be keeping you all from the party. Just one or two other points, Mr Finton.' He drew out the chair beside Treasure and tentatively sat on the edge of it, as though to demonstrate that it wasn't his intention to stay. 'People up here would be most likely to think of Miss Weggly as your secretary wouldn't they? Your main secretary, that is?'

'They could do, I suppose, yes.' Finton even so sounded doubtful. He was standing beside the trolley at the near end of the table, pouring himself some champagne.

'Because she typed the letters to the constituents? Was in on your Saturday surgery? Made the appointments for that, perhaps? Went with you to local meetings?'

'She did all those things, certainly. At various times.' Finton moved up the table and sat down opposite the policeman. 'So yes, your point's a fair one,' he conceded.

'And do you think it has anything to do with why she was killed, Mr Furlong?' Treasure asked slowly.

'It's one possibility, sir. Quite a strong one. At the moment.'

'And pushing our luck, before you go, are you going to tell us how she died, or do we have to wait for tomorrow's papers?' the banker pressed good-humouredly, looking up from the still empty glass he had been fingering on the table.

'I don't think that'll be in the papers tomorrow, sir. Her death may be. We shan't know how it happened till after the post-mortem. Not for certain, anyway.'

'So how about a reasonable assumption to be going on with?'

Still sitting on the edge of the chair, Furlong rocked his shoulders quickly before he replied: 'It seems her neck was broken when a heavy window was slammed down on it.'

'She was guillotined?' exlaimed Kuril, sinking into the chair at the top of the table. 'Oh, God. How bloody awful.' He took a deep swallow from the drink he had just poured.

'Not quite guillotined, sir. She wasn't decapitated.'

'But her neck was broken? It's enough. Poor kid,' Kuril finished with a shudder.

'It was slammed down on her, you said?' This was Treasure. 'It . . . it couldn't have been an accident, I suppose? A broken sash-cord.'

'It wasn't an accident, sir. And it's not likely the window would have been heavy enough. Not on its own.'

'What about suicide? No, I suppose not.' Finton answered his own question before anyone else could do so.

'Any reason to think she could have been suicidal, sir?'

Finton shook his head. 'Quite the opposite. She was on top of the world the last time I saw her. Full of the joys.'

'Have you any idea yet who could have done it?' Treasure asked.

The Chief Inspector folded his arms tightly on his chest and leaned forward. 'We might have, sir.'

'And there'll be other reasons why you're sure she was murdered.

'That's right.'

'She was . . . very attractive, of course,' said Kuril haltingly. 'Was she . . . was she sexually assaulted, can you say?'

'The police doctor said he didn't think so. That was just before I left the scene of the crime. Again, the post-mortem will show for certain.'

'And was Plum Street burgled as well?' asked Finton.

Furlong stared at the questioner with what could have been either speculation or surprise.

'Of course, we've all assumed she died at her office,' Treasure put in promptly. 'I suppose that's right, is it?'

'Quite right, sir. And it was a reasonable thing to assume, even though I hadn't mentioned it,' said the policeman, grinning disarmingly at Treasure. 'It wasn't in the office part, though. It was upstairs in the sitting-room. But somebody may have rifled through one of the filing cabinets downstairs. Or it could just have been left open. We'll know better tomorrow.'

'So someone might have been searching for non-existent letters about non-existent building devlopments?' said Treasure quietly.

'My word, that sister of hers has a lot to answer for. Spreading dangerous lies like that,' Finton declared angrily.

'Which you think could have acted as an incitement to murder, sir?'

Finton cleared his throat. 'Not far beyond the bounds of possibility, is it? In the circumstances, not far at all.' He looked around at the others as if for support.

'For someone with a vested interest in those golf courses, sir?'

'And that covers a lot more people than you think,' was the MP's unexpected and not immediately clear response.

'Someone who rated Miss Weggly's life lower than planning permission to build golf courses?' said Treasure doubtfully. 'There can't be many people whose values are that warped.'

'Mark's right, of course,' Kuril agreed. 'Getting the planning permission through is a simple commercial consideration for Henfold. Who could imagine any rational individual having a life or death attitude about it?'

The silence that followed was brief but awkward while everybody, including the speaker, realized how burning a question might have been begged.

'The attitude of a maniac won't be rational,' Treasure offered sombrely.

Furlong looked across at the politician. 'As for Mrs Task

spreading dangerous lies, sir, of course she didn't make her accusations till the meeting had been on some time. The newspaper she said called her—'

'You don't need to hedge about that. We know it was the *Gazette*,' Finton interjected with authority.

The policeman ran his tongue over his upper lip before replying: 'I see sir. The *Gazette*. Well, whoever it was, we think he may have phoned one other person before the meeting. Possibly even several others.'

'Your theory being that one of those people believed the allegations were true? That Miss Weggly was the secretary involved, and that she had to be silenced?' said Treasure, then shook his head. 'Only holds water if you accept that murder was done so that letters could be suppressed?'

'So that Mr Finton couldn't be wrongly accused of having them?' the policeman added in the same unbelieving tone—or nearly.

The MP looked as if he was about to protest.

'It's preposterous, of course,' insisted the banker, doing it for him. 'Apart from anything else, there weren't any letters.' He looked at the policeman. 'You don't have the name of anyone else who was phoned?'

'Not for certain, sir, no. We're working on it. The fact is though, it wasn't someone from the *Gazette* who did the phoning.' He looked at Finton. 'Even though the caller said it was.'

'But George Pike from the local paper, he—' Finton began.

'Yes, but he was guessing, I'm afraid, sir,' said Furlong. 'In a way he got it half right. The freelance reporter who's usually a stringer for the *Gazette*, he was at the meeting. Man called Glossop. He came in late, and left immediately after Mrs Task made her retraction. No other London paper was represented, so Mr Pike just put two and two together. By the time he started double checking, every paper in London knew what Mrs Task had said, and retracted. It was on one of the wire services. Not that anyone seems to have been much interested at that point.'

'But none of this proves it wasn't the *Gazette* that did the phoning in the first place,' Finton insisted.

'I think it does, sir. Their news editor's been very helpful. He swears it wasn't them, nor anyone local working for them.'

'And you believe him?' asked Kuril.

'No reason not to, sir.'

'Couldn't they just be protecting their sources too, exactly as Mrs Task said she was doing?' Finton demanded.

'Except they've no source to protect, sir. Or story. Mrs Task has told us the caller said he was from the *Gazette*. The paper denies he was. They also deny ever having received a call from someone saying she was Mr Finton's secretary.'

'So it wasn't Pike's deduction you've been working on?' said Kuril.

'No, sir. It was the information we got from Mrs Task. We think Mr Pike was misled. It was coincidence this Mr Glossop was at the meeting, and that he usually represents the *Gazette*.'

'The one other person you think the hoaxer called. Can you give us the name?' asked Treasure.

'Sorry, not yet, I'm afraid, sir.' The speaker paused, and took a small notebook from his pocket. 'One last thing, do any of you know Major Claude Oliphant?'

'Yes. He's Lord Delgard's agent,' Finton volunteered looking at Kuril. 'Mr Kuril and I know him. Was he the one you think was phoned?'

'We don't know, sir. Maybe we never shall. You see, he was found shot dead in his car at seven thirty-two this evening. In the car park between Plum Street and Westgate.'

A big wood spark exploded in the fire, and gave dramatic punctuation to the last announcement, not that it had needed any.

'Suicide?' asked Treasure.

'We think probably so, sir.'

It was Treasure again who broke the following brief silence. 'Was that after he'd made a . . . a visit to Miss Weggly?'

'That's possible too, sir.'

'You mean he killed her? Then shot himself?'

'It may be that's what happened, sir. Too early to say, of course.'

CHAPTER 10

'Missed that hen pheasant by a mile,' grumbled Lord Delgard as he and Treasure fell in together on the wide, deeply rutted footpath. The pinewood they were traversing was close planted, dank and lowering. Gunner was lumbering stoically through the mud and puddles behind his master. Both men had shotguns stuffed into the crooks of their arms and broken open at the breeches. 'Getting too slow for this business,' the older man added.

'I wouldn't have said that. Not on the evidence so far this morning. I saw you pot that bird I missed. Second barrel, and right off your line,' said Treasure, easing the strap of the canvas bag slung over his shoulder. His one-eyed, nearly octogenarian companion had brought down more pheasants than anyone else so far this morning, and about twice as many as he had bagged himself. He looked ahead through the trees. Several of the other members of the eight gun shoot were in front, following behind the larger and motley party of paid and unpaid beaters—Molly Treasure, Maggie Halliwell and Ted Legion were volunteer members of the last group. 'Julius said the next stand is half a mile away,' the banker commented, watching a cocky robin hop on to a nearby fallen trunk, unperturbed by the formidable fire-power passing through its territory.

'Yes, we have to cross the estate road yet,' said Delgard.

'Timber's thinner that side. Ground opens up a lot there too. Old Algy normally allows transport between stands. Land-Rover gets in all right.' He looked about him from side to side as if he was hoping that a vehicle would materialize from behind a tree. 'Rain's playing the very devil with everyone's bridleways, of course. For more than three weeks now,' he went on. 'Walking's good for you, of course. Heel, Gunner!' he bellowed without looking around, and on the accurate supposition that the bulldog's lacklustre progress would be no advertisement for the final sentiment expressed.

The Algy referred to was another viscount, the owner of the estate twenty miles north-east of Thatchford on which the shoot was taking place. But Julius Kuril was the real host to the party since he had leased the Saturday shooting rights for the whole season.

The rain had stopped earlier on, but the predicted hazy sunshine had yet to manifest itself. The droppings from the trees were keeping everyone zipped up inside their waxed clothing.

'I gather Oliphant would have been with us this morning,' said Treasure. He had learned as much from Kuril, who had decided that the murder and suicide didn't presage the need to cancel the morning's sport. Out of good manners Kuril had telephoned this view to Delgard first thing, asking for his concurrence and getting it.

'Yes. Kuril invited him,' Delgard replied, looking and sounding uncertain, though he had clearly been aware that Oliphant would have been present. 'Know Kuril well, do you?' he asked suddenly, as if on impulse.

'Fairly well, yes. He comes from this area, I believe.'

'Indeed.' The response could have been an acknowledgement either of the fact or of the speaker's affecting to be learning it for the first time. 'Decent fellow, is he? Honourable? Trustworthy? Morally sound?' He had punched out the phrases like regular beats on a drum.

'Those are fearsome questions.'

'I know that. Wouldn't bother asking them otherwise. Surely it's part of a merchant banker's job to assess people's probity?'

'Of course.' Treasure was tempted to add that keeping one's counsel to oneself was another part of it. Instead he said: 'Anyway, my reply to all four questions is yes. Unqualified. In my belief, Kuril's dead straight in business. I know nothing of his private life, but I assume that's not what you're asking about. He also has a quite exceptional brain.'

'Good. I've got to rely on him, you see? Can't believe he and I were brought up subscribing to the same codes of conduct, if you follow me? Old-fashioned thing to say, but there it is. Nothing to do with race or religion. I don't discriminate there. Never have. My father did. Fashion in those days. Great mistake.' Delgard sneezed loudly.

'Bless you,' said Treasure.

'Much obliged,' the other replied before sneezing again. He produced a white handkerchief that was about the right size for a formal flag of truce and blew his nose into it. The resulting noise was close to the opening two notes of the Last Post, played on a not very muted trumpet. 'Kuril's integrity over this golf course business is important to me. Vitally,' Delgard went on, after a long sniff that flared his nostrils and inflated the red veins on a nose already swollen by the earlier blowing. 'Got to believe he'll keep his word.'

'Well, I'm quite sure he will.' Treasure this time responded more abruptly than before, a hint of impatience in the tone.

'Glad to hear it.' Delgard shifted the Purdey gun to the other arm, then cleared his throat. 'Didn't doubt it, of course. Still good to have an objective opinion.'

'Quite.' Treasure hadn't really minded Delgard consulting him about Kuril's moral standing, except he felt uncomfortable about it happening when the two of them were in the process of enjoying Kuril's hospitality.

'Yes, good of Kuril to have invited Oliphant today,'

Delgard offered a moment later, as though he was reading the banker's thoughts. 'Yes, very generous.' He made another grumbling noise in his throat. 'Thoroughly bad business, of course. He was a damned good shot, Oliphant. Hm. Good soldier too. Can't credit what's happened. Wouldn't have questioned his courage, would you? Not really, despite—'

'I'm afraid I never met him,' the banker replied. Nor had the question seemed appropriate in another sense: courage was not a virtue he was prompted to ascribe to a murderer.

'You didn't? No, of course you didn't. Stupid of me. Seems he'd been angling to be secretary of the golf club. Already. Mrs Halliwell told me as much last night. Now there's an able woman.' Delgard glanced sideways at his companion. This involved some serious head-swivelling since Treasure was on the wrong side for Delgard's good right eye. 'Oliphant never mentioned it to me.' The speaker halted his stride abruptly. 'Better go this way. Worse here than last week.' He stepped to the side, leading them across a drier but treacherous-looking detour before they would regain the path. 'Tractor's done that. No excuse. Damned careless.' He pointed to the deep, waterfilled gouge they were bypassing with difficulty. 'Might have helped him, you see? Oliphant, I mean. Word in the right ear. Should have asked me.' After their energetic scramble, pursued by Gunner, but not hotly, Delgard looked back at the ravaged section. 'That'll have to be bulldozed and graded.' He gave a disparaging sniff to cover his opinion of the unprofessional conduct of tractor operators. 'Worried I might have thought him disloyal, I expect. That's what my wife says. Watch your step again here.'

'You'd have had a word with Julius Kuril, you mean?'

'Kuril and others, yes.'

Treasure had followed his companion's footsteps with relative ease, and despite his being unfamiliar with conversational ballooning, as practised in the Delgard ménage, he had followed the account of the wretched Oliphant's career aspirations with a similar facility. 'But would you really have thought him disloyal for wanting the golf club job?' he questioned again.

'No. Of course his work as my agent was a doddle. Practically. Well, perhaps that's unfair. Made himself useful in many ways. And I didn't pay him much.' The veiled and culpable glance at Treasure, who had now moved to the side that more easily accommodated veiled, culpable or any other kind of glances, suggested that Delgard might have been going to say how much he'd paid, but he didn't.

'Was he a golfer?'

'Fair to middling. Competent organizer, too. You have to be in the army these days. That's what it's all about. Organization. War by computers.' Delgard's mouth indicated he held that practice as much in disdain as the local standards in tractor driving. 'He was my last ADC. And the youngest. Long time ago, that was. Didn't organize his private life well, though.'

'I understand his wife left him?'

'Yes. Five years ago. For an absolute bounder. That was the nub of it. Made Oliphant look every kind of ass. Never got over it. Bowled him out completely. Fell into bad habits afterwards.'

'Drink?'

'Gambling. Didn't think I knew, but I did. Owed his bookmaker. That'll be the root of it.'

'But it scarcely accounts for his doing in Finton's secretary and then shooting himself.' Treasure frowned as he settled his cap further on to his forehead. 'If he thought she really was going to stop the golf course plan going through, there was some evil sort of logic in his doing her in, I suppose? Protecting his new job. But why did he shoot himself afterwards?'

Delgard got out the handkerchief again and blew his nose loud enough to alert any bird or groundling within several hundred yards. 'He might have thought he was defending me. Guarding my intentions over Vormer. Over its future.'

The tone was severely matter-of-fact. 'Loyalty takes different forms. Even when it's misplaced.' He stuffed the handkerchief back into an outside pocket. 'Oliphant anyway thought he'd made a hash of his life. Since the divorce. Could suddenly have lost interest in going on altogether. Sort of thing happens. Gets triggered in some way. So he did one positive thing before he went. To atone. That's as he saw it.'

'To kill the woman he falsely believed would wreck your plans?' The scenario as painted sounded more than a bit fantastical to Treasure, and Oliphant's remedy too drastic by half. Still, there had to be some explanation for what had happened.

'Not just my plans. What they'll provide for the area. He knew the importance. Sounds far-fetched in the light of day. But that newspaper hoaxer phoning Oliphant set him off.'

'So you believe he phoned Oliphant too?'

'Certain of it. Pity the swine didn't speak to me. Tried, of course.'

'And got your sister, I believe?'

'Yes. After my wife and I had left for Thatchford. Didn't tell her exactly what he wanted. She thought he was interested in the park. Gave him Oliphant's number. Natural thing to do.' There was a longer, sidelong look at Treasure, speculative this time. 'Gather you'd met this detective before? Furlong?'

'Peter Furlong? Yes. Pure coincidence. He was in charge of an investigation some time ago involving a pharmaceutical company I'm concerned in. Bright chap. Told me he's now second in command of the Serious Crimes Squad here. He'll be a credit to your county force, I'd say. Are you the Lord Lieutenant?'

'No. Gave that up years ago.' The bull neck under the glowering face sunk even lower into the worn collar of the black shooting jacket. 'Meant going to too many pettifogging functions. No good at my age. Hmm. This Furlong was on to the whole business quick enough last night.'

'He lives just north of Thatchford, and was home when he heard about the murder. Yes, it seems he got to the scene ahead of his subordinates. Energetic chap.' Treasure smiled. 'I think it all rated extra attention because a prominent politician was involved.'

'Indirectly.'

'Not all that indirectly. The poor woman was Finton's local secretary.'

'Is Finton prominent?' This was more than merely debasing.

'Reasonably so. He's a PPS with a current chance of promotion. And a government reshuffle seems imminent.'

'So one reads.' Delgard was evidently not disposed to engage in a discussion of Finton's merits, or, perhaps in the nobleman's estimation, his lack of them. 'Furlong made up his mind, has he?' he asked.

'About Oliphant murdering Miss Weggly and then shooting himself? I don't know he's accepted that completely, but it's a tempting obvious solution, given the facts. And the circumstances.'

'Oliphant had the Weggly woman's office file on Kuril? Had it in his car with him?'

'The Henfold file from Miss Weggly's office, yes,' Treasure corrected. 'One could assume that naturally pointed to his having killed her, pinched the file, found there were no indiscreet letters in it after all, and ... and did for himself in despair at having bungled things. It was the file that led the police to her place, after they found Oliphant dead in his car.'

'Because of an anonymous call to the police station?' Delgard questioned.

'Yes. The caller refused to give her name. Said she was just a passer-by who'd seen him slumped in the car, opened the door and saw he'd been shot.' Treasure paused, stroking his chin in a speculative way. 'Your own explanation for the suicide at the end fits the situation even more aptly, of course.'

'And you believe that's what happened?'

'If not exactly that, then something like it.' But Treasure's response had lacked total conviction. 'Murdering for a useless file would certainly have been overdoing it. Maybe the victim said something that convinced Oliphant she really was in a position to turn the Council against the plan? Which meant his prospects for a better paid job were caput. Or again, that your own plan had had it.'

Delgard considered for a moment. 'Funny way of murdering someone. With a window. When he'd got a gun.'

'The gun would have been noisy.'

'And the window risky. Hit or miss,' the old soldier almost barked. 'Ever tried killing anyone that way?'

'No. Nor any other way as it happens.'

'Quite. Wrong generation, of course.' The comment had been dispassionate, not disparaging. 'Oliphant was the same. Although he'd served in Northern Ireland. Hmm. Sort of thing that could happen in house to house fighting, I suppose? In the case of this woman, you'd have to get her head sticking out first. Or make her stick it out. Not so easy.'

'He could have been threatening her with the gun?'

Delgard made a doubting sort of noise. 'What if she'd screamed? Or jumped out?'

'The room was on the upper floor.'

'What's underneath?'

'I've no idea. I haven't been there.'

'Quite. Better to jump than get shot. Even if you break a leg on a dustbin. Raining, of course. Heavily too. If she'd screamed would anyone have heard, I wonder?'

'Possibly not. That's according to Furlong. Miss Weggly's place is the only part of the terrace occupied at night.'

'Yes, well, it's offices above the shops in Plum Street these days. We used to own all the leases. Sold them twenty years ago.' The speaker's eye took on a reflective look. 'Shopkeepers lived above in my father's time. Don't any more.'

'Well, Miss Weggly did. The back of her place looks out over a small yard and then the back of a disused warehouse. She kept her car in the yard.'

'Ah, warehouse used to be a tobacco factory. All the backs on the west side of Plum Street look on to that,' Delgard put in with authority.

'I see. Well, there's a lane beside Miss Weggly's that runs from Plum Street to the waste ground car park where Oliphant died. Someone in the car park just might have heard a scream. Nobody seems to have heard the gun that I assume went off in the car.'

'Not easy.' Delgard seemed to be referring again to the murder by dropped window and not to the relative audibility of screams or gunshots. 'You know the sister's opinion?' he questioned suddenly.

'Mrs Task's? Yes. She says nobody should have believed that Miss Weggly was the secretary involved. The one that the hoaxer said was doing the informing. She thinks he didn't say it was the London secretary specifically because he didn't know Finton had two secretaries. She insists most people don't. It never occurred to her even that he could have meant her own sister.'

Delgard's eyebrows lifted, the one over his right eye more so than the one over the eyepatch. This produced a lopsided result that intensified the quizzical effect. 'That explains the way she sounded off at the meeting,' he said.

'Yes. It seems she'd never accepted that her sister was secretary to a Tory MP.'

'Comes down to blind bloody-mindedness on her part, then? God bless my soul.' Delgard kicked at a twig in front of him. 'So she put her sister in jeopardy purely out of self-indulgence? Corrupting thing, arrogance.' He thrust a hand deep inside the long wet jacket and began making strenuous and complicated undercover rearrangements to his inner, lower garments and middle extremities. 'Heel, Gunner!' he boomed once more when the delving was complete. 'That animal's a bloody fool in traffic,' he added, this time looking about him for the dog.

They had halted before a metalled estate road. It ran straight and conspicuously empty towards misted horizons in both directions, and, despite Delgard's misgivings, offered no motorized threat to man or beast.

Gunner, whose progress was slow but determined, began crossing ahead of the others without a sideways glance either way, just as his master uttered: 'Fool or not, you know, it still comes back to courage. Guts.' The last word broke like thunder and prompted Gunner to execute a defensive sort of rumba movement with his rear quarters, before slightly increasing his pace.

Treasure had naturally assumed his companion's last comments had been about the dog. While he thought Gunner's demeanour typical of his breed, the creature hardly seemed to rate the wholesome commendation implied.

'You need to put the barrel in your mouth. Only way to make sure of a clean job,' Delgard offered next.

It was clear then that they were back to Oliphant, or possibly even that they had been back to him before. Delgard was ballooning again.

'I understood from Furlong that he made a nasty mess of his head,' said Treasure, without relishing a discussion of this aspect of Oliphant's demise.

'Exit wound did. At the crown of the skull,' Delgard corrected as they reached the other side of the road. 'With a German service revolver. Lucky to kill himself.'

'Lucky?' Treasure inquired carefully, out of deference to Delgard's military experience, but curious to know why he seemed to have such a very low opinion of German weaponry: could it be enduring prejudice against an old enemy?

'You know I had to identify the body?' said Delgard.

'I'd heard that, yes.'

'No one else suitable. No relatives, d'you see? Never a nice thing to do. He'd pointed the barrel to the side, under

his chin. Not close up either. Foot away, I'd say. Quite a
big entry hole. Bullet could have hit bone. Got deflected.
Anything.' The speaker shook his head, a deep distaste
suffusing the face. 'Could have ended up alive and then
recovered. After a fashion. With fearful brain damage,
probably. Turning him into a cabbage. Happens sometimes
with tentative suicides. Of the feeble type. Oliphant wasn't
feeble.'

'You mean you'd have expected him to . . . to put the
barrel in his mouth?'

'Quite. Only sure way. Or tight against the side of the
l ead.' He raised his right hand and demonstrated with his
index finger, before bringing the hand down again. Then
his face clouded. 'Is that right, then?'

'I'm sorry?' Treasure questioned.

'Oliphant wasn't left-handed.'

'So?'

'Dammit, didn't strike me till now. Don't think it has the
police either.'

'What?'

'The wound was in the left side of his neck.'

CHAPTER 11

'And the shame on top of everything.' Mrs Rose Weggly
pressed the bunched and sodden handkerchief to her eyes.

'There's no shame, Mum. I really don't know why you
feel that,' Madelaine Task replied with firmness. Tight-
lipped, she turned her head away, outwardly disguising the
fury within her.

'Don't you know?' quavered her mother. 'No shame in
my poor dead daughter being three months gone? With no
husband? No prospects either? Not that I knew of. Or you.
Oh dear.' She drew in a choked breath. 'What did I do to
deserve this? Oh God, whatever did I do? Tell me?' She

began to cry again in earnest, the beefy shoulders on the squat round body shaking uncontrollably. Her head was bent and her clenched fists were held together before her mouth, the handkerchief between them only half muffling the sound of the sobs.

The two women were seated at the kitchen table in the Tasks' modest, Georgian-style detached house on the new estate on the eastern outskirts of Thatchford. Still deeply distraught, and after a fitful night, Mrs Weggly had come down from her room half an hour before this at nine o'clock. She was clad still in her nightdress under a blue quilted dressing-gown. Kevin Task had left to open the shop before his mother-in-law had appeared.

Mrs Weggly had been toying with some breakfast when her daughter had answered a ring on the doorbell to be confronted by an embarrassed detective-sergeant accompanied by a uniformed WPC. Mrs Task had taken the two officers into the front room, out of her mother's sight and hearing—which had been just as well in view of the revelation they had made. The preliminary post-mortem had shown that Janice Weggly had been pregnant.

Anxious as the police had been to know the identity, or even the likely identity, of Janice's lover, they had been sent away unenlightened. Mrs Task had argued that it was nobody's business outside the family, apart from the fact that she had no idea who the man could be, and was certain her mother wouldn't know either. While allowing that the man's identity might possibly, but only possibly, have a bearing on the cause of her sister's murder, Mrs Task had still refused to allow her mother to be questioned. She had insisted that Mrs Weggly was still in a state of shock.

Aware that to gainsay anything Councillor Mrs Task decreed was something to be attempted only at peril to themselves, not to mention the local police force in general, the officers had tactfully repeated their sympathies over the bereavement and departed.

Despite what she had said, Madelaine had lost no time

in telling her mother the news. Mrs Weggly would have to be told some time, and since there was an outside chance that Janice might have told her the name of her lover, Madelaine was determined to be the first to share the confidence. One could go further and say that this single desire on her part had transcended any other consideration. She was certainly not motivated by the idea of passing on the information to a police team engaged in accounting for her sister's gruesome death. The pregnancy had no relevance to that. She knew who had done the murder.

But it soon emerged that Madelaine's motivation was academic. Mrs Weggly had at first refused to accept even that Janice had been pregnant at all. After she had abandoned that stance, it became plain that she was hazarding no immediate guess about the name of her daughter's seducer, as she put it.

'Things have moved on, Mum. Women don't need husbands before they have babies any more.'

'Unmarried mothers.' Mrs Weggly spat out the phrase, then bit on her lower lip.

'One-parent families they're called these days.' Madelaine reached across the corner of the table and put a comforting hand on her mother's arm. It was an uncharacteristic gesture. Madelaine was not demonstrative by nature. As she leaned forward she caught their twin reflections in the hall mirror, visible through the open door.

The two of them were very alike—both short, roundish, and heavy of feature, with small, weak eyes set too close, wiry hair that was difficult to manage, and too much flesh in the wrong places. Janice had hardly been tall, but she had been taller than either of them, tall enough to cope with being a bit overweight. Dumpy Madelaine's gaze stayed on the mirror. Men had never called Janice plump, only voluptuous. She had had soft fair hair too, and what in books they called generous lips, as well as a natural peachy complexion with big, baby-blue eyes. And she'd never needed glasses either. She had taken more after her father, of course. Except that if there was any 'of course' about it, why hadn't Madelaine done the same thing? Madelaine had been asking herself that last question off and on since the age of ten.

People often said that Madelaine and her mother could pass as sisters—naturally they said it to Mrs Weggly as a compliment, but quite often in Madelaine's presence. They had never said it about Janice and her mother because the proposition would have been ludicrous. Yet Janice had been only five years younger than Madelaine. Unhappily, it was nearer the truth that Madelaine and Janice looked less like sisters than they did mother and daughter: mark you, no one had ever said that in Madelaine's hearing, but she was always suspecting people thought it. She had even caught her own husband looking at the two of them and thinking it, or she had imagined he'd been thinking it—unless his thoughts had been centred solely on Janice, which was worse. It had been four months since he'd begun paying Janice extra attention, much more than before—ever since Mrs Weggly's birthday party in August. Kevin had insisted on driving Janice home after it because of the rain and her having come on foot.

'Things may have moved on for you. Not for me they haven't. Not from the old values.' Mrs Weggly was rallying slightly and building on her contention. She wiped her eyes and searched for her glasses in the pocket of her dressing-gown. 'Might as well say you needn't have got married because you haven't got children,' she added bitingly.

'That's a daft thing to say, Mum.' And cruel too, she thought. Madelaine was not really prepared to make allowances for her mother's snide remarks, even today. She and Kevin had been trying hard to have a baby for four years. Her mother knew that well enough, yet she went on telling her precious patients and nosy friends that the couple were too selfish to have a family.

'Why did they need to do a post-mortem anyway?' Mrs Weggly had lifted the teacup just off the saucer and held it there as if she hadn't the strength to take it further. 'Why did they have to cut up that lovely body? My beautiful little Janice. I ask you, what's it got to do with anyone else what she did? Now she's dead and gone?' She set the cup down, contents untouched, and breathed in heavily through her mouth. She was going to cry again.

'The post-mortem is because they need to know exactly how she died,' Madelaine provided in a down-to-earth tone, leaning back in her chair away from her mother and away from being able to see their reflections in the mirror. 'Her being pregnant could be linked to who killed her.'

'They know who killed her.' Mrs Weggly forced the words through her tears. 'That Oliphant killed her, the scum. I'd take a scalpel to him, I would.' Anger had rallied her. 'He killed her all right. The police said so last night. Good as.'

'I know, Mum, but they still need to make certain. It could be important to know who the father was. So if you knew—'

'I've said I don't know. Janice never told me.' She paused after making the interruption. 'Not directly,' she added. Her eyes were studying the teacup, the pained expression softening, first around the mouth, then the eyes. 'No point in guessing. It would have to be someone important, of course. Very important.' Her hand went out to move the saucer a little. 'Doesn't have to be anything to do with her death either.'

It was clear enough to Madelaine what Mrs Weggly was leading up to, and which way her mind was working. She was holding Charles Finton responsible for the pregnancy but she was promoting him from vile seducer to worthy suitor with social and political standing—and prospects, too, if Janice had lived, there being such a thing as divorce.

Madelaine sighed under her breath as her mother went on: 'She would have told me. Outright. In her own time. Once they'd ... once they'd made their arrangements. Janice and I were closer than you thought. Much closer.'

Oh yes, they'd been close all right, the older daughter thought sourly. So close it had been Madelaine and her husband who had given Mrs Weggly a place to live here in their own home, and fixed up a room for her practice at the back of the shoe shop, and taken her on holiday with them every year, and put up with her Tory prejudices, and snide criticisms, and her non-stop, mindless jabber.

Yet minutes before, Madelaine's mother hadn't been begging the Almighty to tell her what she had done to deserve a daughter as good and caring as Madelaine. Oh no. Absurdly, all she'd wanted to know was what she had done to lose a daughter like Janice. Except it was Janice who had been the selfish one, the tarty one, the one who had men eating out of her hand, and getting into her bed. It was Janice who wouldn't have wanted a baby, who wouldn't have been trying to have one, but who got everything that other people wanted—including other people's husbands and now another woman's rightful child.

Madelaine would have done anything, given anything, to have had that baby in her womb, just as she believed Janice would have done anything not to have had it in hers. There should have been some consolation in knowing that Janice had failed in something at least, the self-centred slut. Madelaine was sure too that Janice would have been arranging for an abortion—unless the baby was a passport to a rich marriage. So could there be any truth in her mother's unspoken theory about Finton?

'That's the telephone, Madelaine. Aren't you going to answer it?'

Her mother's voice brought her out of her reverie, away from the fresh fantasies of hate about her sister—about Janice and men, Janice and Charles Finton, Janice and . . . yes, Janice and Kevin. That last was the worst fantasy.

'Hello?' she almost shouted into the wall-mounted telephone next to the cooker. 'Thatchford 8189.'

'Hello, love.'

It was Kevin, sounding anxious. 'What d'you want?' she asked stonily.

'Your mum all right?'

'Yes. What's the matter?' He wasn't the sort to have telephoned about her mother's health, not even this morning.

'Have the police been?'

'Yes. Two of them. They've found out Janice was three months pregnant,' she announced without emotion, watching her mother wince.

'So that's it,' her husband said. 'They've been here too. To the shop. Just a detective-constable. On a routine inquiry. That's what he said.' Kevin paused. 'He never told me she was pregnant. Just wanted to know where I was last night. Between half six and half seven.'

'You should have been at the town meeting,' she chided. She'd asked him to come to the meeting—to support his wife, but he'd got out of it, said he was too tired.

'Well, I wasn't, was I? I was home playing my new CDs. You know that. Did they ask you where I was?'

'No.'

'Well I was there when your mum came back from her whist. That was about half seven. It might even have been earlier. Ask her, will you? She'll vouch for me, I know. Anyway, that's what I told them. Only . . . only there's no one to say where I was when . . .'

'When Janice died? No, I suppose there isn't.'

He was silent for a moment, waiting for consolation and support, but getting none. 'Except it'll be all right,' he said lamely. 'Only routine, the policeman said. They know I had nothing to do with . . . well, the murder?' He paused again. 'Another thing, have you heard about Finton's secretary? His proper one?'

'No. What about her?'

'She's dead. Killed in a car accident. Late last night. On her way back to London.'

*

The Fintons' listed Queen Anne town house in St Wilfred's Close was the centre one of three houses in a venerable, unmatched terrace. The building faced directly across the Close towards the slim, steepled west end of Thatchford's famous parish church—part Norman, part early and middle Gothic, and part soaring, fifteenth-century Perpendicular: St Wilfred's was the glory of the town. The quadrangular Close had a well-tended lawn at the centre with wooden benches on the dissecting paths, and an ancient stone cross in the middle.

The three-storey house with its seven window bays was wider than its neighbours, but constructed, like them, of mellowed stone. There was a walled garden at the rear, with a glazed door leading there from the back of the oak-panelled main hall that ran the whole width of the building.

It was a gracious house, and, Felicity Finton believed, with the right status and atmosphere for her two children to grow up in. The Close outside was untouched by modern development, and no through traffic was allowed there. The garden got sunshine most of the day in summer, there was a tennis court at the end of it, and the soil was rich.

Felicity was properly deemed a zealous housekeeper and gardener, but those mundane commitments were only the trivial, outward symbols of another—one that was much more profound. Her meticulously ordered home and garden mirrored her total dedication to a marriage that was her whole life, and which, if it was required of her, she would have defended literally to the death.

Yet few people would have thought of Felicity Finton as a fanatic, which proved that appearances can sometimes be deceptive.

She had been gardening when her husband had called her inside and told her about Philippa. 'If only she'd stayed the night as she'd intended,' Felicity mourned. She moved her head, neck and shoulders from side to side in a level plain several times, like a trainee Hindu dancer: it was part of her demonstration of bewilderment and sorrow. She was

standing in the hall in wool-stockinged feet, legs set wide
apart, toes turned inward in a schoolgirl habit she had
never broken. She had kicked off her gardening boots on
the mat outside the door, but was still clutching the handle
of a wicker basket full of tulip bulbs. Her gloves and a
trowel were on top of the bulbs.

'I told you, she . . . she decided to take all the work back
to London with her. There was such a lot Janice hadn't
even started,' Finton answered with nervous brusqueness,
shock still apparent in his face. 'She wanted to work on her
own computer.' It was a feeble explanation, full of holes,
and he knew it, but there was no other he could offer—certainly not the true one.

'Aren't they all the same? Desk computers?' Felicity had
been his secretary herself once, but before the days of word
processors. She had been quite efficient too—and very
cheap. She hadn't been doing it for the money.

'No, they aren't all the same.' He shrugged impatiently,
and turned away from her, one hand digging into a trouser
pocket, the fingers of the other rubbing his forehead in
short, irritated movements. 'Well, obviously they're not the
same, or she wouldn't have gone back.' He shifted his feet.
'Oh, what the hell does it matter?' he added testily. 'She's
dead, isn't she?'

'I'm so sorry, Charles.' She had thought of going to him,
then decided instead to sink on to the ottoman that was set
against the wall. She never knew quite how to treat him in
a situation like this. 'It must have been terribly late when
she left,' she said, involuntarily glancing at her watch: it
was just after nine-thirty. 'I mean, I went to bed pretty
soon after we got back. After we'd had the tea. I didn't hear
you come up. Must have been asleep. I didn't drop off as
quickly as I expected because . . .' Something made her
first hesitate over what she intended saying next, and then
to saying something different. 'So how long did she stay?'

The two hadn't breakfasted together or spoken much till
now: he had been up earlier than she, shutting himself up

in the study after making coffee. There were only the two of them in the house. Their sons were at boarding-school.

'She wasn't here that long,' he said. 'Not after you'd gone up. I pressed her not to go. To wait till this morning, at least.' He had too, but with conditions, or rather without his accepting Philippa's conditions—that he would tell Felicity he was leaving her before the weekend was over, and that he would ask her for an immediate divorce.

He had tried to make Philippa see reason for more than an hour after his wife had gone to bed. He had been shaken when she admitted arriving in Thatchford last evening almost as soon as he had himself—just as he hadn't expected to find her, in her car, parked outside his house when he and Felicity had got home from the Kurils' party.

Finton had telephoned Philippa immediately after the public meeting had ended. He had told her about the call Madelaine Task had received from a newspaper and what his secretary had been said to have disclosed. He had been sure Philippa would promptly deny being the one who had called the newspaper—but she hadn't. Instead, she had taken advantage of the situation and said she would deny being responsible only if he invited her to stay the weekend at his house after all, so that they could 'talk things out'. He had agreed, very reluctantly—in a panicked decision he later regretted, particularly when he learned from Furlong that the whole newspaper story was a hoax. His call to Philippa had been on her mobile phone. It was the surest way of reaching her at weekends, but he hadn't asked her where she was at the time—or imagined then that she had been in Thatchford.

It was Felicity who had told Philippa about the murder, while they had been making tea in the kitchen. But Philippa hadn't admitted going to see Janice until she was alone with Finton later. They had both agreed to tell no one about that visit. Philippa was sure no one had seen her in Plum Street and both she and Finton wanted her kept out of the murder investigation. Philippa had sworn that Janice had been alive when she left her at around six-forty.

The purpose of Philippa's visit to Janice had been baldly to accuse her of sleeping with Finton, jeopardizing his marriage and political career. Philippa had pretended, selflessly, to be motivated only by the need to protect the MP's reputation and future. Janice had vehemently denied the charge—as vehemently as Finton himself had done earlier—and in the end Philippa had believed her. The visit hadn't lasted long. Because Janice was committed to attending the public meeting, Philippa had volunteered to spend an hour or so in the office at the Conservative Club in Carter Street where there was work to do covering Finton's surgery next morning. Philippa had later had supper at the pub next to the club. Janice had promised to meet her there after the meeting, but had never showed up. By then, Finton had called Philippa and agreed to her staying the weekend at his house.

Philippa had been in a foul temper again at midnight when she had left for London. Finton had refused irrevocably to leave his wife for her. Philippa had made threats. He hadn't known at the time whether she would see them through. He hadn't thought she would, but he had been glad to get her out of the house. Now it didn't matter what she'd intended.

'It's nearly a two-hour drive,' Felicity said, breaking into his thoughts. 'Well, less, I suppose, at that time of night. To her place. Isn't her flat in Highgate? Or Hornsey?'

'I can't remember. One of the two,' he lied, picturing the place with Philippa sitting up naked on the bed as she'd been just a few hours before. Except a wholly unwelcome image kept superimposing itself over the other—the one where Philippa's broken and blood-stained body was lying impaled in a wrecked car.

'Perhaps she was driving too fast. Did the police give you the details?'

'Yes, lovey, they did.' He had turned and was staring

at Felicity now with an intensity she might have found discomforting if it hadn't been for the spoken endearment and the softening in his voice. 'She went off the road on a bend. Half way along that A1 diversion. This side of Roniton village. She hit a tree, apparently. They don't think any other car was involved.' He was steeling himself to accept that his marriage wasn't in danger now, neither his marriage nor his prospects for promotion. He should never have let Philippa think he was that much attached to her, of course—or he should have broken with her before she became a liability. 'The road's very narrow there,' he went on, 'and muddy, of course.'

'But Roniton's only just down the road! She hadn't gone ten miles.'

'I know.' He turned both hands outwards in a gesture of abject despair.

'Had she been drinking?'

'Not while she was here. She might have been earlier, of course.'

'Poor Philippa. And poor you. All this on top of what happened to Janice Weggly. It's really too awful for you.' She had still been nursing the basket, but she put it down now, got up and confidently went across the hall to him, wrapping her arms around his neck. 'Poor Charles,' she said, kissing him gently.

'I suppose we'll have reporters here any minute.'

'Don't worry, I'll deal with them.' She began to massage the base of his neck.

He was wearing a sweater over an open-necked shirt, grey flannels, and leather sneakers. He was due shortly in Carter Street and usually dressed in a casual way for his surgery—said it put the constituents at their ease to show he was one of them, especially the poorer ones. Except all his sweaters were cashmere and the sneakers were hand-made in Italy.

In material matters, Charles Finton hated settling for anything below the best. Happily his wife's money, or more precisely the money his immensely wealthy father-in-law pressed upon his wife, had long since been protecting the MP from ever having to settle for anything less than the best. It had paid for the house in Thatchford, and the flat in Westminster, sent the boys to the best schools, and enabled Finton to give up his legal career and concentrate on his political one much earlier than he could reasonably have expected to do in the ordinary way—even supposing that his future as a barrister had been a promising one, which it hadn't been. More to the point, Felicity's present income and the fortune she would ultimately inherit—she was an only child—underwrote her husband's well-being for life, whatever happened to his career.

So it was altogether necessary for Finton to keep his marriage sweet, or at least to avoid giving grounds for outsiders to sour it. After the kind of escape he had just had, he determined to be more seriously circumspect in his extra-marital affairs in future. Indeed, he had almost resolved to cut them out altogether. He was nearly certain that Felicity really had begun to suspect that something was going on with Philippa, so it wouldn't have been a lot of good his denying it if Philippa had told all—and the consequences of her doing that could have been disastrous.

'I suppose they're bound to link the two deaths? Both girls being your secretaries,' said Felicity.

'You mean losing one secretary is unfortunate, but losing two looks like carelessness?' he glibly paraphrased Oscar Wilde. 'I expect they'll link them, yes.' He pulled her closer to him.

'It seems an awful thing to say, but . . .' She hesitated.

'Go on,' he said, certain she was going to talk about his affair with Philippa, and preparing himself to deny it.

'You'll say I'm mad, but . . . well, I always had the feeling Janice was . . . was the kind who'd try stealing you from me.' She half-whispered the last words in his ear.

'Janice?' He couldn't believe it. 'You're joking?' He almost meant it too.

'I thought men found her sexually attractive.'

'Well, this man didn't.' It was nothing but the truth.

She buried her face in his neck. 'Oh, darling, I'm so glad. I can't tell you how worried I was. You seemed to spend so much time with her.'

'Working, for heaven's sake.'

'I realize that now. It was so silly of me. It's just that I knew she wasn't like Philippa, not in any way. Dear Philippa was so sweet and honest. I mean, I knew she'd never try anything on like that. You know what I mean?' Felicity whispered again. 'One could see that. But Janice seemed quite different.' She looked up into his face. 'Oh dear, I'm afraid I've been very bad about Janice.'

CHAPTER 12

'That was a super old Bentley Lord Delgard was driving,' said Detective Chief Inspector Furlong, turning the Ford right and heading it up Westgate Street. They had just crossed the bottom of Plum Street which was parallel to Westgate, but one way only going south. 'The Bentley had a special one-off body too,' the policeman added with burgeoning enthusiasm. He was gripping the steering-wheel hard like a racing driver.

'Mulliner body, was it?' Treasure asked from the passenger seat.

'Park Ward, with a 1951 engine and chassis. He was talking about it with the duty sergeant at the station. When he was leaving. The sergeant's a vintage car enthusiast. Well, they both are by the sound of it.'

'Except Lord Delgard doesn't regard his Bentley as a museum piece. Only as a well maintained car that'll have to see him out, as he put it. That's what he said when he was driving me down.'

'Must be a heavy vehicle for an old man to handle, sir.

No power steering.' Furlong waited for a gap in the traffic, then, with exaggerated arm movements, steered the car across into the two-acre waste ground municipal car park at the top of the street.

'I noticed that. Wouldn't suit me, I'm ashamed to say. But he copes magnificently. Strong as an ox,' said Treasure. 'Interesting he insisted on telling you personally about Oliphant being right-handed.'

'Yes, sir. And on your being present to see fair play.'

'Was he doing that? Perhaps you're right. I seem to have become his confidant.'

'And impeccable witness I'd say, sir. He doesn't totally trust the local police force.'

'What about your duty sergeant?'

'He's different, sir. Did time as a soldier in the county regiment.' The speaker frowned. 'When Lord Delgard was Lord Lieutenant, I'm told he had a set-to with the Chief Constable. Over hunt saboteurs.'

'Is your Chief Constable anti-foxhunting?'

'Don't think he's bothered one way or the other, sir. Just concerned to uphold the law. Without fear or prejudice, you might say.'

Treasure chuckled. 'And Lord Delgard is a touch prejudiced.'

'Perhaps, sir,' the other answered diplomatically. 'In a way it was a shame we knew already about Mr Oliphant being right-handed. Afraid it disappointed his lordship. Could have saved you a journey, too.'

'Not really. I didn't take a car to the shoot. My wife and I drove up with Julius Kuril in his Land-Rover. She went back the same way. The route's as good as through the town. Lord Delgard would have taken me on to Stigham Manor if you hadn't volunteered.' He pointed ahead, to the right. 'Does that lane lead into Plum Street?'

'Yes. That's Dunce Alley. Pedestrians only.'

Furlong had driven rapidly to the far side of the car park whose boundary there was the long side of an old, large and featureless, industrial building. He stopped the car facing the southern end of this, near the alley entrance.

'Looks wide enough for a car,' Treasure remarked, getting out.

'Only as far as the back yard of Miss Weggly's place, on the other side of this empty warehouse.'

'Which Lord Delgard told me used to be a tobacco factory.'

'That's right.' Furlong locked the Ford, and led the way, head bent, step springing, legs and arms moving energetically—until he stopped abruptly and swung around. 'Should have said, that's the same bay Oliphant parked in, sir.' He pointed back to the Ford. 'We had the area taped off till lunch-time today. Didn't produce much. If there was anything, the rain washed it away.' He turned again on his heel, military style, and headed again briskly for the alley.

There was no door in the short side of the warehouse, only one boarded-up window high under the flattish end gable. The opposite, right-hand side of Dunce Alley was bordered by an unbroken high wall that later merged with the wall of a neglected-looking terrace house. Although the alley bent a little, Treasure could see people and traffic passing across the end of it in Plum Street.

Beyond the warehouse on the left there was a padlocked gate of wooden slats set into a whitewashed wall not quite as high as the one opposite but with black metal spikes set in the top. The padlock was keyless and worked on a combination. Further along the wall Treasure noticed the ancient outline of a bricked-up window opening.

'Miss Weggly leased the area inside as a backyard, sir. It belongs to the warehouse. That's her place beyond. You can see her car through the gate.'

A BMW 230 was squeezed into the space at an angle.

'Not much room for the car. I suppose she had to drive it in and back it out through the main car park?' Treasure was squinting between the gate slats.

'Yes, sir. Awkward, but still safer than leaving a car out

unprotected all night. That was her sitting-room up there. The right-hand window in the middle storey.'

'The one where she was . . . ?' Treasure's lifted eyebrows completed the question.

'Yes, sir.'

Janice Weggly's place was old, but unlike the house on the other side of the alley the outside looked as if it had been recently done over. Like the other, it was a three-storeyed end house with a cellar, in an altered, patched-up terrace. The roofline was sinking a little in the centre, but the tiles under it were regular, like the repointed brickwork below them. The pair of pretty sash windows on each of the upper storeys visible from the alley dipped towards the middle, but their white-painted woodwork looked sound.

'Middle Georgian. The whole terrace,' said Treasure, half to himself.

'Is that right, sir?'

'I'd think so. With old retail premises it's the upper floors and backs that usually survive as witness. This has a shop front in Plum Street, does it?'

'Yes. The houses were built the same time as the tobacco factory. Miss Weggly's house was originally the factory shop. I'm afraid the shop front isn't eighteenth-century any more, though. Come and have a look. We can go inside. View the scene of the crime.'

'Is that allowed?' The banker was surprised at the offer.

'We've just about finished with the place. I'd like to know what you make of the murder weapon.'

Treasure glanced at the padlock on the gate. 'There's a back door to the house?'

'There is, but no one used it from Thursday till this morning. Miss Weggly broke the key in the lock Thursday lunch-time. She was waiting for a locksmith to get it open. That's according to one of her staff. We put a new lock in today.'

'So her murderer couldn't have got in or out that way?'

'Nor anyone else, sir.'

'And you found nothing of interest in the yard?'

'Nothing. There was a dead cat up this end.'

'What did it die of?'

'Search me. We're finding out, though. I don't think it had anything to do with Miss Weggly's death.' Furlong hurried off down the narrow alley to the street.

'See what you mean,' said Treasure a moment later, while viewing the shop front from the pavement in Plum Street. 'But then the Georgians didn't go in much for typing, duplicating and all forms of word processing.' He had been reading from the neat black on white lettered cards displayed on both sides behind the wooden-framed, bowed shop windows. The upper facia board announced 'Weggly Secretarial Bureau' also in black and white.

The ground-floor interior of the premises was only half screened by vertical strip blinds. It was carpeted, and arranged as an open office plan with no shop counter, only a line of three metal desks with computers on them. The wall space and the area behind the window was occupied by printing machines of assorted sizes, except for the pride of place position in the window itself. There a decorative tank of live tropical fish was standing on a wrought-iron frame.

''Afternoon, Meadmore. Anybody left upstairs?' the Chief Inspector asked the uniformed policeman who was standing in the porch to the left of the window.

'No, sir. Not since three o'clock,' the young man replied, after saluting. 'I've got the keys, sir.' Behind him to the right was a glazed door into the shop with, alongside it, a typical 'thirties-style suburban front door, with a fan of stained glass inset into its upper quarter.

'We're going up to the flat,' said Furlong to the constable, and indicating the second door to Treasure.

'Very good, sir.' The man handed him some keys.

'Is there direct access from here into the shop?' Treasure asked after he and Furlong had entered, crossed a short, narrow hallway inside, and begun ascending the stairs.

'Yes. Behind these stairs.' Furlong was taking the steps two at a time. At the top, he led the way along a corridor and through the first door on the left. 'Sitting-room,' he announced keenly, like an estate agent with a prospective buyer.

It was a small room, gaudily decorated, with lemon-painted walls, orange flowered curtains, and a mottled green carpet. Two over-large armchairs and a matching three-seat sofa, all covered in white imitation leather, left very little space for anything else. The sofa was set against the wall, under the window. The wall opposite had the door at one end, a tiled open fireplace in the middle, and beyond that some staggered wooden shelving supporting a TV set, a glass-fronted drinks cabinet full of bottles, and another glass tank of tropical fish. There was a glass coffee table in front of the sofa with some fashion magazines on it, an ashtray, and a small glass jug full of water.

Furlong went across to the window. He knelt on the sofa before undoing the catch and pushing up the lower sash.

'The bottom of the window is quite high,' Treasure said, also kneeling on the sofa. 'The girl was short wasn't she? Putting her head out was like laying her neck on the ledge. Well, more so than it would be in my case, for instance?'

'More like it'd be for me,' the five-foot-nine policeman answered with a grin, thrusting his head out to demonstrate.

'And if I'd brought the sash down hard again while you were doing that—'

'You'd have been repeating what happened to Janice Weggly. At least as we understand it.'

'That she put her neck out, and Oliphant or someone else broke it with the window?'

'That's right, sir. With enough force to splinter the wood, too.' Furlong's hand went to finger the bottom of the window. 'The PM report says she died instantly. The blow was either professional or just lucky. If it hadn't been, seems it would have paralysed her from the neck down. Then he'd have needed to hold the window on her till it strangled her. It wouldn't have taken long.'

'Long enough, perhaps. For her sake I'm glad it happened so quickly,' the banker commented with a shudder. Like Furlong, he was now resting his elbows on the back of the sofa and studying the car and the yard below. 'Interesting, there must once have been some kind of low building connecting this house and the factory,' he said. 'You can see where a roof must have butted into the factory wall. And there's a bricked-up door space under it. Like the window space in the alley wall.'

'Yes. There's a storage cellar underneath too. It belongs to the warehouse. No interest to us, though,' Furlong replied. 'It's locked and bolted from the other side. Doesn't seem to be in current use. We're checking it out all the same. With the owner's estate agents.' He leaned forward again, his expression becoming more serious. 'And so she stuck her head out in the pouring rain because she wanted to, or because the murderer persuaded her to?' he questioned ruminatively.

'Because if she'd had an inkling of what was going to happen to her, she'd have been fighting like mad.'

'Right, sir. But there was no sign of a struggle. She must have done it voluntarily.'

'I suppose there are plenty of reasons to explain why?'

'Not so many with the rain beating straight in.' The policeman sniffed. 'She was fully dressed too. We assume ready to go to the meeting.'

'What if someone called up to her from the alley, and she opened the window to call back?'

'Whoever it was would have seen the window come down on her and raised an alarm.'

'Unless it was the muderer's accomplice with the whole thing arranged in advance? Mmm . . . no.' Treasure shook his head. 'Too contrived.' He raised his hand to touch the window. 'This frame's quite heavy.'

'Not heavy enough to have done the damage by itself,

sir. Not without human pressure being applied, even if the sash was broken.'

'Which it isn't.'

Furlong pulled his head clear, then motioned Treasure to close the window. The banker did so vigorously. There was a retort like a gun firing.

'It could be a lethal instrument, all right, only you'd have to time and position things right,' said the policeman.

'Which might be difficult, I suppose.'

'Not if he had an arm around the victim. If he was in any way guiding her.'

'Surely she'd still have fought back?'

'I mean guiding her in a . . . in an amorous sort of way, sir,' the policeman offered, it seemed without much conviction.

Treasure's eyebrows lifted a fraction. 'You mean they could have been making love on the sofa, then decided it'd be nicer with their heads out the window in the pelting rain? She was fully dressed, you said? That's not even kinky. It's just daft.'

'My wife said the same thing, sir.'

'I'm not surprised. There was no sign of sexual activity? Of any kind?'

'No, sir.'

Both men had got up and were standing in front of the sofa again.

'Where was the body found?'

'In a heap on the sofa. It had just been pulled back, and the window closed afterwards. Her neck looked very nasty. Squashed.' Furlong made a pained face. 'The head lolling unnaturally. Like a broken doll's. You should see the pictures.'

'No, thanks.' The banker considered for a moment. 'D'you suppose Oliphant could have been the father of the child?' he asked, changing the subject obliquely.

'He could have been, sir. But so could about ninety per cent of the male population. In theory, that is,' the other added quickly. 'That's what the blood group report shows.'

'But it's obviously convenient to assume it was him. Closes the case up with a vengeance. Gives a spare motive, as it were. I mean if she was pressing him over paternity of the child. That's always assuming the coroner's verdicts fit with yours. About both deaths. Is that what you're hoping, Peter?'

'It's what my Chief Superintendent reckons, yes. Can't blame him either. There's just as much unsolved crime up here as there is in London.'

'So you're grateful for obvious solutions?' Treasure moved across the room to take a closer look at the tropical fish.

'And whether you accept the obvious solution as the right one, sir.' Furlong folded his arms across his body and began some earnest to-ing and fro-ing with his head. 'You know the people involved with Miss Weggly, and Vormer House, and the golf course business. Would you say Major Oliphant was the one most likely—'

'To have done her in? Because clearly you aren't, for some reason?'

'How d'you mean, sir?' The questioner sounded uncomfortable.

'Well, if you were, you wouldn't have let me up here for a start. Hoping I'd drop someone else in it.' The banker grinned. 'You forget too, I didn't know Oliphant.'

'But the others?'

'I know none of them well. Charles Finton might have been the one with a motive but that seems doubtful, very doubtful, and even so he didn't really have opportunity. I thought pressing him as you did last night covered that. No. Sorry to disappoint, but if you really want my honest opinion, I think Oliphant has to be your murderer. On the evidence.'

'Circumstantial evidence,' Furlong put in.

'But pretty indicative if not conclusive. Were there none of his fingerprints up here?'

'No. Nor anyone else's. Except a few of Miss Weggly's.
The whole place had been dusted. That could have been
before or after the murder, of course. By the victim or the
murderer, who would have worn gloves anyway.'

'What about the bedroom?'

'In as apple pie order as this room. Come and see.' Furlong promptly led the way into the corridor and across to
the doorway nearly opposite.

'Good lord,' Treasure exclaimed on entry. 'She was inor-
dinately fond of her own reflection.'

'And the colour pink, sir.'

'As well as spotlights and these perpetual bloody fish.
And that's an absolutely massive bed.'

'King size, yes.' The policeman had stood to one side
watching his companion's expression with something
approaching glee.

The room was small, like the sitting-room, but with even
less space left to move around in because of the furniture.
At the end of the bed there was a long, built-in dressing-
table and chest of drawers. The predictable glass tank of
tropical fish was set at one end of this arrangement, next
to a TV receiver. Except for the single window in the
middle, the wall on the far side of the bed, opposite the
door, was entirely taken up with wardrobes, again built in,
and fitted with mirrored sliding doors. There were ruched
pink satin drapes over the window, also along the front of
the dressing-table and around the stool. The flouncy pink
and white duvet, the square pillows and lower bedsheet
were in the same material, and all freshly laundered. The
small spotlights that Treasure had remarked on were
assembled in groups of three on lacquered metal stalks fixed
around the dressing-table, above the door, and on both
sides of the bed.

But the decorative *pièce de résistance* was the ceiling which
was covered in reflective glass.

'I've never slept in a bedroom with an all-mirror ceiling,'

Treasure remarked speculatively. 'Wonder if that does me credit? Must be made up in sections.'

'Yes, sir. Difficult to see the joins, though. The spotlights are worked from the bed. They have dimmers,' Furlong provided in a somewhat awed tone.

'For when they're not needed for serious reading, I expect,' said Treasure lightly. 'Was she supposed to be living alone here?'

'She was, according to her mother and sister. Her two regular employees, interviewed this morning, both think she had boyfriends.'

'With a bedroom like this, and a body like that, I'm not surprised. I assume this is our Janice?' He had picked up the large silver-framed photograph from the bedside table. It showed a full-length colour shot of a naked, buxom young woman with a pretty face, leaning back on her elbows in a provocative pose on a beach somewhere.

'That's her, sir, yes. Natural blonde, as you can see.' The speaker paused. 'Her nightdresses and underwear and er . . . and things, they're pretty revealing too. In all senses. What you might call hot stuff,' Furlong continued in the tone of constrained surprise. He pulled open a drawer and took out some flimsy, mostly black and diaphanous undergarments, exhibiting them briefly like a reluctant auctioneer.

'Evidently not meant for keeping out the cold,' said Treasure.

'There's a leather whip in the wardrobe, too. A few articles of that sort. Thongs and such,' the policeman added, but sounding as if he shouldn't have.

'Hmm.' The banker mused. 'I'd say this was a girl who probably took her sex life quite seriously. Question is, did she have a regular lover or did she play the field?' He looked up, studying his reflection on the ceiling as he went on: 'And I suppose a typing agency could be a front for something else? Are there other bedrooms?'

'Two upstairs, one not completely furnished, the other pretty conventional.'

'Judged by the standard in here, you mean? What about the bathroom.'

'It's on this floor, next door. Re-fitted recently. Nothing out of the ordinary. Want to see it?'

'Not really. I wonder who decorated this room, did the electrics, and so on? I'd guess not a local firm.'

'No, it wasn't. London shopfitting contractors. People who did the ground floor did this floor at the same time. One of the ladies mentioned that this morning as well. She'd never been up here, but she knew Miss Weggly got it done that way so it'd be tax deductible.'

'Well, that could have been one of the reasons. A bedroom like this might get a single girl talked about, if it was done by the local builder. What are these employees like? Glamorous?'

'Not specially. Worthy, I'd say. Both middle-aged, and gone back to secretarial work after bringing up families.'

'I see.' Treasure glanced again at the photograph, then looked about the room. 'You said the place might have been done over by the murderer?'

'We assume the murderer. Not up here. It was the locked filing cabinets downstairs. The ones with the client files in them. They were disturbed. As if someone had been looking for something in a hurry.'

'Were the files broken open?'

'No. Miss Weggly's own set of keys was in one of the locks. Both her employees identified them.'

'So it could have been her who'd been doing the looking? Were the client files personal or company?'

'Both. But most of the personal clients are to do with companies the agency works for anyway.'

'You said last night Oliphant had the Henfold file with him in the car, and the cover was wet. Would there have been a Julius Kuril personal file as well?'

'There might have been if the agency had done work for Mr Kuril separately.'

'And had it? Did you ask?'

'Yes. Both the other ladies said they thought there could have been another file. But we didn't find it. Not here or in the car.'

'Nor any letters about house-building on the golf courses?'

'No, sir. There's a separate group of files for Mr Finton. Constituency and private. One for Councillor Motwell's business, too. But there's nothing in any of them about golf course houses. If letters do exist they didn't have to be filed here, of course.'

'Because there was another secretary?'

'Who died last night, sir.'

'In tragic but accidental circumstances.'

'We assume that, yes.'

'Is there any doubt?'

'None, probably. We haven't had the post-mortem results yet, nor the accident report.'

The banker thought for a moment, then shrugged. 'It still seems to me everything fits in the way that suits your Chief Superintendent. Except for how Oliphant got her to put her neck on the block.'

'And why he did, sir.'

'You're still not convinced about him?'

'We need to be sure.'

Treasure nodded. 'Frankly, I'd take the solution offered.' He looked at the bed again. 'Seems she changed the covers on Fridays.'

'That's right. The last lot were in the machine in the kitchen. They'd been washed and dried. No way of telling when. And it's not the kind with a lint trap either. For catching debris.'

'So everything's been washed away?'

'That's right.'

'Bad luck. Could we have a look at that yard before we

go?' Treasure asked as they were descending the stairs.

'Sure,' said the policeman, but as he was unlocking the back door a strangled female voice started squawking through his pocket radio.

'Better help yourself, sir,' said Furlong a moment later, after a brief exchange with the disembodied banshee. He waved the banker through into the yard. 'I'm going to use the telephone in the office.'

The concrete floor of the yard was badly cracked. There were wide undulating tidemarks of grime in places, and more enduring deposits of thicker, wettish dirt in the cracks, with moss growing at the bottom of the walls and around the cover of an evidently disused coal hole near the door. But the area had been cleaned of the more transitory sort of detritus by the rain—except for what Treasure identified as the shrivelled remains of a small, transparent plastic bag which had attached itself to the treads of the nearside front wheel of the car.

'Found something interesting?' asked the policeman when he reappeared.

'Not really.' Treasure straightened up, rolling his other find—a blue elastic band—between his fingers. He offered it and the bag to Furlong who took them without then appearing to know what to do with them.

'We've not bothered much with the yard. No evidence anyone's been in it since Wednesday,' said Furlong. 'The car was brought back from service then and hasn't been out since. We checked the mileage reading with the garage. Miss Weggly only used it at weekends, apparently.' He re-examined the elastic band, then put the two finds in his pocket before continuing in a more urgent tone. 'Look, sir, I have to go to Vormer House. I can still drop you off first at Stigham Manor if you like. But when I mentioned you were with me at the moment, Lord Delgard asked if you'd come too. There's er . . . there's been a development.'

CHAPTER 13

'Fellow wouldn't do it, you see? Shoot himself with his left hand. Not somebody right-handed. Never heard of such a thing,' Lord Delgard complained as he stumped along the west wing corridor in Vormer House, ahead of his two visitors. 'In here,' he directed next, throwing open the parlour door. He stood aside for the others to pass, then rasped, 'Shift yourself, Gunner,' at the dog, which had been following at his heels but was now standing irresolute in the opening.

'It wouldn't be the moment for totally rational actions, perhaps? When you're about to do yourself in?' said Treasure.

'All the more reason for body responses to be involuntary. Not deviant.' After he'd said this, Delgard looked mildly surprised, it seemed, at its profundity. 'Reflexes stay normal if the mind's deranged,' he went on, warming to his treatise. 'Not a time for new tricks. That entry wound should have been on the right. Stake anything on it. Take a pew, both of you. My sister'll be here in a minute. Glad you came too, Treasure. Yes.'

'Peter Furlong passed on your invitation.'

'Quite. This is an informal meeting. That's what you said, Furlong?' Delgard's good eye beamed hard at the policeman, leaving no room for equivocation.

'Yes, sir. And, as promised, I'm having your point rechecked. About the Major using the wrong hand. The first report definitely shows his left hand prints were on the gun,' Furlong offered, a touch apologetically. Afterwards he followed Treasure's lead and sat down—but not in a wing chair like the banker. He chose a short-backed, upright armchair, settling himself not very far into it, his head and shoulders just perceptibly starting to rock in time with the loud tick of the grandfather clock in the corner.

'Drink for either of you?' Delgard inquired, looking up suddenly and opening his hands in a hostlike gesture. He was standing with his back to the fireplace where logs were burning cheerfully. After the two men had refused his offer he went on: 'By the by, my sister was in the town last evening after all. She forgot. Easy thing to do. Done similar things myself. Often.' He stared at Treasure, then turned his head to do the same at Furlong, almost daring them not to agree on an explanation which made up in simplicity what, on the face of it, it might seem to lack in total plausibility. 'Ah, and here she is,' he completed as the door opened. 'Tell you herself.'

The visitors rose to greet the Hon. Bea, and Furlong was introduced to her by her brother. The lady had entered looking flushed and—to anyone familiar with her normal appearance—a good deal subdued. Gunner, sitting next to his master and the fire, had slowly heaved himself up expectantly after the others rose, slumping down again when it was clear no one was going anywhere.

When Bea had taken her usual seat on the sofa she said quietly and without prompting: 'I'm sorry, Mr Furlong, in the confusion last night I seemed to have misinformed your . . . your assistant—'

'Detective-Sergeant Pettifad, ma'am.'

'Is that his name? I'd forgotten, I'm afraid. Well, he came to ask if there'd been a telephone call earlier in the evening. From the *Gazette*.' She folded her hands in her lap.

'And you were very helpful. Told him there had been one, ma'am, for Lord Delgard, and that you'd put the caller on to Major Oliphant.'

'It had seemed the right thing to do at the time. Putting him on to the Major, I mean. Except . . .' she paused, touching the side of her mouth with a large green handkerchief bunched in her hand.

'My sister thinks that the call might have made Oliphant do in the Weggly woman, then shoot himself. Reasonable conclusion. Could be right, too, but nothing there to blame herself for. Told her so,' Delgard put in firmly.

'Quite right, sir.' The policeman hesitated, and shifted on the end of the chair before adding tentatively: 'It's what you told the sergeant next, ma'am. That's what needs clearing up.'

'I know. I said I didn't go out. In the confusion I'd quite forgotten I did. Go into the town, I mean. It's because it ended up as a fool's errand, I expect.'

'I see, ma'am.'

Bea had looked from one to the other of her three listeners after beginning her explanation, but her gaze now stayed on her brother as she went on slowly: 'I'd hired a videotape for the evening, but as soon as I turned it on I realized it was a film I'd seen before. Quite recently. So I decided to drive down to the video shop to change it.'

'That's Newman's Video Hire at the top of Plum Street, ma'am? On the left?'

'That's it. But I was too late. They close at seven-fifteen. I should have telephoned first to say I was coming. They're usually very accommodating. But being Friday, the girl probably wanted to get home in any case. It was pelting with rain. I remember that well enough.' She took a cigarette from the packet in her cardigan pocket, lit it from a red-covered gas lighter, and inhaled deeply. The hand holding the lighter had trembled a little.

'And you got to the shop at?'

Bea frowned. 'It was several minutes after seven-fifteen. Say twenty past. Anyway, it was an abortive outing. As I said, that's probably why I forgot about it.'

'Quite so, ma'am.' Furlong paused briefly before adding in a quiet and concerned tone, 'But we understand you made another stop in Plum Street? Before you came home?'

Bea took another long drag from the cigarette and exhaled again: 'I'm not sure if . . .' She had been looking at her brother again when her words stopped.

'You implying someone saw my sister, Furlong? You

never mentioned that on the phone? But if it's the case, let's have the detail straight. No beating about the bush,' Delgard demanded.

Treasure thought it would no doubt take a thousand years to develop and refine the peasant-crushing, aristocratic arrogance needed to get away with a question as bold and outrageous, if potentially disarming, as that one—with the questioner's demeanour the while indicating a militant sort of innocence that bordered on righteous indignation.

But the Chief Inspector seemed unconscious of the affront—or to be ready to wear it—when he answered compliantly: 'A local couple with their two teenage daughters, sir. They were driving down Plum Street and say they saw Miss Delgard's car draw up outside Miss Weggly's place. They then say they saw her hurry across the pavement into the porch and in through a front door.'

'How'd they know it was my sister? How could they see properly when it was raining hard?' Delgard thrust both hands into the deep side pockets of his long jacket where they immediately became engaged in some energetic burrowing.

'Their car was going quite slowly because of the conditions, sir. The couple know Miss Delgard very well by sight, or so they say. And the daughters had both been Girl Guides.' He gave Bea a respectful smile as he continued. 'It seems they recognized their former County Commissioner without difficulty.'

'And reported her to the police? Good lord—'

'Not exactly, sir. Not directly,' the policeman interrupted Delgard's testy observation. 'Not in the way it might sound. It was a casual remark by the mother this morning, about Miss Delgard being out in all weathers at er . . . at her time of life. Only she said it to the wife of one of our constables. The officer happened to be part of the house to house inquiry this morning in the Plum Street area.'

'Who are these people?'

The arc of Furlong's forward rocking extended slightly

before he replied: 'I'm afraid that's the only thing I can't tell you at the moment, sir.'

Treasure concluded that there was a limitation on peasant-bashing after all, and Delgard had just met it.

'The Colligans, I expect. They're a very nice family,' said Bea, stubbing out her cigarette. 'And they say they saw me go into Janice Weggly's?' she completed, resignation in the tone.

'That's it, ma'am. Through the door to the flat upstairs. Are you . . . are you able to confirm that at all?'

Bea had leaned back and was studying her thumb as it rubbed the inside of her forefinger. Then she looked up. 'I think I'd better, Tug.' She put this as a comment not a question, before turning to the Chief Inspector. 'You see, I was only trying to avoid admitting it to keep the family name out of what's happened. I don't believe I've done anything improper.' She breathed out deeply, it seemed in relief.

'I understand, ma'am.'

'Now look here, I have to—' Delgard began.

'No. Leave this to me, Tug, please,' his sister interrupted loudly. 'I fear evasion's not our strong point,' she continued, leaning back on the cushions and now a good deal calmer than she had been before. 'It was that phone call from the newspaper that upset me, of course. I felt I ought to do something about it. While there was still time.'

'The caller did more than just ask to speak to your brother?'

'Certainly he did. He told me what it seems he'd already told Madelaine Task. I didn't know that at the time. Or about his calling her at all. He said he was from the *Daily Gazette*. That they'd had a report about Charles Finton's secretary intending to . . . to spill the beans about house-building on the golf courses. That's if the planning permission was cleared for approval, as I felt it would be, at the meeting last night.' The speaker paused, one hand going to stroke the cameo brooch at the neck of her blouse. 'He asked if I thought the scandal would mean that planning permission wouldn't go through. I was horrified at the prospect. It seemed to toll the death knell on everything my brother had agreed to, after all that anguishing.' She reached in her pocket for another cigarette. 'If a scandal were to happen, I thought it would be bound to affect him, to threaten the most generous action the people in this area could possibly come to enjoy. Ever.'

'And that's why you went into town, ma'am?' Furlong put in, again quietly.

'It was. I tried to telephone Major Oliphant first, but he wasn't in. That was why I thought the newspaper couldn't have spoken to him as I'd suggested.' Her eyebrows lifted. 'And I really did want to change the videotape. The shop was closed, as I said. I think it was only then that I finally made up my mind to try to see Janice. To persuade her not to do such a frightful thing. Or perhaps . . . I don't know.' She shrugged her shoulders.

'You knew Miss Weggly, ma'am?'

Bea nodded vehemently. 'Since she was a child. Her sister too.'

'And that she was Mr Finton's secretary?'

'Certainly. It happens her poor mother and I had been discussing that earlier in the day.'

'And you found the door to the flat open?'

Lord Delgard cleared his throat with a kind of roar that made the dog jump. 'Bea, you don't have to answer any more questions, you know,' he said. 'You needn't have answered any, come to that. What d'you think, Treasure?'

The banker hesitated a moment, then answered: 'Miss Delgard wanted to keep your name out of the present investigation. That's understandable. But the best chance of achieving that now may be to tell Furlong everything. She's already said she's done nothing improper. I'm sure Furlong accepts that. This began as a privileged meeting, otherwise I shouldn't be here. Furlong's applied a good deal of dis-

cretion already. If Miss Delgard has anything more to add
I'd say now's the time.'

Delgard nodded slowly at his sister, but there was still a
reluctant frown on his face.

'The door to Miss Weggly's flat was open, ma'am?' the
policeman asked.

'It was ajar, yes. I was surprised. I called as I went
upstairs. There was no answer. I'd not been there before.
To the flat. Only to the shop part. The lights were on
in the first room on the left. The curtains closed. It's a
sitting-room. Well, you must know that. Janice's body was
on the sofa under the window. Her neck was badly broken.
The head was . . . it was bent over at a grotesque angle.'
Bea swallowed hard. 'She was quite dead.'

There was silence for several seconds before Furlong
asked: 'Did you check that Miss Weggly was dead in any
way, ma'am, or did you just assume she was?'

Bea looked down at the cigarette in her hand, then up
again at the speaker. 'I assumed nothing. I made the proper
examinations in the circumstances. She was certifiably
dead, though probably not for very long. I was a nurse in
the war, Mr Furlong. In the London blitz. And for some
years after that. One learned to diagnose death, and to
recognize it on sight.' She gave a brief, grim smile. 'In this
case I'm afraid the set of the neck said everything.'

'I see. Could you tell me what you did next, ma'am?'

Bea crossed her substantial legs, leaning forward to pull
the tweed skirt well down over her knees. 'I left immediately.' She blinked twice, quickly. 'No, I didn't call an
ambulance, if that's what you're wondering. It was clear
Janice was beyond any help in this world. About that I had
no doubts, not at the time or since.' She paused, again
going through the unnecessary repeat exercise of arranging
her skirt. 'On the other hand, I confess I panicked. I
thought Janice had committed suicide or else that she'd
been murdered, probably the latter. In either case I knew
a police investigation would follow. If her death was to do

with her threatening to blab about some secret arrangement over the house-building, it was unfair to get my brother involved. I was certain he knew nothing about any such arrangement. But if it was I who found the body? Well . . .' She ended with a shudder.

'I understand, ma'am. Or at least . . .' Furlong was hesitating over what to say next. He looked from Treasure to Delgard before he asked: 'Did you touch anything in the flat, ma'am?'

'Only Janice. I tried to take her pulse, of course.'

'Did that mean moving her?'

'No. I only felt her wrist and neck.'

'Did you know how she'd died?'

'It was obvious her neck had been crushed in some way. It wasn't clear to me how that had happened. Not at the time. I didn't think she'd hanged herself because . . . well, for obvious reasons.'

'Except that at first you thought it could have been suicide?'

'Only fleetingly. If it had been suicide someone would need to have brought her from where it happened and put her on the sofa.'

'Quite so, ma'am. But that wasn't immediately clear to you?'

'No, Mr Furlong, and I doubt it would have been to most others either. It was an extremely shocking thing to come upon out of the blue. Very unnerving.'

'Have you any idea why the front door was open?'

'None. I was grateful that is was, at the time. The two doorways are under a porch, but the wind was in the east yesterday. I remember the porch was nearly as wet as the street.'

'You didn't try the door to the shop?'

'No. The shop was in darkness. Or semi-darkness. The window lights were on, but the place was evidently closed, whereas, as I've already said, the other door was ajar.'

'And you saw no one else either inside or outside the flat?'

'No one.'

'And when you'd left the flat, and recovered from your shock, you didn't then decide to call the police?'

Delgard made one of his erupting noises, the sign of an impending verbal protest.

'It's all right, Tug,' his sister put in quickly to forestall him. 'It's a very proper question. I'm just sorry I don't have a very proper answer.' She stared straight at Furlong as she continued: 'I plain funked doing that, Mr Furlong. I accept it was irresponsible of me. But having got away without being seen, at least that's what I'd thought, it seemed better to leave things as they were.'

'Still keeping the family name out of it, ma'am?'

'Yes.'

'Even though you'd known Miss Weggly since she was a child, and been talking to her mother earlier in the day?'

'Yes.' She gave a loud sigh. 'Put that way it makes me sound very callous. Unfeeling.' Her voice broke dramatically on the last word. 'I'm very ashamed of my . . . my inaction,' she completed.

'More to the point, ma'am, you were giving extra time for a murderer to get away,' Bea's interrogator added severely.

'Oh, come on, man,' Delgard broke in. 'You know perfectly well Oliphant did it. And he was in the car park a stone's throw away, probably dead already.'

'Probably, sir.' Furlong pushed his hand up the side of his cheek as if testing the closeness of his last shave. It wasn't difficult for him to understand why Delgard should now be so certain of Oliphant's culpability when he had been decidedly sceptical about it a few minutes earlier. 'Just one or two final questions, Miss Delgard,' he said, eschewing broaching the last point with Delgard himself. 'If Miss Weggly had been alive when you reached her, what exactly had you been intending to do? Just now you mentioned doing something before it was too late. To dissuade her, or perhaps something else, you said.'

'I wasn't intending to murder her, if that's what you're suggesting,' Bea replied, some spirit returning to her voice. 'I wouldn't have harmed her in any way. I only wanted to find out if she really was going to spill the beans. And if she was, to try stopping her.'

'Not to find out if . . . if she had any beans to spill? If these alleged letters existed?'

'Oh, that too, I expect.'

'Or did you have reason to know that the letters did exist?'

'Certainly not. How could I?'

'Were you also aware that Miss Weggly wasn't Mr Finton's only secretary? That he had another one in London?'

'Yes. Her mother mentioned it to me. It was the young woman who died in the road accident last night, wasn't it?'

'That's right, ma'am. So did it occur to you that it could be the other secretary the phone caller had meant? That the alleged secret letters could be in her charge, not Miss Weggly's?'

'No, I didn't think that. It seemed to me Janice was the one who'd be dealing with things up here. With anything to do with the constituency.'

'I see. And did you know anything about Miss Weggly's private life? Who her men friends were, for instance?'

'No. We weren't at all close. Merely long-term acquaintances.'

The policeman stopped rocking, and folded his arms in front of him. 'Thank you, ma'am. You've been very helpful. I'm afraid we're going to need a formal statement from you later. For the Coroner's Court, you understand?'

'Of course.'

'Does that mean Miss Delgard's in the clear?' Treasure asked.

'I'm afraid that's hardly for me to say, sir.'

'But damn it, she only held back to protect me,' Lord Delgard insisted.

'Quite so, sir.' But the tone was matter-of-fact, not indulgent.

'I'm sure you think I've been very foolish, Mr Furlong?' offered Bea.

'No, ma'am. Imprudent perhaps.' He stroked the side of his nose. 'And a bit unlucky with it.'

CHAPTER 14

Molly Treasure looked up from painting her nails. 'But I'm sure he just meant she was unlucky to be spotted by the Girl Guides or whoever it was. Having to own up to being in the flat. He couldn't have believed she'd done the murder, surely?'

'Well, I thought it was an enigmatic sort of comment. Coming on top of saying he couldn't promise the old girl was in the clear,' Treasure replied. He put down the copy of *The Times* he had been only half reading. 'Of course, he bowled everybody over when he announced Bea had been to Janice Weggly's.'

'He never mentioned that to you when you were driving to Vormer?'

'Certainly not. Only that she'd been seen in the town. Bea evidently hadn't told Delgard either.'

The two, both clad in white towelling dressing-gowns, were in what Sheila Kuril had described as the principal guest suite at Stigham Manor—a title well justified by the comforts it boasted. The corner bedroom was large, with garden views to the east and south. It was cosily furnished in the Early American style with pretty chintz covers, a handsome mahogany four-poster bed, a chaise-longue under one of the windows, and a pair of original Grandma Moses paintings on the wall opposite the bed which, though not in period with the rest of the setting, were sympathetic to it. Treasure was seated in a tall-backed, winged arm-chair. His wife was at a slender-legged dressing-table set before a window with flowered curtains now closed behind it.

It was six-thirty. The couple had spent the previous half-hour together in a foaming jacuzzi in the bathroom—where the fitments were firmly state of the art, not antique. They were about to dress for dinner which was to be informal.

'But Peter Furlong already knows who did the murder?' Molly questioned.

'Only in a wishful thinking kind of way. He considers the set-up was too pat. Circumstantially. Too easy for the police to accept.'

Molly's eyes opened wider. 'How conscientious can you be, for heaven's sake?'

'Very, in Furlong's case. He's just as foxed as Tug Delgard about the gun being in Oliphant's left hand. He showed me around that flat for his benefit, not mine. I think because he has severe doubts. Based on instinct more than fact. He's a curious sort of copper.'

'So he was expecting you'd say something that would spark a different scenario?'

Treasure scratched an itch on his bare leg. 'I suppose so, yes. There was no other reason to let me into his confidence.'

'And all because you're involved in the golf development, but not part of the local mafia like the others?'

'That and because he and I happen to know each other.'

'And he trusts you?'

Treasure shrugged. 'We get on well enough.'

'And do you also feel instinctively that Oliphant didn't do it?'

'That's overstating it. I'd say he may not have done it. And one has to face the fact that there's no physical evidence to prove he was ever in that flat. No fingerprints. Nothing of that sort. Nobody saw him go in or out. And his shooting himself around the time she died just could be coincidence. Just.'

'And he was holding the gun in the wrong hand,' said Molly. 'All of which is making our pet Chief Inspector uncomfortable? Well, if you ask me, I think he wants jam on it. It can't be that difficult to shoot yourself left-handed.' She demonstrated the point by swapping the nail polish brush from the right to the left hand and pointing it close to her left cheek.

'Still awkward if you're holding a heavy revolver,' her husband replied. 'And irrational in the circumstances, too.'

'Hmm. And how did Oliphant get hold of the Henfold file if he hadn't been in the Weggly flat? Wasn't the cover supposed to be wet from the rain?'

Treasure thought for a moment. 'The wetness had no special significance on a night like yesterday. And he could have picked the file up some other time.'

'Borrowed it or stolen it? But it was none of his business, was it?'

'One doesn't know. There just might have been a legitimate reason for his having it. Anyway, it was kept in a cabinet in the agency on the ground floor, not in the flat. He didn't need to go upstairs to get it.'

'But he could still have gone into the shop or the flat without anyone seeing. It was pouring with rain. It was the time in the evening when there's hardly anyone in the streets, not in little towns like Thatchford, even when it's fine. And you said yourself it'd be easy for anyone to slip into the porch from that alley without being seen.'

'If someone came that way, certainly. Bea was seen, of course.'

'Because she drove down Plum Street, parked her car outside, probably banged the car door shut, and thumped across the pavement to the Weggly place. And all at the very moment when that hawk-eyed lot were driving past, qualifying for proficiency badges in observation. Or playing "I Spy".' Molly examined the nails of the hand she had finished. 'Bea Delgard is a marvellous old girl who'd never hurt anyone,' she added stoutly.

'But who took a hell of a risk not reporting what happened immediately.'

'For a very good reason. To protect her brother. She's full of unselfish good intentions. You know she drove up to the shoot just for the lunch today? Brought that huge hamper of goodies from the Vormer House kitchen. She was humping it over to the picnic area by herself. It was just when the beaters were getting there. I saw her, too late to help. She does it every Saturday, apparently. Cooks a lot of the stuff herself.'

'It's probably because Julius has been inviting Tug to the shoot. As a permanent guest since the start of the season. The old boy told me.'

'And Bea providing the grub balances things? Sounds a cushy arrangement for his lordship, and a lot of work for his sister. Except, of course, she reveres him, in a strangely unsentimental way. It comes out in so much of what she says, though. About what he's done for the community. You don't think Peter Furlong seriously suspects her of anything?'

'At one point I really thought he might be building up to arrest her. So did Delgard. He got very uptight.'

'But didn't you say whoever yanked down that window needed a lot of brute strength.' Molly looked up quickly. 'Ah, I see what you mean.'

'Exactly. Probably a lot less brute strength than humping the hamper. And according to Furlong, hitting the victim in the right spot was more important than strength anyway.'

'And Bea was a nurse?'

'Yes. Given the opportunity, one assumes she'd have known exactly where to aim. As for the power behind the blow, she may be getting on, but she rides still, and seems remarkably fit. I'd say she's very strong indeed. So's Tug.'

'Not as strong as Major Oliphant.'

'You never met Major Oliphant,' Treasure countered promptly.

'Neither did you, but it stands to reason. He was a soldier. In his prime.'

He shook his head. 'Retired soldier, and middle-aged actually.'

'And he had a motive to do in Janice. His job was at stake. Or the one he was expecting if the planning permission went through.'

'That was only at stake if Janice really did have some damaging letters and intended using them. But he could see they weren't in that file.'

'She could have kept them somewhere else. In fact it's pretty certain she would have. I would,' Molly said with assurance. 'Wouldn't other people have had access to filing cabinets in the agency?'

'I've no idea. Possibly. Except Julius insists the letters never existed anyway.'

Molly finished doing her nails, then turned to brush her hair. 'What if no one had told him about them?' she said. 'I mean, he's the big boss after all. It could be his underlings were plotting the whole thing as a surprise, without telling him in advance.'

'Not over something as fundamental as building hundreds of houses on golf courses,' her husband answered flatly. 'Anyway, there aren't any underlings in the sense you mean. I told you, Henfold is run by a tight little management group.' He picked up the paper again and turned a page of it. 'No, I really believe the whole letter business was a hoax.'

'So why was it worth it? What was it supposed to achieve?'

'To muddy the waters enough at that meeting so that a majority of the people there would vote against the plans. Except it didn't work.'

'All right, so Oliphant murdered Janice for some other reason. Jealousy? Something to do with her baby, perhaps?

Maybe he was her regular lover and then discovered she'd been cheating on him.'

Treasure grinned. 'Julius knew him well. He swears he couldn't have been her demon lover. He's quite adamant about it.'

'How could anyone possibly tell about something like that? Still waters run deep.'

'Well, Oliphant's were fairly stagnant, according to Julius. And he didn't fit with diaphanous underwear and mirrored ceilings either.' The banker picked up the telephone which had started ringing while he had been speaking. 'Hello? Oh, hello, Sheila. D'you want Molly?' He looked across at his wife. 'Oh, it's an outside call for me? . . . Yes, thank you. What do I do? . . . I see. The left-hand button?' As his hostess had instructed, he pressed the first of three buttons below the dialling figures on the handset, and the incoming call was transferred. 'Hello, Mark Treasure here . . . Is that Fred Larkhole? . . . Oh, Sid Larkhole? But you're related . . . His son? I see. So do we know each other . . . ?'

'I'll handle the questions, Ken,' said Furlong to the large, raincoated figure waiting with him on the doorstep of the house in St Wilfred's Close.

'Right, sir.' Detective-Sergeant Pettifad leaned back and continued to whistle 'Comin' through the Rye' under his breath. He wasn't Scottish, nor noticeably musical either.

'Nice house. Been here a long time though, I expect,' the Sergeant offered some moments later when the doorbell still hadn't been answered. He spoke quite slowly, the ponderous jowls giving weight to the intelligence. Then he screwed up his eyes, the better it seemed to search the panelled door for signs of woodworm or other evidence of decay. 'Takes a lot of upkeep, house like this,' he further vouchsafed in a seriously confidential manner. The hand that had briefly smoothed the polished brass door boss, now returned to stroking the heavy dark moustache, which in profile pro-

truded further than the flattened nose, and well beyond the
upper of Pettifad's two chins. A shoe was then extended
towards the immaculately painted black foot-scraper on the
right. The iron implement was not one that callers were
expected to do anything so worldly as to scrape their feet on,
unless those feet happened to be bare, clean and otherwise
guaranteed not to harm the pristine and venerable surface.
Pettifad's toecap tentatively touched the metal crossbar,
then came away again as if reacting to an electric shock.
He gave Furlong a told-you-so kind of nod and went back to
hissing the second line of 'Comin' through the Rye'—which
Furlong identified as the first line of 'My Bonny lies over
the Ocean', but he wasn't musical either.

Pettifad was twenty years older than the Chief Inspector,
half a head taller, and four stone heavier. A good deal of
his extra weight resided in a beer belly that the raincoat
did nothing much to disguise. A conscientious officer but
one still lucky to have made the rank of sergeant, he had
latterly been employed almost exclusively on desk work. He
had been assisting Furlong this week because influenza had
fairly laid low three of the regular sergeants in the Serious
Crimes Squad.

'Good evening, Mr Finton. Sorry to disturb you, but I
wonder whether we could have a quick word, sir?' said
Furlong as soon as the politician had opened the door.

''Evening.' Finton seemed to be considering the question.
He parted his lips, hesitated, then closed them without
uttering again. He followed this by looking at the time,
and eventually conceding: 'I suppose so. I hope it really is
quick.'

'Thank you, sir.' The policeman paused. 'If we could
come in perhaps?'

'Oh . . . yes, of course.' Finton stepped back abruptly.
He was formally dressed in a grey, pin-stripe business suit.

'This is Detective-Sergeant Pettifad, sir. Would your wife
be available for a word as well, by any chance?'

'In the drawing-room. Over there.' The speaker looked

at Pettifad without seeming actively to enjoy the experience.

'Good evening, sir. Dried up at last then, thank the Lord,' the Sergeant volunteered, looking upward speculatively as he crossed the hall, as though to suggest that but for the providential change in the weather, rain might even now be penetrating through the ancient ceiling.

Felicity Finton got up from the grand piano set to the right of the double doorway as the others entered. The drawing-room, like the hall, was panelled in scrolled oak with a boldly carved frieze above. It was an elegant room, its focus a well-lit landscape in the Constable manner hanging above the wood and Italian marble fireplace. Probably in deference to the delicacy of the panelling, there were no other paintings in the room, but some goodish pieces of furniture—notably two eighteenth-century gilt upholstered armchairs, a Chippendale-style beechwood sofa, and a pair of ornate mahogany side tables, one on either side of the fireplace. A substantial oriental rug, with an intricate design depicting small cavorting animals, occupied most of the central floor space, which still left a wide border of polished wood around the walls. There was a central crystal chandelier, but most of the illumination came from shaded light brackets set on the frames between the panels.

'It's Mr Furlong again. Good evening,' said Felicity, moving towards the visitors with three over-large strides, her arms held stiffly, away from her body and slightly behind it as if caught in a slipstream. 'More questions, is it?' she added brightly, and swaying sideways after coming to a halt in front of the callers.

'He's promised not to be long, darling,' her husband offered pointedly and without bothering to identify Pettifad or even it seemed, to recognize his presence.

'Yes. It's about Miss Boyden-Pent, ma'am,' said Furlong.

'Not Janice Weggly?' Felicity replied as if she had been in some way disappointed. She did some *mea culpa* patting to the front of the pale blue, long-sleeved dress she was wearing as she added: 'Won't you sit down? Both of you?' She nodded at Pettifad who reacted to the invitation by smiling broadly, removing his raincoat and rolling it into a tight ball. This much accomplished, he then lowered himself heavily on to the beechwood sofa, causing the others involuntarily to tense for sounds of cracking.

The sofa held, but in the ensuing silence, Pettifad's stomach rumbled loudly. 'Pardon,' he said, grinning broadly at everyone and adjusting the raincoat on his lap.

The Chief Inspector waited for the lady to sit before settling himself, more gingerly than his assistant, on the edge of a curricle chair. 'Was there anything you wanted to add about Miss Weggly, perhaps, ma'am?' he asked.

'No-oh-no,' Felicity rattled out shrilly, like a Morse code signal. 'Except—' she glanced at her husband—'except to know if you're certain yet that he killed her? Major Oliphant, I mean.'

'Not yet, ma'am. Not for certain, no. That won't come till after the Coroner's Court, of course.'

'Of course,' Finton who was still standing, echoed impatiently. 'Now then—'

'Though there was one point I should have covered earlier,' Furlong interrupted. 'When I saw you both this morning. About Miss Weggly.'

'Yes?' the politician questioned, his impatience more marked than before, or perhaps it was irritation with his wife for elongating the interview when it had scarcely begun.

'It concerns Mrs Finton, sir.' The policeman turned his gaze back to the woman. 'Did you go from here to the meeting last night on foot or by car, ma'am?'

'I walked. I knew my husband would have a car there for afterwards. We were to go on to the Kurils'.'

'I see. Can you remember what time it was when you left here?'

'Yes. It was quarter to seven. It's only a ten-minute walk to the Community Centre. I use a short cut.'

'So you got there before seven? Before the start of the meeting?'

'Bit later than seven, actually. But the meeting hadn't started. It was late. They usually are, aren't they? The Council sort? They don't seem to be able to help it.' She gave a toothy, neck-stretched, mouth-wide-open smile, while her whole upper body was making an energetic circular movement.

'That's right, ma'am.' Furlong also lamented the tardiness of municipal meeting makers. 'It was raining heavily, of course. Did you get very wet?'

'Oh, I was well wrapped up. Had my long Barbour jacket and a golf umbrella, and my indoor shoes in my pockets. The wet never bothers me. My hair's usually a mess anyway.' She ran her hand through the lank, offending feature.

'And the short cut you took, ma'am. Did that take you through Plum Street?'

'Across the middle of it, yes.'

'Not past Miss Weggly's place?'

'Oh no. That's further down.'

'I see, ma'am. You say it's a ten-minute walk from here to the Centre, but last night it took you more than ten. Did you stop anywhere?'

'Look here, I think you'd better say why you're asking my wife these questions, Chief Inspector,' Finton put in testily, his jacket open, thumbs moving to the waistcoat pockets, the watch-chain glinting as fiercely as its owner's eyes.

'It's because Mrs Finton may have seen someone around Miss Weggly's, sir. By all accounts, there weren't many people in the street.'

'No, there weren't,' Felicity agreed, looking from one to the other. 'Sally Culper remarked on it too. I don't believe we saw anyone in Plum Street.'

There was a heavy silence.

'That'd be Mrs Culper the curate's wife, would it, Mrs Finton?' asked Pettifad, speaking for the first time since the stomach rumble. 'She was with you, was she?' He looked at the Chief Inspector, heavy eyebrows raised to signal an apology for intervening, except none was needed.

'Oh yes, didn't I say? I caught her up on the way. Just round the corner. She was going to the meeting too. But she had to drop some magazines in to old Mrs Hislop at the top of Westgate. We stopped to have a word. You know how it is?'

Furlong cleared his throat. 'Yes, thank you, ma'am. About Miss Boyden-Pent's visit here last evening—'

'What didn't you cover on that this morning?' Finton broke in loudly, looking at the time.

'Only a small matter, sir. You mentioned you all had a cup of tea together.'

'That's right.'

'And Miss Boyden-Pent didn't take any alcohol while she was here.'

'None at all.'

'It's just that we now know she had a large gin and tonic in the bar of the Eagle and Child, next door to the Conservative Club, between nine-thirty and ten o'clock, and two glasses of wine with her supper there before that.'

'Well, she didn't mention any of that to us,' said Finton.

'Did she tell you she'd been in Thatchford since before seven last evening, sir?'

'No. She didn't mention what time she'd arrived.' The politician shook his head. 'Are you sure she was here that early?'

'Quite sure, sir. She got to the Club soon after seven. What we're wondering is, since she was up here, why didn't she go to the meeting in the Community Centre?'

'Oh, that's easy. She was hugely conscientious. She'd come up to help me over the weekend, and she knew there was plenty of my work to do in the office at the Club. So far as she was concerned, Janice Weggly was covering the meeting.'

'She knew that, sir?'

'I'm pretty certain she did.' He swallowed. 'Yes, I must have mentioned it to her earlier.'

'Did her drinking cause the accident, d'you suppose?' Felicity questioned.

'She was on the limit, certainly, ma'am. Maybe not quite over it. It was something else she'd taken we're bothered about. Something that in combination with the drink could account for what happened.'

'Oh dear, she should never have driven off like that. So late. Such a long way.' Felicity ran her clasped hands along her skirt to the edge of her knees. 'What was it she'd taken? An antibiotic? Something of that sort? A medicine?' She leaned forward earnestly.

'Phenobarbitol, ma'am. Only a sedative dose. As much as anyone might take to get to sleep. It wasn't a suicide dose or anything like that. Except she'd have been crazy to take it at all on top of alcohol before setting off on a long night drive. It just doesn't make sense. Do you know if she had barbiturates on prescription for any reason, sir?'

'I've no idea,' Finton replied stonily. 'You'd have to ask her doctor.'

'We have, sir. His name and address were in her Filofax. He'd not prescribed anything of that kind.'

'So when is she supposed to have taken this . . . er . . . this sedative dose?'

'That's the problem, sir.'

'You mean you don't know?'

'The opposite, sir. Judging from the degree of absorption into her system, she took it around eleven-thirty last night.'

'You mean, after she'd arrived here?'

'That's it, sir. You didn't notice her take a pill? Or dissolve one in her tea, maybe?'

Felicity gave an anguished whimper and rose to her feet. There was a horrified expression in her eyes. 'Oh God,' she cried, 'oh, my God.' Then, hands clasping her cheeks, she rushed from the room.

CHAPTER 15

At first sight, the Ploughman's Arms seemed a suitable enough place for a clandestine meeting—if for nothing much else. It was three miles south of Stigham Manor in open farming country at the windswept crossing of two very minor roads. There were a few isolated cottages in the general vicinity but no village. The inn was small, and almost determinedly uninviting, with a peeling, poorly lit sign announcing its identity above another smaller, less dilapidated one that affirmed the place was a free house—a fact Treasure took only as confirmation that no brewer considered The Ploughman worth owning. An unlit notice at the roadside announced that coaches were welcome, but in so desolate an area this was evidently more to signal a hope than a serious expectation.

The pub yard at the side was empty except for a small dung-coloured Ford that had seen better days. Treasure drew the Rolls up level with the other car but more than a safe door's width away from it. As he walked across the forecourt a dog, close by but invisible, started a slow bark, deep-throated and more unwelcoming than threatening. An intended halo of coloured lights around the inn door in the centre of the building had been reduced to a string of spent bulbs and a single functioning bordello-red one at the apex. This generated some comic ambiguity, but nothing much in the way of decorative effect or any lively improvement on the general illumination.

The inn's lacklustre interior was predictable. Beyond the entrance there were inner doors on either side of the small stone-flagged lobby. These must once have led to separate public and private bars—for as Treasure next discovered, the single concession to modernity further inside had been the botched removal of the partition separating those fallen bastions of class distinction. Now the undivided, three-sided bar counter was set against the far wall, framed and backed by the familiar set-up of bottles, glasses, beer-taps and advertising material, excepting that even here a parsimonious landlord continued to allow only a speakeasy level of lighting. An immense, clear glass, empty bottle with a narrow neck was the largest item on display. A notice stuck to it read 'Give to Help the Aged' but, as yet, nobody had.

At least the banker had no problem in identifying the man he had come to see. Sid Larkhole was the The Ploughman's only customer. He was seated in his overcoat away from the bar at a round wooden table in the corner to the right of the door, next to an unlit fruit machine, and nursing an untouched half-pint glass of beer. He got up as soon as Treasure appeared and hurried towards him.

'Found your way all right then, Mr T.? Thought you would. Nice of you to come.' He offered a limp hand for the shaking, the wrist upraised like a dog's paw. 'Saved my life you have, squire, I can tell you. Drinks are on me. What can I get you, then?'

'Oh, a half of bitter would be fine.'

'Another half of best draught, missus,' Larkhole called to an invisible barmaid. He steered Treasure to the isolated table like an obsequious usher at a funeral.

'I've very little time, Mr Larkhole, but what you said on the phone sounded important. Just tell me first though, is your father still alive? I ought to know, of course.'

'No, still dead, I'm afraid, Mr T.' Larkhole gave a wheezy laugh at his own small and not entirely tasteful witticism. This ended in a heavy bout of coughing which injected some patchy colour into the otherwise uniformly off-white pallor of the badger-like face. 'He passed on three years ago. Eighty-two, he was. Lived with my married sister in West Ham.' The speaker cleared his throat again, wiping his mouth with a handkerchief frayed at the corners. 'Ate some jellied eels that didn't agree with him, he did. Died the same night. Collapsed while he was on the . . . well,

you know.' Larkhole gave a loud sniff, then shook his head.
'We thought of suing. The stallholder. For damages. But
at that age you couldn't be sure what a jury'd decide. More
than a bit dodgy. And what with the diabolical cost of a
brief these days . . .' But the far-away look in his eyes
showed he was still regretting not having tested the point.

'Well, I'm sorry. Your father was a very loyal Grenwood,
Phipps employee,' Treasure volunteered expansively, pulling out a chair and sitting on it.

'Oh, he lived for the bank, Mr T. Lived for it. Anybody'd
tell you that.' Larkhole looked about him as if expecting a
chorus to materialize to support the contention. 'Even after
he'd left. Used to read bits out from that house magazine
you sent regular.' Now he leaned forward, eyes narrowing
before the imparting of a special confidence. 'Thought very
highly of you, Mr T. You in particular, I mean. All the
commissionaires did.' He fell back in his chair, ran a finger
along the centre parting of his well oiled hair, and picked
up his glass.

'Oh, I was very junior in his day, you know.'

Larkhole lifted the same thin finger in protest. 'But
marked down for high office. The highest, my old Dad
always said. He was right too. Company doormen always
know a thing or . . . Ah, thanks, Ma.' He had broken off
to address the small, wizened old woman in the long woollen dress with an uneven hem who had shuffled over with
Treasure's beer. She was trayless, and held the glass out
before her in both hands like an uncertain celebrant with
an overfull chalice.

'Thank you,' said the banker, watching as the crone bent
slowly over the table and then even more slowly set the
glass down in the middle of it. 'Not many customers this
evening,' he added with a smile, while Larkhole took too
long selecting coins from a folding leather purse he'd produced from a side pocket.

'Going to clear up tomorrow,' the woman responded in
a reedy voice. She used the side of a bare hand to whisk a

beer spill from the table on to the floor, contemplating the result with some satisfaction.

'Early yet, I expect,' said Larkhole loudly, handing over the money.

'Well, it's the only draught bitter we got,' the recipient answered defensively, and with the same inconsequence as before. She counted the coins carefully. 'Just right. Ta,' she said coolly, as though she might have been expecting a handsome tip. She pushed a wisp of grey hair behind her ear, turned about, and made off in the direction of the bar, or the place beyond or even possibly under it where she had come from earlier.

'So how did you know I was here?' Treasure asked when he and Larkhole were alone again.

'It was in the evening paper, squire. Report on the meeting last night. With a picture of you. And the others.'

'I haven't seen it. And I suppose they also reported—'

'The two deceased?' Larkhole interrupted. 'No, only the one. Major Oliphant. But the other, the Weggly lady, that was on the local radio tonight. Nasty, that. Well, they both was. Cheers, then.' He slurped some beer from the top of the glass.

'And you know something nobody else knows about Major Oliphant?'

'Too right I do, Mr T.' He put the glass down and pulled his chair closer to Treasure's, carefully scanning the still manifestly empty bar before continuing in a lowered tone, 'He didn't do for himself, if that's what they think. It wasn't suicide. No way.'

'The report didn't say suicide, surely? There has to be an inquest.'

'Good as said it. Foul play not suspected. Well?' Larkhole's nostrils tightened without much disturbing other facial features, except the nose distanced itself slightly from the immobile pencil moustache. 'Only leaves one thing if they say that, don't it? I mean, it can't be natural causes, not from a gunshot, can it?'

'Accident?' Treasure hazarded pedantically, though without conviction.

His companion's teeth snapped at the air, like a terrier catching flies. 'I was there, Mr T. I saw it happen. Except I didn't twig. Not at the time.'

'You saw what?'

'The gun go off. I was in my car in the car park, wasn't I? The bottom end, by the entrance. I was following the Major.'

'Why? I mean—'

' 'Cos I needed to know where he was going next. Which was nowhere in the end, poor sod. Begging his pardon.' Larkhole moved a hand upwards as if he was about to make the sign of the cross—which would have been unusual for a lapsed Calvinist—except the hand then dived inside his overcoat and engaged itself in some searching underarm explorations.

'But you saw him die? So why haven't you been to the police?' Treasure took a tentative first sip of the beer and found it surprisingly good.

'Ah, professional problems there, Mr T.' Larkhole sucked his teeth. 'It's my line of work, see? Nothing dishonest mark you. It's just my governor wouldn't like me mixing it with the Bill. With the police. If you follow me?'

'No, I don't. You'd better explain. And preferably from the beginning. About your relationship with Oliphant, for instance.'

'That's easy, Mr T. I collects debts. Well, really I put the frighteners on punters for a loan shark. There's nicer names for what I do, of course, but this being between friends . . .' He gave a self-deprecating smile.

'By frighteners you mean you threaten violence, or apply it, or both?'

'Do I look like a muscle man, Mr T.? No, what I do is go to see the punter who's got behind with the repayments. I tell him about the godawful things that'll happen to him if he don't ante up toot sweet. It usually works.'

'And if it doesn't?'

'I have to try again.'

'Using violence?'

''Course not, squire. It's all mullarky, that part. Just threats.' He moved his half-empty glass along the table in front of him.

'I see.' Treasure decided to give the last assertions the benefit of the doubt. Certainly Larkhole didn't have a thug's physique. 'And Oliphant was one of your punters?' he said.

'Right. Into my governor for a tidy sum.'

'How much?'

'Shouldn't say.' He paused. 'But it was into five figures.'

'Over ten thousand?'

'With interest, more like fifteen,' he offered. Client confidentiality had been abandoned to a sterner imperative.

'And you were here intending to see him about it?'

'I had seen him, Mr T. Last night around half six. In his cottage.'

'With what result?'

'A good one. Scared the sh . . . the living daylights out of him.'

'How?'

Larkhole shuffled in his chair. 'By threatening to see this Lord Delgard he worked for.'

'Nothing else?'

The other's gaze went gently heavenward, in a supplicating way. 'Nothing much, no,' he answered carefully, then looking at Treasure again he added: 'It was his lordship that bothered him, really. See, he'd been gambling money that wasn't his. That was before he come to Mr H. for help. Mr H. being my governor.'

'Gambling with Lord Delgard's money?'

'That's about it, Mr T.'

'And you say you got a result?'

'Oh, he was going to pay up all right. By Friday. There's always someone people like that can turn to. In the end.

But they got to be really desperate. Threatened.' The gaze dropped briefly floorwards on the last word.

Treasure had raised his glass half way to his lips. 'So why were you following him?'

This time Larkhole became the tolerant teacher indulging the backward child. 'To see if he was going to get it straight off, of course. In case I could collect before Friday. I work on commission and bonus, don't I?'

'But what if he'd gone to someone's house? You could hardly have—'

'Ah, but he didn't, squire. Anyway, I needed to find out. He got on the phone as soon as I left him.'

'How did you know that?' The banker took another long draught of beer.

'After I left I went back round the house and saw him at it. Through a gap in the curtain.' He noted his companion's disapproving look. 'Well, all's fair, innit? I mean, the Major'd let Mr H. down good and proper. He was weeks behind. Months, really. You got to think of it from the moneylender's point of view. Well, as a banker you can see that. No? OK, so you wouldn't. Sorry, squire.' He had held up his hands in a gesture of surrender at Treasure's reaction to the last comment. 'Of course it's not quite the same for a banker. A proper banker.'

'Not nearly the same, Mr Larkhole,' said the current Chairman of The British Merchant Banking and Securities House Association, and over-loftily—but silently thankful that he was in the overt, regulated end of what was still the usury business.

'Anyway, Mr T. I couldn't hear what was said. Only I saw he got ready to go out straight off.'

'So you followed him. To the car park. I know where he put his car there, by the way.'

'At the end of that building? Well, he stayed in it, too. So I thought most likely he was waiting for someone.'

'What time was this?'

'Seven o'clock when we got there. Quarter past when

someone got in his car. Through the front passenger door. Came from the top end of the car park. I don't know who it was.'

'Man or woman?'

'Most likely a woman. I can't be certain, though. It was pelting still. Whoever it was had an umbrella. Big one.'

'A golf umbrella?'

'Could have been.'

'Did you notice the colour?'

'Not a chance, squire. I was fifty yards away. Maybe more. And the rain was coming down like—'

'All right. So what happened next?'

'Almost straight after, there's a flash of light in the Major's car. Like they was lighting cigarettes.' Larkhole nodded to bolster his contention. 'That's what I thought they were doing, see? As if whoever got in was after a light. For a smoke. Because whoever it was got out again straight after, umbrella up, and going like the clappers. Well, you'd expect that, in the rain.'

'Going in which direction?'

Larkhole's face clouded. 'To the top end, I think. I wasn't really watching. Not after whoever it was got clear of the car.'

'But was she a big woman?'

'Honest, I couldn't tell, Mr T. Bigger than me, probably.'

'And do you remember if a car left the park soon after?'

'No, but I been wondering about that. I was by the entrance, the wrong end for the official exit, and I was watching the Major. See, I thought maybe his caller would have brought him money. Not cash. It'd been too soon. A cheque perhaps. If the Major drove home I was going with him. But he didn't shift.'

'How long did you wait?'

'Fifteen, maybe twenty minutes. Till the flaming police car come. Blimey, that give me a turn, I can tell you. Drove straight up to the Major's car. There was only the driver. I got away when he went to see to the Major. Out through

the bloody entrance I went. Copper never saw me, I'm sure
of that.'

'And you think that flash of light was the gun going off?'

'Had to be, squire.'

'But you didn't hear an explosion?'

'From inside his car? From that distance? In the rain?
With my windows shut, and my hearing not exactly spot
on?'

'All right, but you realize there's no question you should
have gone to the police before now? Whatever your
employer's attitude.'

'Not on, Mr T.'

'Well, I'll have to tell them if you won't.'

Larkhole's eyes narrowed. 'That's different. Or could be.
But not if you just tell 'em it's me that's told you. Not right
away, anyway. I'd deny it, see? Then it's your word against
mine. The DPP don't like that. No corroboration.' He
finished his beer. 'And all they got to know for now is it
wasn't suicide. That's so they know what they're about.'

'So why don't you tell them?'

'Because I can't prove nothing. Because I was up here
pressuring the Major for a loan shark. I ask you, Mr T.,
who's going to believe it wasn't harassment? They'll say he
shot himself because of something I said.' He twice pinched
the end of his nose, quite fiercely both times. 'I er . . . I
better tell you. I been inside, see? Done a bit of time. Not
for nothing violent. But they'll know I got a record.' He
pulled the corners of his overcoat across his legs. 'Only I
know the truth of this one. And the truth's worth two thousand nicker to me, and that's a fact. An honest two thousand too. Ten per cent of what's salvaged, like.'

'I don't follow you? You mean your employer will have
a claim on Oliphant's estate? I hate to disillusion you, but
I wouldn't count on his—'

'No, better than that, squire. It's the insurance. My governor had the Major insured. Accident only. For twenty
grand. He always does that with the dicey ones. Which is

most of 'em, of course. To be on the safe side, like. The premium's peanuts, and the punter pays it anyway without knowing it. Mr H. is the only one can benefit. Only there's no pay-out on a suicide. Well, that's fair, I suppose,' he ended, with considered magnanimity.

'But there would be on a murder,' said Treasure slowly. 'Provided the murderer doesn't prove to be the beneficiary.'

'That's it, Mr T. That's it in one. No wonder you got to the top.' He had missed the speculative hint in the banker's last comment.

'So what do you really expect me to do?'

'Why, tell 'em you got an informer, squire. Someone who knows it was murder. They work with snouts all the time. Tell 'em what I saw. So they can get out and collar whoever done it.'

Treasure grinned. 'You have a touching faith in the capacity of the police to catch felons.'

'They caught me all right. The time I ended up in the Scrubs,' said Larkhole ruefully. 'And that was only for petty extortion.'

'But you're giving them no lead on this, other than the belief that you witnessed a murder.'

Larkhole looked mildly affronted. 'Oh I am, Mr T. The same kind they had on me that time. For the extortion. Petty extortion,' he corrected himself firmly. He leaned right across the table, hunching his shoulders together, clasped hands pushing down towards his ankles. 'The Major made a phone call from his house at six-forty-six last night. Made a note of the time, didn't I? Whoever he called arranged to meet him, then killed him. Has to have done.' His teeth made the fly-catching snap again. 'They can trace that call, squire. It'll be on the record, that will.'

CHAPTER 16

'You appreciate your informer could have done in Major
Oliphant himself, sir?' said Furlong, sitting bolt upright on
a black plastic chair on the other side of the table from
Treasure. The banker had just finished a rapid account of
what Larkhole had told him.

'With Oliphant's own gun?'

'Which is only what he's alleging someone else did.'

'Except if he was responsible he'd be bonkers to put the
thought in anyone's mind that it was murder. Well, at
this point, surely?' Treasure objected again. 'Not when the
chances are the police and the coroner are going to settle
for suicide?'

Furlong's eyebrows lifted as if to imply that the last comment could only be a guess—and possibly a bad one.
'There's a benefit in it for him though, you said, sir?'

'Two thousand pounds? Hardly enough if there was a
risk of his branding himself as a murderer.'

'Perhaps he hasn't thought of it that way. Or perhaps
that's why he wants his identity kept secret.'

There was a coolness in Furlong's manner, and he looked
tired, his usual energy and ebullience noticeably absent.
Treasure had been conscious of this—and something else
—from the moment the Detective Chief Inspector had
shown him into this depressingly windowless, cream-
painted interview room on the ground floor of the
Thatchford Police Station.

The banker had called the station on his car telephone a
few minutes before this, from the yard of the Ploughman's.
He had said he needed to see Furlong with urgent information on the Janice Weggly case. He had been put
through to Detective-Sergeant Pettifad who offered to see
Treasure himself immediately, explaining that his chief was

in an important meeting and couldn't be disturbed. Even so, when the banker arrived it was Furlong who had come to greet him.

It was the policeman's friendliness that Treasure felt had evaporated, along with the lively manner. He was sensing strongly that Furlong was a lot less comfortable about their relationship than he had been earlier.

'At least you now know for certain that Oliphant was in fairly deep financial trouble,' said the banker, running the fingers of one hand along the edge of the black-topped, oblong metal table, then flicking the corner several times with this thumb.

Besides two unoccupied chairs, the only other furniture in the room was a smaller side table with a telephone and an elaborate recording machine on it. Treasure assumed that the machine hadn't been switched on without his being told, but it was symptomatic of what he thought of as Furlong's present attitude that he even imagined that it might have been.

'We pretty well knew he had money problems before, sir,' the Chief Inspector offered in a dismissive tone. 'From what Lord Delgard told us.'

'But what Delgard said was supposition, wasn't it? That's what it sounded like when he spoke to me.'

'I'm not sure that what your unnamed informant has said counts as anything better, sir. If you'll forgive my saying so.'

'Oh, come off it, the man's admitted he's employed by a moneylender to pressure late payers. They'd practically given up on Oliphant.'

'So he's told you, sir,' came the wooden response.

'Well, I believe him. Can't see a reason not to. There might have been grounds for Oliphant saying he'd make good by this Friday, of course.'

'Your man believed that at the time?'

'To the extent of it being something he had to put to the test, at least. He says people like Oliphant usually have a very last resort.' Treasure pouted between the sentences. 'It was why he followed Oliphant, of course.'

'If he had no fairy godmother, after all, it explains why Oliphant might want to kill himself, sir,' offered the policeman speculatively. 'Washes out any reason for his being murdered, of course. Except in the mind of anyone who'd stand to gain if it wasn't suicide.'

'And you think my . . . my snout would have invented this character in the car park, the whole gun flash sequence and so on, just for his own profit?'

Furlong fingered his tie, it was dark blue with a small red armorial crest repeated all over it. 'He may not have invented seeing the gun flash, sir. That's one of the reasons why it'd be helpful if he could be interviewed by the police. Professionally.' The last word had been treated to an ominous inflection.

'Well, I'm sorry the privilege has been wasted on me only so far,' Treasure responded with some acerbity. 'But frankly there wasn't a cat in hell's chance of his coming to you.'

'And we're very grateful, of course, sir.'

Treasure gave a cynical grunt. 'But you feel that other than his seeing the gun flash . . . ?' He left the rest of the question unspoken.

'All the rest could be invention, sir. He'd have nothing much to lose by it, and quite a bit to gain.'

'The nothing much being, as you've said, that he could be indicting himself as a murderer.'

'Though there'd be no witness to that, and no corroborating evidence.' Furlong leaned back in the chair, balancing it on its two back legs. 'But if his testimony is reliable, it proves Oliphant never left the car.'

'That he never went into the Weggly place? Couldn't have murdered the woman, and, incidentally, couldn't have lifted that file himself. Not then anyway.'

The policeman nodded carefully. 'That's why we really have to get the man in, sir. To test his story.'

'I've told you, there's nothing I can do about that for the

moment. I don't even know how to reach him. He's going to call me tomorrow night at Stigham Manor.'

'You think he's staying in the area?'

'I've no idea. I imagine he did last night.'

'And you didn't take the number of his car, sir?'

'I'm afraid it didn't occur to me. In any case, it may not have been his car. The one in the car park.'

'I could insist you tell me his name, of course, sir. By not telling me, you realize you're obstructing the police in the execution of their duty? I could ... I could have you detained for that.' He had paused during the sentence while appearing to be studying the air duct grille in the wall behind Treasure, and with an altogether undue amount of care.

The banker's expression hardened. 'If you want to play games, that's up to you, Peter. But I'll risk it, because I made a promise. In good faith. Believing the information would be enough to be going along with. I've told him I won't give you his name for twenty-four hours, and only then after asking for conditions to be attached. I'm sorry I forgot to mention those before.'

The now red-faced Furlong looked ready to accept the delay if not gladly, then with fortitude. 'I expect he asked for more time than twenty-four hours to begin with, sir?' he said.

'A lot more, as a matter of fact.'

'And the conditions are?'

'That you won't call him as a witness, or make him give a formal statement.'

'He's not got a hope, I'm afraid.'

Treasure shrugged. 'I told him that. But I promised to put his conditions all the same. His viewpoint's understandable, of course. If he's officially involved at all he's going to be in trouble with his boss.'

'Hm,' was the policeman's short comment on the less than inalienable rights of informers with criminal records.

'His information could be key though, couldn't it? If it's

true. And I must say I believe it is. Not an elaborate lie, just to make two thousand pounds.'

'Still a lot of money to some people, sir,' Furlong observed dourly, gently implying he was one of those people, even if Treasure wasn't. 'And his boss is going to make a lot more than that, which should reduce the inconvenience of having his runner involved. But, yes,' he completed reluctantly. 'I accept the information is important, if the man is telling the truth.'

'Added to which, he still didn't have to come forward,' said Treasure with a final effort at justification.

'Which he hasn't done yet actually,' Furlong put in pointedly before continuing: 'I wonder if there's any way he could have known we've been following a different line from the suicide theory?' He had been watching Treasure's eyes as he spoke.

'The Honourable Bea, you mean?' the banker said, then since there was no response he added: 'If he knew anything about her, it certainly wasn't from me.'

'I'm sure of that, sir.' Furlong dropped the front of the chair forward and his arms on to the table. 'All right, we shan't press for his name now, or call him as a witness later, if we don't need to.' He took a long breath. 'That's if we make an arrest in the next twenty-four hours. By this time tomorrow.'

'Good.'

'Involving an unshakable confession supported by two witnesses more acceptable than your man will be to the Crown Prosecution Service.'

'That's a pretty one-sided deal.'

'We're talking about murder, sir.'

'Two murders?'

'Possibly.'

Treasure frowned, gave a short, impatient sigh, and checked the time with his watch. 'Look, Peter, I'm sure there are sound police reasons why you've now set me at arm's length over all this, but I've put myself out quite a bit, initially at your instigation. It was you who suggested to me Oliphant might not have committed suicide. If he was murdered, I'll do everything I can to help you find out who did it. But it's bloody irritating to be told I'm laying myself open to arrest if I—'

'I'm sorry, Mr Treasure, I really am,' the policeman interrupted, getting to his feet and looking embarrassed. 'I wasn't serious about detaining you. You've been very helpful. I can't tell you much more than I have at the moment, except the meeting I was in when you arrived was with my Chief Superintendent, from Divisional Headquarters, and . . . and someone from the Crown Prosecutor's Office. I've got to rejoin them now.'

'Does that mean an arrest is pending?'

'I can't say any more, I'm afraid, sir. And I'd ask you to keep the information you have on the case strictly to yourself for the time being.'

'Including the meeting with my informant, of course?'

'Especially that, sir. Strictly to yourself.'

'All right. But if you're going to arrest who I think you are, I believe you'll regret it.' Treasure stood up too. 'For heaven's sake, Peter, why not act on what my chap said? Oliphant made a phone call at quarter to seven last night. Can't you at least find out who he called? Surely you can make British Telecom tell you that?'

Furlong's head and trunk bent forward, not in the characteristic way, but slowly, and went just as slowly back to the upright. 'Mr Oliphant made no phone calls himself last evening, sir,' he said. 'The one your informant saw him taking must have been incoming. We think he must have had two of those. One purporting to be from the *Gazette*.'

'And the other?'

'We've a shrewd idea who that was from, except it's been denied so far.'

'Anyway, sorry I'm late,' Treasure apologized again to the three others who were standing, with drinks in their hands,

before the fire in the big hall at Stigham Manor. He had
come straight in from his car, and explained that he'd been
to Thatchford to pick up a sweater he'd left at the police
station earlier in the day—a story that was true, so far as
it went. Only Molly felt surprise at what she knew had to
be an evasion.

'You can't be late. The host isn't here yet.' Sheila Kuril,
the host's wife, contrived this piece of social logic with controlled irritation in her voice. 'He and Maggie have been
walled up in that study for the last half-hour.' She plucked
at the frilly collar of the elaborate flowered silk blouse she
had on over a red flared skirt, and which her frown suggested she now wished she hadn't bought, let alone worn.

'Serious business, I expect,' said Molly in a placating
way, smoothing a bare arm. She was wearing a simple blue
and white silk dress, but shapely and sleeveless, with a very
straight skirt.

'Well, they're sure as hell not making love. They'd have
been out here sooner,' Sheila rasped, still plucking. 'And I
don't know either why we're standing about in this cavern
now we're only six for dinner. Would you rather go to the
drawing-room?'

'No, it's nice here,' Molly insisted. 'Credit to you, Sheila.
It's warm, but grand as well, in an understated way,' she
completed, looking about her approvingly.

'And in any case you prefer big stages, don't you, darling?' said Treasure, putting his arm around her shoulder.

'Well, thank you, Molly,' Sheila commented over-
gratefully. 'It's Julius's idea always to use the hall. Makes
him feel like a baron,' she ended, her ire diminished because
feeling like a baroness wasn't exactly repugnant to her.

'Can I get you a drink, Mark?' asked Ted Legion, after
handing a glass to Molly. He seemed to have taken charge
of the drinks trolley in the host's absence, and had been
busy there when Treasure came in.

'I'll help myself, thanks,' the banker replied, not certain
for the moment what he wanted. He walked over to the

trolley, and while he was making up his mind the study door was opened sharply, and a flushed and angry-looking Maggie Halliwell came out. Kuril followed behind her, but not closely, and, as Treasure noted, in a studiedly relaxed manner.

'Drink, Maggie?' the banker called as she stepped across the hall in his direction.

'Thanks. Scotch, please. J&B. A big one. With plain water. I'll be back in a moment.' She hurried past him and disappeared up the broad stone stairs.

'Sorry, everyone. There was a complicated fax in from the Sydney office. Maggie's the Australian authority,' Kuril explained, watching the lady's retreat. Then, a twitch of his mouth showing he was conscious of an oversight, he moved across to shake hands with Legion. 'Didn't know you'd arrived, Ted. Should have dragged you in on the debate.'

'The Sydney office working Sunday's now?' Sheila asked, consulting the diamond-clustered watch on her wrist. It was a not very subtle indication that she doubted the existence of any fax—complicated or otherwise.

'We Australians never let up,' Legion joked.

'Are you in property development too, Ted?' Molly asked when their host went to join her husband at the drinks trolley.

The big man beamed. 'It's been one of my various interests, yes. What you and I might call a resting activity.'

Molly's eyebrows lifted. 'You don't mean you're an actor too? I'm so sorry, I should have—'

'In radio,' he interrupted bashfully, head and eyes directed at the floor in front of Molly's feet. 'I'm a Jack of all trades in the radio business, Molly.' Both his large hands cupped the crystal tumbler he was holding as if they had to be careful not to crush it. 'Manager, producer, news and sports commentator, actor, advertising salesman, you name it, I've been all of them. Sometimes simultaneously. You have to be if you run a small broadcasting station where I come from.' He looked up. 'Of course, coping with the real estate comes into that somewhere too.'

'And we now have something more interesting in that line set up for him over here,' Kuril put in, as he and Treasure rejoined the circle. 'More appropriate to his future rank, too. Isn't that right, Maggie?'

The woman addressed had just reappeared on the stairs. She seemed to have regained her normal composure, helped by the tailored blue linen dress she was now showing to better purpose than before. If the dress was both essentially feminine and crisply efficient, Molly, for one, felt its merits reflected those of the weaver.

'Do I take it you're making an official announcement, Julius?' Maggie asked carefully. She had spoken after taking the glass Treasure had ready for her. Her eyes darted from Kuril to Legion and back again.

'Sure. Want to make one yourself? Everybody's welcome,' Kuril replied, but his words suggesting that there might be a true cause underlying the banter.

Maggie indicated refusal with a slow sideways movement of the head.

'Isn't it a little premature, Julius?' Legion put in, looking embarrassed.

'Not as between the members of this tight little circle,' Kuril replied. 'Ted's joining the Henfold board.'

'Congratulations,' said Treasure, while thinking it might have been appropriate for him to have heard the news before this—then on reflection deciding it was probably none of his business, or not directly so anyway.

Molly and Sheila repeated the good wishes.

'Ted's going to front the operation in this area,' Kuril enlarged.

'So you won't be going back to Australia, Ted?' asked Molly.

'Not on a permanent basis, no,' the big man responded.

'What about your family? I've forgotten, are you married?'

'Er . . . well, no, Molly. Not exactly. Fact is, I . . . I just got divorced.' The reply was subdued as the speaker glanced across at Maggie. Her response was a blank stare over the top of her whisky glass.

'Well, now we have a celebration, it's a worse shame the Fintons had to pull out,' said Sheila. 'And I really can't imagine how Felicity came down so fast. With whatever it was Charles said she has. Come to that, he didn't say exactly what it was, did he? Altogether too vague.' She looked around at the others. 'I mean, she seemed fine when we last talked on the phone. That was around five this afternoon.'

'Maybe it was a migraine,' said Molly.

'Well, if it was, it's probably over by now,' Sheila more insisted than speculated. 'Maybe I should call them and see how she is? If she's better I'm sure they'd still want to make it. I can easily have dinner set back a little.' She was nothing if not a determined hostess.

Kuril cleared his throat. 'No, don't do that. Charles called again just now,' he said, his glance avoiding Maggie's. 'I'm afraid he's very upset. So's Felicity. She's not ill. It's over the death of his London secretary.'

'So they just need cheering up? Well, did you say—'

'It's not as easy as that,' Kuril interrupted his wife. 'Their lawyer was there. They were just leaving for the police station. Felicity's somehow tied in with the girl's death. Only indirectly, it seems. The lawyer wants her to make a voluntary statement to the police.'

'That sounds quite serious,' said Treasure, quickly calculating whether that had been the reason why Furlong had been so uncooperative, and deciding it probably wasn't. 'Is that all there is to it?'

'I gather so,' said Kuril, this time looking at Maggie. 'Anyway, the Fintons won't be joining us. So how's everybody's glass?'

'Empty,' Maggie replied, holding hers out immediately.

She had shown singularly little interest in the Fintons'
problems.

CHAPTER 17

'Brandy?' Kuril asked.

'Small one, thanks,' Treasure answered. He was admiring a slim painting on the study wall near Kuril's desk—a
vivid beachscape, windswept, with stark human figures in
the foreground. 'This is new. Another John Wonnacott,' he
remarked.

'Yes. Of Essex flatlands. He gets better all the time, I
think. Sure you won't have a cigar?'

'No, thanks.'

Kuril balanced the long Havana he had just lit on an
ashtray while he poured the drinks. 'I think he's the most
inspired of our perceptual painters. And the most
ambitious. That one's very complex. As a composition.
Unusual shape, but it works, don't you think? Gutsy too,'
he went on, the enthusiasm mounting. 'Got it last week in
Cork Street. Just couldn't pass it up.'

'It's terrific, yes. You're getting quite a collection of his
now. For appreciation or just love?'

'Both, I suppose. Not really my style to buy a picture
that isn't going up in value. Same with a development site,
but they don't call you a Philistine for that.' The expression
on the long face matched the cynical claim. 'I can never
really see the difference between the two.' He walked over
holding two balloon glasses, the cigar jammed between his
teeth and bared lips. He handed one of the glasses to
Treasure.

'I think you do see the difference. But you prefer people
to think you don't. Isn't it perverse to want to be judged a
Philistine? If that's what you intend. Cheers.' Treasure

took a sip of the brandy while continuing to admire the picture.

The other members of the dinner-party were making up a bridge four in the drawing-room. This was largely at Sheila's instigation. Treasure had not wanted to play and had said as much. Despite Legion's repeated offer to stand down so that Kuril could join the four, the host had been even more adamant that he and Treasure needed to discuss the funding of the Prague development.

'"By their deeds you shall know them." Is that right?' asked Kuril, studying the picture, while pursuing Treasure's point.

'More or less. Fruits, not deeds, I think. "By their fruits you shall know them." But the sense is probably the same. Why d'you ask?'

'Because it's true. Or ought to be. People in this country judge you too much by your background, not your achievements. I don't have any background. Not in the right sense.'

'That's not strictly true. You didn't have an easy childhood, but from what you've told me, you were scarcely deprived.' He was surprised and uneasy about Kuril's sudden bout of self-deflation.

'That's a relative judgement.'

'Sure. And if you don't think I'm doing you enough honour, or giving you enough credit, your origins don't seem to have held you back any.'

'Not in money terms, perhaps.' Involuntarily, Kuril's eyes cast about some of the objects in the expensively furnished room.

'Or social ones.'

'Don't you believe it.' He motioned Treasure towards the leather chair at the end of the long table, pulling another out for himself. 'If you're new rich, with no education, it's reckoned you can't be an æsthete, so you have to be a Philistine with no taste. There's nothing in between.' He blew out cigar smoke, then waved it away from Treasure's direction with his hand.

'That's tosh, of course.'

'Agreed, but you have to prove it is. And you don't do that with words.'

'By their fruits? I see.' Treasure nodded as he repeated part of the Biblical quotation. 'But the luscious kind that cost a lot of money? Charitable actions, for instance? Like saving Vormer House and contents?'

'If you think that's a charitable action.'

Treasure ran his tongue along his upper lip. 'On balance I'd say I could persuade myself it was, yes. And certainly more . . . more the action of an æsthete than a Philistine.' He grinned. 'Even allowing for un ultimate modest appreciation in the residuals. The golf club and surrounds.'

Kuril's eyes narrowed slightly. 'So you think it'll all improve my reputation with Tug Delgard and his kind?'

'If it needed improving.' Treasure took a larger sip of the brandy. He disliked being an audience for the soul-searchings of multi-millionaires expatiating on their wealth or status. Inevitably they ended up justifying the first or trying to enhance the second.

'I wonder how much it would take for me to blow it again. To undo all the good?' Kuril inquired slowly, examining the end of the cigar, then looking up suddenly.

'Quite a lot, I should say. And I'm sure you've no such intention. Look, didn't you want to talk about those new Prague projections?'

Treasure certainly wasn't itching to discuss business with Kuril, but he had felt duty bound to make the offer. That subject apart, he had more important matters to consider than his host's estimation of the frailty or otherwise of his own social standing.

What was increasingly burgeoning in the banker's conscience was the conviction that Bea Delgard was about to be wrongly arrested for the Weggly murder, and that what he had told Furlong about Larkhole's testimony was likely to increase not diminish that possibility. Furlong could easily now construe that Bea was also responsible for Oliphant's death. Treasure was fairly sure that the policeman had accepted already that it was she who had made that second telephone call to Oliphant. Now it would be easy for him to believe that she could have persuaded Oliphant at that point to meet her in the car park.

For his own part, Treasure was sure Bea hadn't spoken to Oliphant, even though she had admitted trying to do so—and that proof of her innocence of both murders was tied in with something he had seen during his visit to the Weggly place earlier that day, if only he could make the link.

'Prague was an excuse. I wanted to get out of playing bridge. Same as you,' Kuril replied to the last question, breaking in on Treasure's inward preoccupation. The speaker flicked imaginary ash off the pristine lapel of his mohair jacket. 'Except you were more honest than I was about it,' he went on. 'Brought up to tell the truth, of course, in the public school tradition.'

'You have quite a reputation for honesty, and I don't believe a white lie would tarnish it much,' Treasure replied promptly. He wondered if Kuril had been angling for him to say something of the kind, which almost certainly meant that the self-justification was about to begin in earnest, with a diatribe about a man's honesty and integrity not being dependent on his background or his wealth. 'I wonder how the Fintons got on with the police?' he said, pointedly changing the subject. 'I got the feeling you purposely avoided discussing their plight at dinner?'

'Yes, I did. Except it's actually what I wanted to talk to you about now,' the other replied, to the banker's surprise. Kuril held the base of his brandy glass between thumb and forefinger and circled the liquid around inside as he continued: 'Charles told me more than I felt I could decently pass on to everybody. Not yet anyway, although I'd had to tell Maggie. For a start, Charles said Felicity drugged Philippa Boyden-Pent's coffee last night.'

'Good God.'

'By mistake. Well, it would have been, wouldn't it?' Kuril looked up at Treasure who wasn't sure if the last comment had been intentionally enigmatic. 'Felicity dissolved some phenobarb in her own coffee, and Philippa drank it thinking it was hers. It's as simple as that. The phenobarb came on top of the booze Philippa had drunk earlier, which was a fair amount in the course of the evening. They think she just fell asleep at the wheel later.'

'Felicity has admitted the mistake to the police?'

'That's what Charles said on the phone. He's gone bananas over it, of course. Felicity came straight out with the explanation, apparently. That's after the police told her Philippa had taken phenobarb. Might have been better if she hadn't.' He shrugged. 'But she was in shock, and just blurted out the whole thing.'

'Well, at least it should stand to her credit,' said Treasure firmly.

Kuril's eyes narrowed. 'Except there are complications. Charles was having an affair with the girl. Quite a lot of people knew it too.'

'I see. But not his wife, presumably?'

'No, but he's scared she'll find out now. She's loaded, you know?' He gave a cynical smile. 'I think I told you, it's the reason he couldn't very well do without her. Anyway, he thinks the police may know already. About Philippa and him.' Kuril put his glass down on the table, and rubbed both hands together slowly in front of him. 'If they do, he's convinced they'll believe Felicity drugged Philippa on purpose.'

'Or that Charles drugged her, with Felicity taking the blame to protect him,' Treasure added quickly.

'I hadn't figured that.' Kuril took a long drag on his cigar. 'She'd do it too. In certain circumstances. I mean, if she'd found out about the affair and . . . and say Charles wanted to break it off, or said he did, and Philippa was making trouble.' He paused for a moment, taking the cigar from his mouth. 'Except I honestly believe the whole thing was an accident.'

'If it wasn't, then it was a pretty hit or miss way of setting up a murder.'

'That's right. And according to Charles, Philippa didn't decide to leave till well after Felicity had gone to bed. He and the girl later had a slight disagreement, as he put it, and she decided to leave after that, entirely on impulse. If he'd intended to drug her, to cause a driving accident, or if Felicity had, they'd have needed to know she was going much earlier. When they were having tea.'

Treasure shook his head. 'The police will only have the word of the two of them to support what happened. The Fintons could have invented the whole sequence. Fortunately, what they say is the truth actually sounds the most plausible explanation. And since Felicity has volunteered it was her fault.'

'You think it'll be OK?'

'Yes. It'll be better if the police don't find out that Charles and the girl were sleeping together, but even if they do, it doesn't mean they'll alter their view of the facts. And if that's the worst that comes out—'

'Well, I'm afraid it may not be,' Kuril put in, with a resigned expression. 'I said there were complications. In the plural. Felicity told Furlong she went to the meeting last night with a Mrs Culper, a local clergyman's wife she's friendly with. Said she caught up with her in the street, very near her house, at quarter to seven. Well it seems that wasn't true. Not exactly anyway. The two women met at the time Felicity said, but not where she said.'

'Is the difference important?'

'The police may think so. Felicity let them think she'd come straight from her house, and overtook Mrs Culper almost straight away.'

'So?'

'They asked Mrs Culper for confirmation, and didn't get it. She'd called at the Fintons' at twenty to seven, hoping

Felicity was going to the meeting by car. Hoping to get a lift. She rang the bell several times.'

Treasure frowned. 'And I suppose there was no reply?'

'That's what she said, apparently. And Felicity overtook her later at the top of Plum Street. That's quite a distance from St Wilfred's Close.'

'But what Felicity said could still be true,' the banker offered slowly. 'So she didn't hear the doorbell. So her idea of distance is vague. And if she'd consciously been planning to deceive, and that Mrs Culper is a friend, surely she'd have—?'

'Made some advance attempt to have her back up the story?' Kuril interrupted. 'Perhaps. The fact remains, the police are entitled to believe Felicity could have been at Janice Weggly's place. Some time before quarter to seven. Even well before.'

'So she could have murdered the girl? But why would she?' Then enlightenment showed on his face. 'Oh God. You don't mean Charles Finton was bedding Janice too?'

Kuril blew out some smoke. 'No, he wasn't. But Philippa Boyden-Pent for one thought he was. She went to see Janice when she got here last night to tell her to keep her hands off him. The point is, Janice was alive when she left, which Charles says was just before seven. That's what Philippa told him. Felicity obviously wasn't there at the same time as Philippa, and she was certainly with Mrs Culper from ten to seven onwards.'

'But the police don't know about Philippa's visit?'

'Not yet. They will soon. Charles had promised Philippa he wouldn't tell anyone she'd been to see Janice. This was after he told her about Janice's death. They neither of them wanted Philippa to be mixed up with that, of course. Not in any way.'

Treasure nodded. 'And it was hardly in Charles's interests to tell anyone. Certainly not to give her reason for going there. Presumably he'll say it was about secretarial work?'

'Yes. And, of course, now it doesn't matter who knows Philippa was there.'

'Possibly not.' But the banker had his own reasons for sounding less certain. 'Unless someone else knows why she was there, and tells the police. But I agree, what matters most is Felicity wasn't there.' He paused, squeezing his brow between thumb and forefinger. 'Of course, the police will only have Charles's word that Philippa went to Janice's, and more important, that Janice was still alive when she left. They may think he's just cooked up this fresh twist.'

'Because if they find out Philippa was with Janice they'll think she murdered her?'

'It's possible. But it's more likely they'll believe Felicity could have done for both women. Out of jealousy,' Treasure replied, with what to him seemed an obvious deduction. 'After all, each of Charles's secretaries thought he was sleeping with the other one. Why shouldn't his wife have thought he was sleeping with both? It's the conclusion other people may draw now. People who get hold of the real facts. Or think they have.'

Kuril nodded sharply several times, pushed back his chair and got up. 'You're right, of course. Made exactly the conclusion I thought you would. And I'm afraid that's the core of the problem,' he said, walking over to the fireplace with his nearly empty glass.

'For Felicity?'

'For Charles as well.' He rested his free hand on the stone mantelpiece, while his dark eyes searched the burning logs. 'Both his secretaries are dead. One pregnant and murdered. The other, his lover, killed by his wife's carelessness.'

'Which is putting it in the most charitable way,' Treasure commented quietly.

'Exactly. If he and Felicity come out of this technically innocent, it could still ruin him politically. The tabloids will have a field day on him. You know what they'll claim? Another sexually insatiable politician. Love-nest in con-

stituency, that kind of thing. Incidentally, from something
the police said, Charles knows already he's the right blood
group to be the father of Janice's baby. It's . . . it's a very
common group.'

'And was he the father, d'you suppose?'

Kuril turned about to face Treasure. 'No.' He paused for
a second. 'As a matter of fact, I was.' He regarded the
banker with an expression that was mostly questioning but
also partly amused in a puckish way. 'Now I've shocked
you?'

'No. Surprised me, that's all. Is it something you have to
admit?'

'Just possibly.' Kuril shrugged. 'And, in the circumstances, I'll probably do it anyway. For Charles's sake. It
was my mistake. No reason why he should have to pay for
it. He's not big enough to survive the sort of scandal he
could be facing. I can draw the heat off.' He drew on his
cigar, then exhaled slowly. 'Janice was my whore. That's
all. Had been for more than a year. I didn't think she had
. . . higher aspirations, but she did.'

'The baby? It wasn't an accident?'

'Not on her part.'

'And she wanted you to divorce Sheila and marry her?'

'Yes. You could say she turned out to be an old-fashioned
girl. As well as a scheming little bitch.' Kuril's face was
wooden as he uttered the last sentence. 'When I told her
there was no hope of marriage—' He broke off with a short
chuckle when he caught sight of Treasure's changed
expression. 'Oh, don't worry, I didn't kill her. If you
remember, I was with you and Molly at the . . . the relevant
time.'

Treasure nodded and relaxed again. 'What do you mean
by saying you may have to admit responsibility? If it's not
quite certain, surely—?'

'Janice's lawyer knew the situation. That was part of her
scheme too,' the other man interrupted. 'We were in the
process of making a settlement. It's a woman lawyer, inci-

dentally. Not local and not Janice's regular legal adviser. She wasn't at all malleable even before the murder, and I don't know what kind of discretion will apply if and when the police get to her. Maggie's been working on her this afternoon. Believes it's only a matter of money. Getting her fees paid and so on. I'm not so sure. She has a lot on us. For instance, she could even prove I paid for the improvements in Janice's flat. Indirectly.'

'I see.' The banker couldn't stop himself wondering who chose the bedroom décor, Kuril or the girl, or perhaps the taste was mutual. 'And coming clean, as you put it, isn't going to spoil your own long-term political ambitions?'

The other man made a dismissive gesture with his free hand. 'From your encouraging words just now, I'm prepared to risk it. After all, I'm saving the reputation of one of the Party's up and coming leaders. That ought to count, even in the medium term.'

'What about Sheila?'

Kuril walked back to the table and picked up Treasure's glass with his own. 'I think we're due for a refill,' he said, before moving on towards the drinks tray. 'Sheila will . . . will stand by me. In the time-honoured public manner of wronged but forgiving wives.'

'She knows already?'

'Sure. And I've been pardoned—for getting found out. You should understand, Sheila can't be bothered with sex. It's not one of her on-going activities.' He pronounced the last sentence with an American accent. 'I'm left to my own devices in that area. On condition it's treated strictly as playtime. Nothing serious or involving. Which is exactly how I prefer it too.' He paused, and looked up in the middle of pouring the brandy. 'Therapeutic and circumspect, you might say,' he added with a self-indulgent smile.

'In those terms, wasn't Janice Weggly a bit close to home?'

'Which home? Our real home's in London. I use this one more than Sheila, of course. But Janice never came into it.

That's one of the unspoken rules. I always play away from home. Both homes.'

'But wasn't the place in Plum Street a bit public?'

'Not if you had access through the warehouse cellar.' He grinned. 'One of our subsidiary companies owns the place. Another one owns the freehold of the car park site, and nearly all the houses on the west side of Plum Street. We've been quietly collecting property round there for years. We'll be going for planning permission eventually. For a super-market. Anyway, the front door to the warehouse is in North Street, at the top of Westgate. Very circumspect.'

'Do the police know Henfold owns the place?'

'Shouldn't think so. Nobody else does. Nothing dishonest involved. It's simply not in our corporate interests to have such information disclosed. If it doesn't have to be.' He chuckled. 'They can find out if they dig hard enough, of course.'

'And that you have the key to the cellar?'

'Same again.'

'Could the murderer have used the cellar route?'

'Oliphant? Not a chance. For a start, mine's the only available key.' He breathed out sharply. 'Damn Oliphant.' He came over with the replenished glasses, and sat down again. 'On Thursday Maggie made terrific progress for me with Janice's foxy lawyer.'

'A money settlement?'

'Sure. There was still plenty of time for an abortion. Janice would have had one too if . . . well, if Oliphant hadn't gone round the twist and . . .' He shrugged and left the sentence uncompleted while he drank some brandy.

'And Maggie was handling the negotiations?'

'Of course. I've no secrets from Maggie. Her loyalty's total. And her discretion. It was she fixed me up with the warehouse arrangement.' He grinned. 'But she's furious about what I'm planning to do now.'

'Which was why she came out of here tonight looking so upset?'

'Yes. I've never known her so angry. Figures any scandal affecting me directly can still screw up the planning permission on the golf course development. I don't believe it. Do you?'

'I don't really see why it should do, no.'

'Maggie says the local councillors are narrow-minded. Especially Winkler the Liberal Democrat. I don't believe it. Not that narrow.'

'Mrs Task will have anger to add to her grief,' Treasure said coolly, and aware that in terms of sentiment his host had so far seemed singularly untouched by the murder of his mistress.

'Well, you can hardly blame her for that, I suppose,' the other replied with a practical judgement still bereft of emotion. 'But the Labour councillors would have voted against anyway. The Tories will carry it, I'm sure, with the Liberals,' he completed. 'And Maggie will come round to my view. Has already, probably. She trusts my judgement.' He stared over the top of his glass at Treasure. 'And I'm delighted if you still think I'll not be blowing my reputation with Delgard and his like.'

'Over what may come out over Janice Weggly? Probably not. Your business integrity won't be put in question.'

'Only my sexual habits. Something that doesn't count for so much these days?'

The banker nodded. 'And I agree the effect of disclosure won't be as dramatic for you as things could have been for Charles Finton. Also it's probably better to come clean of your own accord. Better than risking an uncontrolled leak, I mean.' He paused and looked at the time. 'Julius, you'll have to excuse me now. I need to make a phone call.'

'Not to the police, I hope?' The question seemed to be in jest.

'No. And, I hope, very much in your interests. I just wish you'd hold up on any . . . revelations, till this time tomorrow at least.'

Kuril's hands parted in a gesture of compliance. 'Can I know what this is about?'

'Sorry, not for the moment. You'll have to trust me.'

'OK. And I'll still do as you say, if it makes you more comfortable.'

'It does.'

CHAPTER 18

'And Julius revealed all, just to get your gut reaction?' asked Molly next morning.

'That's what he implied. Except I don't really believe he'd have altered his intentions whatever I'd said,' her husband replied. 'I think he was practising on me, that's all.'

Treasure was driving the car slowly along the perimeter road inside Vormer Park, to the south of the house. The two had been to the early service at St Wilfred's Church in Thatchford. It was a little after eight-forty, and since it was fairly certain that there would be no breakfast on offer at Stigham Manor until nine at the earliest, they were going back by what Molly called the scenic route. There had been more heavy rain in the night and the roads were still puddled, but it was fine now, if a good deal colder, with a bleary sun trying to break through the morning mist.

'You think he really intends to go public with the dirt?' Molly went on.

'Not necessarily.'

'But telling you is virtually—'

'No it isn't,' he interrupted. 'He naturally assumed I wouldn't tell other people.'

'You've told me?'

'You're not other people.'

'I am when it comes to telling me about your snout.'

'That's different. There's a reason for that. In any case,

Julius probably assumed I'd tell you. In confidence. It makes us both accessories.'

'To what?' Molly demanded idignantly.

'Nothing serious. Just his honestly expressed, prior intention to own up. Eventually. Something he can claim if he gets found out in the meantime. He's a wily bird.'

'Sounds pretty devious to me.' Molly's face clouded. 'You mean if the murder is put down to Major Oliphant after all, and if the Fintons aren't accused of anything ghastly, because both Charles's secretaries are dead—'

'And if Maggie can square the Weggly lawyer, then Julius can keep his secrets to himself,' Treasure completed for her.

'Himself and us?'

'Yes. And Sheila, and Maggie, of course.'

'Hmm. But if it has to come out, for instance, that Julius was the father of the Weggly child, I mean in a way that he can't deny? Then he say it wasn't a secret because he'd told you? Us?' Molly didn't sound overly impressed with their weekend host's moral stratagems. 'Can we stop a minute?' she asked. 'The best view of the house is just coming up.'

'Sure.' He braked, then steered the heavy vehicle carefully on to the wide grass verge beyond a copse of silver birch and rhodondendron on the left. He ended the manœuvre so that the car was parked with the bonnet pointing towards the road opposite, which joined the one they had been on, making a T-junction.

The spur road led down through the softly landscaped valley and up again to Vormer House—not in the haughty, dead straight way of some formal avenue approaches to grand houses, but first in a westerly curve and gentle descent through green meadowland, its course punctuated by clumps of birch and alder or by a majestic specimen walnut, lime or beech, most of the trees still mustering a cover of autumn leaves. Midway between the perimeter and the house, the way swung right to run level and straight for a short distance eastwards across the centre of the vista until it came to follow the nearside of an oval lake. Next it crossed a stone bridge over the stream at the lake's extremity before hugging an isolated section of drystone wall that might seem to have been put there for purely picturesque reasons—had it not been for the sheep presently huddled in its lee. Not until after this did the road run north, in its final short and straight ascent to Vormer's courtyard gate.

To the viewers nearly a mile away, the house looked no less stately for seeming as natural a part of the landscape as the centuries old oak trees in the original parkland behind it, and which it still easily predated.

'The whole thing really is glorious,' said Molly. 'Will the golf spoil it?'

'Hardly touches what we're looking at now. The courses will be well to the west. To the left over there. It's mostly pasture at the moment. That little temple you can see beyond those trees is where they're putting the clubhouse and the rest. Delgard knows what he's doing.'

'So his sister's right to support him so strongly?'

'Yes.' He pouted. 'And I'm convinced she didn't commit murder to prove the point.'

'Except the police really don't accept Major Oliphant did it. Not any more?'

The banker's forehead wrinkled. 'That's true. But it doesn't mean Bea's their only other suspect.'

'Thanks to your mystery informer?'

'You could say that.'

'And that's still all you're going to tell your nearest and dearest about him?'

'Until tonight, yes. I don't want both of us open to a charge of obstructing the police.'

Molly wrinkled her nose. 'Wish I could remember his name. I just wasn't paying attention at the time. I'm sure there was a bird in it. Sparrow? No, swift-something?' When her husband didn't take the bait, she stopped fishing,

crossed her legs, and added instead: 'Peter Furlong was so
certain about Oliphant at the start, wasn't he?'

'Yes. He was settling for the obvious on Friday night.
Police forces are overstretched, of course. They can't afford
to ignore gift horses when they're offered. And Oliphant's
apparent actions were certainly . . . explicable. When he
was told Janice had letters that could destroy the Vormer
survival plan, he rushed out in a fit of madness and
destroyed Janice.' He paused. 'Destroying himself afterwards when he saw he'd done the wrong thing for what he
believed was the right reason. It all fitted.'

'Except the letters never did exist?'

'But Oliphant never knew that, and the police didn't
either at the start. They can't even be absolutely sure of it
now.'

'But you are?'

He hesitated. 'I think so.'

'And the police view only faltered because Janice was
pregnant?'

'When Peter Furlong figured her death didn't necessarily
have anything to do with letters or golf course plans.'

'That it was just as likely to be because she was black-
mailing the father of her unborn child?'

'Except you and I know the father is so relaxed about
it all he says he's ready to accept paternity just to save
embarrassment for Charles Finton.'

'So we're back to the letters as a motive? I suppose
Felicity has to be the other prime suspect, does she?'

'Yes.' He was silent for a moment, contemplating the
idyllic scene stretched out before them. 'One can't help
feeling it would have been better if Friday night's solution
had endured.'

'But not if a guilty—'

'Sod it!' came a clear, shrill cry from outside the car. It
interrupted Molly's homily, as she and her husband
watched a bespectacled, fleshy female, clad in white shorts,
blue sweater and trainers, slide abruptly into view on the

road from beyond the rhododendrons. It was Madelaine Task, and she was lying flat on her back, legs in the air, one arm flailing ineffectually, the other bent over to shield her head as she came to a stop level with the car.

'Any serious damage, d'you think?' asked Treasure a moment later as he was helping the still dazed councillor awkwardly to regain her feet.

'Only my pride, probably,' she answered bravely in a shaky voice and with a still commendable attempt at humour. 'Slipped on something. Felt like oil. Can't have been from that. They don't leak, do they?' She nodded towards the Rolls-Royce while rubbing her head and trying to straighten herself. Looking very white, she continued to lean heavily on Treasure while tentatively bending and stretching her right knee. Her right leg was the limb most smeared with the brown stain that was also streaked along her shorts and up her sweater. When she put her foot to the ground she winced and only half suppressed a whimper of pain.

'Your ankle, is it? Could it be broken?' called Molly who had also got out and was holding a rear door of the car open. 'Come and sit down in here.'

'Ankle and head. Don't think either's bust. Ankle feels more like it's strained. Could be all right in a minute.' Mrs Task was hopping slowly towards the car with the owner's support.

'Did you jog all the way here from the town?' asked Treasure.

'No, my car's on the other side of Vormer House. In the visitors' car park.' She turned about, and with Molly's help fell back on to the rear seat. 'Oh, that's a bit better. My . . . my head's throbbing like hell.' She looked down dazedly at the seat. 'Am I staining the leather?' Next she examined her hand which was smeared with brown as well.

'Nothing that won't come off. And sit back properly, if you can. Rest your head,' said Molly who had now got in beside her through the other door. 'It's not oil. It's sheep droppings. Organic,' she completed confidently, as if this offered some definite kind of all round consolation.

'Oil's organic, too,' said the victim in a weak voice.

'But much more penetrating,' Molly went on in compensating style. She was wiping dung off Mrs Task's exposed lower limbs with handfuls of tissues from a box in the seatback.

'We'll wait a bit. Then when you feel better we can run you to your car,' said Treasure. 'If you can't drive it, Molly can follow us in it to your house. Unless you'd rather we got you to a hospital? Or your doctor?'

'No, really, I'm going to be fine,' came with evidently forced conviction.

Treasure noted Mrs Task's still pale complexion and the involuntary shiver she gave as he spoke. 'Well, better not to catch cold, anyway. There's a rug in the boot you can wrap around you,' he completed, going to fetch it.

'Thanks. Sorry to be so much trouble.'

'Glad we were on the spot,' said Molly. 'Do you jog here every morning?'

'Only weekends,' Mrs Task replied, while not very expertly taking off her glasses with both hands. 'Not always then, either. At the moment it's . . . it's any valid excuse to get away from the house. The house and my mother. She lives with us.' She gave a deep sigh.

'She's pretty grief-stricken, I expect,' said Treasure, wrapping the rug around her legs. 'Your sister's death must have been a terrible shock for her. For you too, of course. We're very sorry.'

'My mother blames me for what happened,' Mrs Task responded dully, polishing the glasses with a tissue. 'And she's getting to me.'

There were curious admissions to make to comparative strangers, except Molly had sensed that the speaker was on the brink of tears—that the shock of the fall coming on top of the family tragedy might be acting as an emotional trigger.

'Mothers do sometimes take such things out on their grown-up children,' the actress said with feeling. 'Deep down she possibly feels some equally unaccountable kind of blame herself.'

'My mother's been blaming me and excusing my sister since we were little. Over just about everything.' This came in as soulful a tone as Mrs Task's previous comment. She tucked the rug tighter around herself, leaned back, and half closed her eyes.

'I understand,' Molly responded. 'If your sister was as angelic a child as my sister was—'

'Janice was a little bitch from a very early age. And she always got away with it,' Mrs Task, suddenly very alert, broke in on Molly's sympathizing with an unexpected, hysterical note of venom in her voice. 'My mother's even blaming me for Janice having a baby. It's her twisted way of blaming me for not having one, see? I make allowances, but she can be dead cruel when she tries. Dead cruel.' The speaker became curiously subdued again after the last outburst. She ran the hand holding the glasses across her temple. 'I don't know why I'm talking to you like this. I'm really not with it. We'll all miss Janice, of course,' she added, with evidently forced conviction. She leaned forward to examine her injured foot, and began rotating it more easily than before.

'Was it that hoax phone call that's bugging your mother? The one you spoke about at the meeting?' Treasure asked.

'Yes. She talks about practically nothing else.' Mrs Task looked up at the banker who was still standing outside on the grass. 'Why did I tell the whole of the meeting about it, she keeps asking. As if Janice's killer got the idea from that. From me. That bastard Oliphant wasn't even at the meeting, for God's sake. And he got the same call. Must have done. After Miss Delgard. She put them on to him. She's said so. Only it's obvious Oliphant must have thought Janice was Finton's secretary. So he went and killed her. It had nothing to do with me.' The sentences came out with a rush, like an overly pent-up protest.

'And you didn't think of her in that way? As his secretary?' asked Molly.

'Never. She was never his proper secretary. He used her agency, that's all really. It didn't even cross my mind the man on the phone meant Janice. I'm still sure he didn't either. Whoever he was.'

Treasure cleared his throat. 'And from what one hears, it's hardly possible that anyone at the meeting we were all at could have killed your sister. I mean, after hearing your announcement. The ... er ... timing ...'

'That's right. It would have been too late. She was dead already,' Mrs Task interrupted gratefully. 'Of course she was. I keep telling my mother that, but she won't listen.' The last words seemed to catch in her throat, and suddenly she did burst into a fit of uncontrolled sobbing. 'I'm so sorry,' she uttered some moments later, still deeply tearful. She took some fresh tissues from Molly. 'I don't know why ... I mean ... I haven't been like this before.'

'Because you've been bottling things up. Putting on a brave face. Well, let it out now. We shan't mind,' said Molly, putting a comforting arm around the young woman. 'You'll feel a lot better in a minute. Then I think we should get you home.' She nodded at Treasure who closed the rear door and got into the driving seat. 'Will your husband be there?' Molly asked.

'Yes, I suppose so.' Judging by the tone of the response the fact wasn't one that had filled the speaker with a wholesome expectancy. 'Thank you for being so understanding. Both of you. I think you're right. I have been holding it back.' She wiped her eyes with the tissues. 'Anyway, I'll be all right now. And my foot. I'm sure I can drive. If you could just drop me back at the car.'

'Good,' said Treasure from the front. 'And you really must stop having misgivings about what you said at the meeting. About the phone call. It was fair political comment at the time.'

'I wish I could believe that. I told you what my mother thinks. She's got me so worried.'

'But I don't suppose you mentioned the call to anyone before the meeting, did you?' asked Treasure.

Mrs Task shook her head. 'Only to other councillors. The ones I was with.'

'And was that when you'd arrived at the meeting?'

'Just after, yes.'

'And none of them left the hall and came back later?'

'How d'you mean? Oh, I see. No, they didn't.' Mrs Task looked puzzled. 'Anyway, no one on our side, the Labour side, would have wanted to stop Janice showing letters about the house-building. Even if they thought it was she who had them. It would have helped us to have any letters exposed.'

'But you didn't think of her as the one who had them in any case,' said Treasure as he moved the car on to the road.

'That's right.'

'Curious about that caller,' he went on. 'It seems he wasn't from any newspaper.'

'So the police told us.'

'Did they ask you if there was anything odd about the call?'

'No.' Mrs Task shook her head. 'There wasn't either. Not really.' She frowned. 'The line was a bit fuzzy. That's all.'

'And you still believe Major Oliphant killed your sister?' said Molly, still sitting beside Mrs Task on the rear seat.

'Yes. The police don't, though. Not any more. They've been pestering us night and day for stuff on Janice. As if it was her fault. Something she'd done.'

'Did Janice have any strong likes or dislikes?' Treasure asked from in front.

'Yes. She was crazy about men,' Mrs Task responded acidly.

'And tropical fish?' said the banker with a short chuckle.

'Oh yes. She was gone on those fish.' But the admission had come grudgingly, the tone more guarded.

Nor did Mrs Task volunteer anything else till they reached her car.

Several minutes later the Treasures watched Madelaine Task drive away from Vormer car park in the direction of Thatchford. This was after they had helped her into her car and satisfied themselves that her right foot was up to coping with the pedals.

'What did you make of the *cri de cœur*?' asked Treasure as he turned the Rolls in the opposite direction.

'Understandable in the circumstances. She found us a sympathetic audience.'

'She was a quite different person from the fiery, confident politician of Friday night,' Treasure observed ruminatively.

'She's gone through a lot since then. Still is going through it, by the sound of it.'

'You didn't think it was all a bit put on?'

'Well, not the fall for a start,' said Molly in an indignant tone.

'No. Of course that was genuine all right. Nasty too. I just thought she got better sooner than she let on, with the later histrionics just possibly laid on for our benefit.'

'So what are you suggesting?'

Treasure sniffed. 'That like Julius and his good intentions, she was busy making us character witnesses to her . . . well, in her case, innocence.'

'Innocence? You're not seriously suggesting she could have murdered her sister?'

'I think she was very possibly capable of it. She hated her enough.' He settled more comfortably into the driving seat. 'But if my snout is telling the truth she's in the clear. Trouble is, I've got to be sure he is.'

CHAPTER 19

Larkhole parked his car in front of the shop—the end one in the terrace of four in the short main street of Cudlam-on-the-Wold, a small, unpicturesque village that did nothing to justify the length or allure of its title. The shop contrasted sharply with the more predictable trades of the other three—a general store, a bakery, and a greengrocer's. All four businesses were private, with living quarters above. Only the premises of J. Slugersby & Son, Aquarists, seemed to have been redecorated less recently than any of the others: a lot less recently.

This would be the third retailer of tropical marine fish that Larkhole had called on since ten o'clock when the first one had been advertised to open: that had been in Nottingham, quite close to the 'bed and breakfast' where he had spent the night. But it had been a general pet shop, with just a few tanks of tropical fish. The second of the addresses he'd copied from the Yellow Pages had been in Warkborough where he had also drawn a blank. That one had been an extension of a garden centre with tropical fish as a promising sideline—or so the keen but ageing dolly-bird assistant had explained. Before pressing on to the third shop, Larkhole had weighed the possibility of the ageing dolly-bird becoming a keen sideline in an amorous context, but reluctantly decided that she was too upmarket for him.

Cudlam-on-the-Wold lay equidistant from the other two towns and closer to Thatchford than either. No aquarists had been listed in Thatchford. It seemed that dedicated purveyors of tropical fish settled in outlying, cheap rental districts, relying on customers to seek them out: it was a new trade to Larkhole, in the sense that no one in it in his time had ever defaulted on a loan from Mr H. Judging by

the outward appearance of J. Slugersby & Son, it was very
unlikely that anyone, even Larkhole's employer, would offer
a loan against such a rundown-looking business. Even so,
it was clear from the things in the window—they hardly
merited calling a display—that the owner was an aquarist
with no sidelines. Larkhole would have come to Slugersby's
earlier except the place didn't open till eleven. If no one
here provided the information he was after, he'd have to
start again on a fresh group after lunch: none of the other
pet shops on his list opened on Sundays until the afternoon.

He tried the shop door. It yielded with difficulty and a
disquieting judder. An electric bell started to ring as he
entered, before the noise it was making degenerated into
a hoarse, un-bell-like gargle. Inside, the atmosphere was
over-warm and faintly eerie. After stepping along a narrow
defile beyond the doorway, the visitor found himself in an
area walled on all sides, it appeared impenetrably, by row
upon row of small, water-filled oblong tanks. The glass
tanks were fitted with wires, bubbling steel tubes, the kind
of underwater foliage you find in tropical oceans—with bits
of rock and general detritus to match—and finally a very
few lively, colourful fish, seemingly content in their attenu-
ated, watery homes-from-home. The dim overall illumination was provided by small individual strip lights set behind
each tank: it was this that deepened the weird air of the
place.

'Want to look round?' asked a disembodied male voice
from the depths of the shop. 'Help yourself.'

'Yes. Thanks. Thanks,' Larkhole repeated, the final
expression more confident than the others. He adopted an
ingratiating smile and leaned forward myopically in the
semi-darkness, till gradually he made out the outline of a
narrow shop counter, tightly jammed between the tanks on
the rear wall, and some human movement behind it. Then
he glanced from side to side and nodded in an altogether
approving way. 'Very nice. Oh, very nice,' he observed
with the authoritative air of one well qualified to assess the

interior of a retail aquarist's shop—as though he might even be an official inspector of such establishments. Still nodding, he turned a professional gaze on to the nearest tank, studying it intently—until it became apparent that there were no fish in it.

'Something in particular, was there?'

The voice now sounded from the area close to but well above Larkhole's ear. He looked around and upward. Even the light from the tanks was now obstructed by the figure before him whose upper silhouette was the more fearsome for that. The man was immense—in all directions he was immense, and his person smelled strongly of embrocation. Larkhole wondered for a moment why it didn't smell of fish. 'Mr Slugersby, is it?' he inquired, with the degree of deference that a Stanley might afford a Livingstone.

'That's me. Call me Joss. Me dad's Jim. Stock's low at the moment. There's not the trade, see?' The speaker stepped back a fraction, and to the side, so that the diffused light illuminated his features for the first time. He looked to be in his late thirties—with shaven head, piglike eyes, a broken nose, and an upper lip covered by a ringmaster moustache, waxed at the ends. He was wearing a singlet, blue jeans of prodigious girth, a vacant expression, and a large gold ring in his right ear.

As he had been speaking, he had bent down and pushed aside the cover on one of the lower tanks, then dipped an enormous hand into the water. The hand reappeared with thumb and forefinger holding, by the tail, a minnow-like fish, grey in colour, and of no apparent distinction. Uncovering an eye-level tank, Slugersby in turn thrust the hand into this. In a moment a small but dangerous-looking white crab ceased disguising itself as a bit of coral in the tank and lurched forward, two of its pincers reaching for, then pulling the flailing minnow from the man's fingers before it was ignominiously devoured.

Larkhole cringed. He was a sensitive man where dumb animals were involved.

'His dinner-time,' said Slugersby.

'You always feed them by hand?'

'No. I just enjoy it more that way,' the big man replied, dipping for another minnow in the lower tank.

'Ah,' said Larkhole, which seemed the only answer for someone not wishing to give offence. 'Since I was passing, I wondered if you could help me and the wife? Bit of a social problem.'

Slugersby, another minnow in his fat paw, hesitated in his movement while he digested the information. 'Social?'

'A friend gave the wife a fish. A tropical fish.'

'Marine or fresh water?'

'Ah—'

'Me dad and me, we only do marine.' The writhing minnow went the way of its late brother—or sister.

'Marine,' Larkhole repeated firmly. 'The wife keeps a tank of marine tropical fish. Yes. The only trouble is this er . . . this specimen came anonymous, like. It was a party we gave. The wife's birthday party. You know what happens? People drop presents on a seat in the hall and you can't tell after who brought what. Awkward. This was in a plastic bag. Elastic band round the top.'

'What kind of marine fish?'

'A . . . a red one, I think. Or it might have been blue.' Red and blue seemed to be the predominant colours of the creatures in the surrounding tanks. 'Not very good with colours myself. Colour blind,' he added, in an inspired after thought.

Slugersby's moon face remained as good as expressionless. 'Bought here, was it?'

'We think so. Probably. By one of the people in this photo. It was in the local newspaper yesterday.'

Slugersby took the cutting from Larkhole and returned with it to the back of the shop. There was some natural light permeating through to where he went to stand beyond the counter. 'Know this bloke all right. Lord Delgard, that is,' he said. 'He don't buy from us. Came to a bout once, though. That were two year ago. For charity it was.'

'A bout?'

'All-in wrestling.'

'You . . . you do wrestling too? Expect we've seen you on the telly.'

'Yeah.' He was holding the square of newsprint taut between both hands. 'And all these was at your wife's party?' The tiny eyes had gone smaller still. They gazed at Larkhole, the lids screwed up denoting either disbelief or wonderment, it was difficult to tell which.

'Not Lord Delgard. Not his wife either. The others, though. It was for . . . for charity.' It was another inspired piece of invention.

'Go on? A birthday party for charity?' The invention had registered and rather surprisingly impressed. The eyes swivelled back to the newsprint. 'This one was in here Friday.' A huge index finger stabbed at one of the heads in the photograph. 'Bought a lionfish. Spotfin lionfish, same as that one.' He pointed to a tank next to the counter. In it was a red fish with a crustated head, fierce-looking fins and a ridge of spikes down the back. 'I gave the warning, all right,' Slugersby added carefully.

'What warning?'

The movement of the wrestling aquarist's thick cheeks, plus a slight downward turn of the mouth and moustache was as near a registering of emotion as the whole face seemed capable of evincing. It was an expression similar to the one worn at the execution of the two minnows. 'Other fish in your wife's tank still all right, are they?' he questioned slyly, and without directly answering Larkhole's question.

'Yes. They're . . . they're fine.'

'Big ones, are they?'

'Er . . . mostly, yes. Why? Don't lionfish like little ones?'

There was a low rumbling sound resembling the distant approach of a London Underground train, except it was coming from deep inside Slugersby and just before his mass-

ive frame, the bare fleshy arms, the flabby chest-folds held
in by the singlet, the immense stomach, all began to quiver
like a well set jelly turned out of a complicated mould. The
owner of all these appurtenances was succumbing to a bout
of uncontrollable mirth.

'Oh dear. Oh my lor',' he managed to utter eventually.
'That's rich, that is. They love little uns,' he continued.
'And quite a lot of big uns as well.' His last quip sent him
back into a fresh round of laughter, though it didn't last as
long as the previous one.

Larkhole's teeth snapped together decisively. He had got
what he had come for. 'It was definitely the third from the
right in the picture. The one who bought the lionfish?' he
pressed, retrieving his exhibit.

'Right,' Slugersby replied, wiping his mouth and eyes
with a red check handkerchief. 'Took it away in a plastic
bag like you said.'

'Done up with an elastic band? A coloured one?'

'Right again. We reckon that's our trademark.' The
speaker's delivery had slowed. 'Blue elastic bands. Me dad
got a job lot of them in a bankrupt sale years ago. Thousands of 'em.' He was looking at Larkhole with an apprais-
ing and fresh interest, as though there was something about
him he hadn't noticed before—possibly something sus-
picious.

'Would you swear to what you've just told me?' Larkhole
had opened a pocket notebook and was starting to scribble
words in it with deliberation and more difficulty because of
the limited light.

The wrestler's eyes narrowed again, and he folded the
beefy arms in front of him. 'Depends,' he said carefully,
then after a pause he added: 'Divorce inquiry is this?'

Larkhole stopped writing and looked up with every
appearance of having been caught out. 'Cor, you're a sharp
one and no mistake, mate. Been ahead of me all the time,
have you?' he offered in an obsequious and complimentary
manner.

'Knew you wasn't what you said,' the other replied, pleased with himself. 'Used to do a bit of the old domestic inquiry stuff meself once. Mean going to court, will it?'

'Might do. Generous expenses, though. Very generous.'

'Always ready to help put a wrong right, of course,' said Slugersby magnanimously. Then he added: 'How generous?'

'To what extent do the mobile phone companies have to cooperate with the police? I mean in a situation like this?' Treasure asked as he and Furlong were going up the stairs to Janice Weggly's flat in Plum Street.

The Detective Chief Inspector gave a pained look, though since he was in front of the questioner the effect was lost. 'Depends on whether you're assessing the cooperation as a copper, a responsible citizen, or a subscriber conscious of his rights, sir.'

'I see what you mean. I suppose if I'm paying for the service I'd expect my privacy to be protected, even if that didn't balance with the public interest?'

'Exactly, sir. In some cases particularly when it doesn't balance with the public interest. But in this case, I think we'll be getting what we need without a court order.'

'Quickly as well?'

'Oh yes. We should hear in the morning. That's where telecommunications companies can always score, of course. All their working data's retrievable instanter. You had the numbers of all the mobile phones. We've pretty well guessed the times of all five calls. So in the end the company only has to confirm information.' He had stopped when they reached the landing and turned to face Treasure. 'If you're right, it'll be a useful bit of deduction. Like your knowing what killed that cat.'

'Starting with a lucky guess in both cases.' Treasure gave a disparaging smile before adding: 'Meantime, Bea Delgard is—'

'Safe at home, not being put upon by policeman,' Furlong interrupted with a grin.

The two men were on warm terms again. Larkhole's anonymity was still being respected by Furlong, but less grudgingly than on the evening before.

'Do we want the bedroom or the sitting-room, sir?' he asked.

'The kitchen first, Peter.'

It was four o'clock on Sunday afternoon. Following a call from Larkhole at midday, Treasure had telephoned Furlong to say he expected to have new information for him by early evening which would exonerate Bea Delgard from any involvement in the deaths of Oliphant or Janice Weggly. In return he had pressed the policeman to indulge him in two connections—by arranging for some facts to be checked, and by meeting him again later at the Weggly place for a brief demonstration.

A uniformed policeman had still been on duty at the door in Plum Street when the two men arrived. Because of the new direction the case had taken during the previous twenty-four hours, the premises had still not been handed over to Janice Weggly's family.

'Did you get anything on car alarms on Friday evening?' Treasure asked, crossing the small but well-equipped kitchen and turning on the cold water tap.

'Yes. And we didn't need to knock on any extra doors either. In the house-to-house inquiries yesterday morning, two local householders had reported hearing an alarm going off. One of them couldn't remember exactly when it went off, but the other was fairly specific.'

'Should have been close to five past seven,' said Treasure.

'That's what you said on the phone, and that's pretty well what the witness had volunteered. He said it was just after five past. He'd heard the seven o'clock news on BBC radio which only lasts five minutes, and was letting his dog out just as the next programme started. He lives on Sowergate, the street that runs across the bottom of Plum

Street and Westgate. He thought the alarm probably went off in the Westgate car park. It stopped after about five minutes, he said, so he wasn't sure whether the owner had switched it off or whether it had stopped automatically.'

'But he didn't report it at the time?'

'No. Too far away, probably. He'd have left it to someone closer. Except there wasn't anyone. Not a householder. Only three families actually live in Plum Street now, and they're all at the very top. A passer-by could have reported it, of course. Anyway, no one did.'

'And the other person who remembered the alarm?'

'Was the wife of one of the families I just mentioned. Only she wasn't at all sure about the time.'

Treasure turned away from the sink. 'Could you slip this elastic band round the top of this thing?'

'Certainly.' The policeman had watched the banker take a kitchen-size transparent plastic bag from his pocket, then two-thirds fill it with water.

'Right,' said the banker. 'Since you're playing the victim in this demonstration, you'll be in here when the action starts. I'm your visitor, so I'm going to the sitting-room. I've just asked you for plain tap water to put in the whisky you've offered me. You've come out here to fetch the water in that little glass jug we saw on the coffee table. So could you stay here for the minute it'd take you to do all that?'

When he reached the sitting-room, Treasure crossed to the sofa, knelt on it with the plastic bag beside him, opened the latch and pushed up the window. Then he grasped the bag in both hands and after taking aim, hurled it at the BMW that was still parked in the yard.

The bag hit the car windscreen, bursting on it with a loud plop. Instantly, the car alarm sounded, filling the room as well as the area outside with a high-pitched, staccato wail. Treasure shut the window and was standing in the centre of the room when Furlong burst in.

'Victim thinks her car's being stolen,' the policeman said, still moving. 'She puts jug down in the handiest spot, jumps

on to sofa, throws up window,' he continued, fitting actions
to his words.

'Thrusts out head,' Treasure joined in, reaching over the
other man. 'And then, wham!' He started to bring down
the lower sash, but stopped it well above where Furlong's
neck was positioned immediately under it.

'Is that a reasonable explanation of how the victim was
made to volunteer herself for the chop?' said Treasure, his
voice raised above the noise of the alarm.

Furlong pulled his head in and shut the window. 'It's a
convincing hypothesis, sir,' he said.

'And that alarm is set to stop in five minutes, then it
re-sets itself?'

'That's right. I'd better have it stopped before that,
though.' He was half way to the door before he stopped to
add: 'If all those calls came from just one of the sources
you've suggested, the evidence is going to be hard to deny.'

'But meantime, we can follow the plan as agreed?'

The policeman hestitated for a further moment. 'You still
don't want to tell me how exactly this meeting of yours this
evening can hurry things up?'

'Not without risking a lot of reputations if it doesn't,
including my own. And I'm deadly serious about that.'

'All right, we'll do it your way. I shan't have the information from the phone company till mid-morning
tomorrow, of course.' Furlong checked the time. 'Your
meeting's at six, you said, sir?'

Treasure nodded. 'And we're not driving back to London
till after dinner.'

CHAPTER 20

'Julius did say six, didn't he?' asked Maggie Halliwell as she entered Kuril's study, closing the door behind her. 'I was going to apologize for being late.' She looked at her watch. It was five past the hour.

Treasure got up from where he had been sitting in one of the armchairs set beside the fire. 'Come and sit down. Julius rang a moment ago. He's still at Councillor Motwell's. Be here as soon as he can. Will you have a drink?'

'No, thanks. It's a wee bit early for me yet. Is the Council news good, did Julius say?'

'Very. Motwell's taken the necessary soundings. From all interested parties. There's no question the planning permission will go through. The Weggly murder hasn't altered the clear message everyone took from that meeting.'

'Nor should it have,' said Maggie firmly, while arranging herself in an armchair across from Treasure.

She was wearing a white lace blouse with a deeply plunging neckline over a mid-length pleated black skirt which stylishly set off her pretty legs and ankles. If the lady was past the first bloom of youth she went to some trouble to maintain a physical attractiveness that complimented her mental capacities. Treasure remembered that at their first meeting he had been prompted to equate the small mouth and the Highland accent with primness—an illogical conclusion that the present delicate display of cleavage was doing a good deal to dispel.

'Anyway, I'm glad,' she went on. 'It's not one of Julius's major projects financially, but it's important to him personally.' She crossed her legs, arranging the skirt over them. 'So really we don't need to be meeting now at all. Not to talk about what we do if the plans are turned down. Has anyone told Ted?'

Before lunch, Kuril had asked Treasure if he could join him with Maggie and Ted Legion at six. This was so that they could decide whether Henfold should make a formal appeal if the golf course proposals were rejected by the Council. Kuril had already arranged to meet Motwell before this at five.

'Sorry, I should have said, Ted rang too. From his hotel. He's been . . . held up as well. Be here in time for dinner.'

'Oh?' Maggie seemed surprised. 'So that just leaves the two of us. Look, would you mind terribly—' she was making as if to rise but she stopped at Treasure's interruption.

'As a matter of fact, I'd appreciate a private word,' he said. 'Very private. About the Weggly baby,'

Maggie leaned back in the chair again. 'What about it?' The dark brown eyes opened a fraction wider as they stared back stonily into his.

'Julius told me he's the father. And intends to make the fact public to save Charles Finton further embarrassment.'

'And cause himself a muckle of trouble,' the woman replied tersely, the Scottish idiom matching the intonation which had sharpened with her indignation. 'That could ruin him locally, of course. And in a lot of other places too. He's so naïve. And Sheila's too indifferent altogether. People round here certainly aren't broad-minded about things like that. Not nearly as much as those two imagine, anyway. The situation may have been different when the girl was alive. Now she's dead, what's the point? I hope you advised him against doing anything so foolhardy? Charles Finton can look after himself.'

'I doubt that, and if Charles were accused of being an accessory to murder, I don't think Julius—'

'An accessory to murder, you say? Of the Boyden-Pent woman? Is that something you know for a fact? From your policeman friend?'

'It's not fact yet. And it's nothing to do with the Boyden-Pent death either.' He hesitated, folding his arms tightly across his chest before he went on. 'Look, this will need to be between the two of us, but yes, Peter Furlong's working on the theory that Felicity killed Oliphant and Janice Weggly. With her husband as an accomplice.'

'But it was Oliphant who killed Janice. Then he killed himself. Surely to God even the police can work that out?'

'It seems not. They have a witness who saw him shot in his car, by the woman they're sure had just murdered Janice.'

Maggie straightened sharply in her chair, her chin lifting above the slim neck. 'And that's supposed to have been Felicity? But why?'

'Because she believed Charles had been having an affair with Janice.'

'But really, that's preposterous. Charles wasn't having an affair with Janice. I could swear to that myself.'

'Except the police wouldn't believe you. I think Furlong's working on the premise that Charles broke off the affair after Felicity found out about it. That Janice was black-mailing him. Over the baby.'

'Does Julius know any of this?'

'Not yet. When he does, I think it'll make him even more adamant about admitting he's the father.'

'Then we've got to stop him. D'you understand? We must stop him. I—' Suddenly Maggie had become flushed and tense. Then, just as quickly, she seemed to take hold of herself, breaking off the sentence she was delivering and continuing instead with: 'But can they prove a case against Felicity?'

'I got the impression they were well on the way at one point. Beginning with Charles's involvement. They think it was he who made the three phone calls on Friday evening. The ones from the man who said he was from the *Gazette*.'

'Meaning it was Charles who started the rumour about

the letters? The non-existent letters? Why? It makes no sense?'

'I'm afraid it does. From a prosecutor's viewpoint. The letters were a hoax from beginning to end. They were invented simply to make it look as if Janice was murdered for a business reason, when in fact it was because of the baby.'

'A hoax from beginning to end,' Maggie uttered dully, repeating the words still as a statement not a question.

'Obviously the Fintons knew the letters could never be produced,' Treasure continued. 'So they couldn't affect the planning permission in the end. But in the short term they provided a perfect reason for Oliphant to murder Janice and then to kill himself, apparently in a fit of remorse. And the plan very nearly worked too.'

Maggie frowned. 'But who says the girl was blackmailing Charles? And Oliphant did die by his own gun, which he must have taken with him to kill Janice. And even if he killed her in a different way, the gun was there for him to use on himself afterwards.'

'No. The police think he had it with him on the murderer's orders, for an entirely different reason. That was after he'd been made to believe the letters existed.' Treasure leaned forward in his chair. 'But he had no intention of killing Janice himself. He didn't have the chance either. They know that because he was being watched from the time he left his house to the time of his death.'

Maggie reacted to the last statement with a short backward movement—as if she had been pushed. 'I don't understand,' she said. 'When was Felicity supposed to have put Oliphant up to helping her? To doing anything about the letters?'

'With the fourth of five phone calls made by either Charles or Felicity, probably on the same mobile telephone. As I said, the first three calls are supposed to have been made by Charles. To Mrs Task, Bea Delgard, and Oliphant. The last two by Felicity.'

'And have the Fintons been questioned about this?'

'Yes, and they've denied it, of course.'

'But the police don't believe them?'

'They think Felicity rang Oliphant at around quarter to seven, saying she'd had a call from the paper, and asking if he'd had one as well, knowing quite well that he had. She would also have calculated that by then he'd be worried stiff about the letters, and the consequences if they were exposed. She arranged to meet him in the car park before she went alone to see Janice, to persuade her to give up the letters, she told him. He was to bring his gun to lend her, something no doubt he'd have balked at normally, but being half out of his mind he was ready to do anything Felicity demanded. She'd have said she only wanted the gun to threaten Janice, which is the kind of conscience-salver I gather would have suited Oliphant. To do something key to the action without actually getting involved in it. You knew him, of course?' He paused, waiting for a comment.

'He was a nervous creature, certainly,' Maggie offered thoughtfully, but without over-commiting herself to the judgement.

'I see. Well, what the police think Felicity actually did was get there ahead of Oliphant, murder Janice, and join Oliphant afterwards in his car. When he handed her the gun, she shot him with it. He'd probably given it her with his left hand, so she put it back in the same hand without thinking.'

Maggie continued to seem more compelled than surprised by the story. 'But how is Felicity supposed to have overpowered Janice?' she asked. 'Janice was much the stronger of the two.'

'Felicity took her a present. A tropical fish in a plastic bag half full of water. The fish was a peace offering, perhaps. As everyone knows, Janice was crazy about tropical fish. This was an expensive specimen too, and rare. A lionfish which incidentally eats anything live it can swallow, including other fish. They have other unpleasant attributes as well, but they look very exotic. I don't know whether the choice was symbolic?' He looked at Maggie as if expecting a comment.

She raised one eyebrow enigmatically. 'Symbolic of what? Did the fish play some part in the girl's death?'

'Yes, it did,' he answered. 'When Janice was out of the room, Furlong thinks Felicity threw the plastic bag through the window at the car below in the yard. The impact set off the trembler alarm. Janice came back thinking her car was being stolen, put her head out the widow to see, and Felicity practically severed it at the neck by bringing down the sash.'

'Is there any evidence that—' Maggie began.

'Yes,' the banker put in. 'The evidence of what happened is bitty, and partly circumstantial, but convincing in total.'

'And amounts to what?'

'The alarm certainly went off. It rings for five minutes, then stops and resets itself. Two people heard it. Bits of the bag and the elastic band survived being washed away by the rain on Friday night. There was a stray black cat involved too. It had triggered the alarm in the past and learned better than to sleep on the car, but it happened to be sheltering under it. It ate the fish and was killed by the poison in its spines. Another of those unpleasant attributes I mentioned. Bad luck on the cat. Also for the murderer. The police had an autopsy done on the animal. They've also found the aquarist who sold the fish. He says he can identify the buyer.'

'I see.' Maggie breathed in slowly. 'And Felicity's final phone call?'

'Was made to the police. Anonymously, of course. At seven twenty-five. To say there was a dead man in a car in the car park. That's how they found Oliphant. You know the file in the car led them to find Janice's body?'

'How do they know the calls were all made on a mobile

phone? The same one?' she asked in reply, ignoring his question.

'They don't yet. But they will tomorrow morning. One way or another. A mobile fits the circumstances, for someone who was on the move, who couldn't use an ordinary phone and wouldn't want to be seen using a payphone. Unfortunately for the Fintons, or whoever it was, calls made from mobiles are the easiest to trace after the event, because the phone companies' billing records are very detailed. They're also almost instantly available.'

'But if they check Charles's mobile number?' She spoke as if she was thinking of something else.

'And the numbers of everyone else remotely involved who owns a mobile,' the banker answered promptly. 'Mine, Molly's, Julius's, Sheila's, Ted's, yours too. I expect. Felicity doesn't have one of her own, apparently. They collected all the numbers this afternoon. Furlong explained it was for elimination purposes.'

'Ted doesn't have a mobile either. And nobody asked me for my number.' She paused. 'Ted and I were out together this afternoon.'

'Would they have got your number from Julius, perhaps?' He stood up and put another log on the fire.

There was silence for a moment while they both watched the wood take flame. Then Maggie said quietly: 'So Charles is supposed to have made the first calls, then met Felicity and given her his phone?'

Treasure turned from the fire. 'Yes. You see, Maggie, it's all feasible. If one accepts the motive. That Charles was the father of the child. And he could have been, according to his blood group. It's a distinction he shares with Julius, of course. Even so, if Julius—'

'Felicity couldn't have made that last call. She was in the meeting at seven twenty-five,' Maggie interrupted. 'You know that. So must the police.' She was holding his gaze steadily as she went on. 'And she got there just after seven. So she couldn't have met Oliphant at seven-fifteen.'

'You seem very sure?'

'Even though I was in and out of the meeting myself, you mean?'

He shrugged. 'I've told you the police case is incomplete. Possibly some of the times are approximate.'

'But not that approximate. What you really mean is that when the evidence is complete, the case against Felicity and Charles will fall apart, even if Julius hasn't admitted by then he's the father of the Weggly baby?'

'When the evidence is complete,' Treasure repeated portentously. 'Of course there could be surprises then. After all, it was only yesterday they believed Bea Delgard could have been—'

'The murderer? Yes. Which is why you had to play the white knight and extricate her,' Maggie had interrupted again, her tone resentful.

'She's an old lady who shouldn't have been harassed,' he replied.

'And Janice Weggly was a young, scheming little slut with no conscience who deserved everything she got,' Maggie countered sharply. 'She was reneging on the deal she'd agreed over the baby. With no thought for the future of others. A lot of others. She was after Julius, and she meant to get him for herself—or ruin him.' The speaker stood up suddenly, breathing heavily. Then, folding her arms in front of her, she paced to the desk, standing in front of it with her back to Treasure for several moments.

The banker remained standing, and silent, watching her —watching while the anger evident through the tense set of her shoulders gradually but visibly subsided.

She turned about, slowly this time. 'So can we stop pussy-footing,' she said coolly. 'Because we neither of us believe Felicity or Bea killed Janice.'

Treasure smiled. 'Which puts both of us some way ahead of the police, of course,' he said carefully.

'I take the point. Also why you set up this . . . this *tête-à-tête*. Julius isn't coming back soon, is he?'

'Not as soon as he intended, no.'

'I thought not. And why isn't Ted Legion here?' The tone was now matter-of-fact and briskly businesslike.

'I'm afraid I called him and stood him down. I said the meeting was cancelled.'

'I thought so.' She paused. 'Ted's not done anything culpable.'

'Except I believe the aquarist will identify him as the one who bought the lionfish.'

She considered for several seconds. 'You mean you're quite certain of that?'

He breathed out sharply. 'Yes, I'm afraid I am.'

'So what? Ted was in the public meeting when Janice Weggly died.'

'Except it was he made the three phone calls before that. If I'm right, the police are going to know it in the morning. As well as whose mobile he used. Who he was working with.'

'Making those calls wasn't a criminal offence.'

'Not by itself, perhaps.'

She seemed to be about to speak again, then didn't. Instead she walked silently back to the chair and sat down, her hands hanging loosely over the chair arms in a purpose-fully calm manner. 'In your opinion,' she asked slowly, 'when the police have all the . . . all the evidence you spoke of, it'll be conclusive?'

'This time without any doubt,' he answered soberly. 'They'll even know how the murderer got in and out of Janice's place without the risk of being seen. Through the warehouse.'

'But only Julius has—'

'Using the killer's own duplicate key,' he interrupted. 'They'll also have figured why Oliphant's assailant approached his car from the north end of the car park, not the alley. That stems from the same reason, of course. Leaving the front door to Janice's flat open was to make it look as though the murderer had used it. Since Bea was seen to go in that way later she came to be the prime suspect. That was unfortunate.'

'But in the end not for Bea,' Maggie commented drily, then continued. 'With conclusive evidence you think there'll be arrests tomorrow?'

Treasure nodded.

'And who will be arrested?' she asked.

'I would expect you and Ted Legion.'

'Thank you for your honesty. So everything you've been saying about the Fintons you believe actually applies to Ted and me?'

'Yes, I do.'

'Will you tell me why you didn't say so before this?'

'Because the police still believe the Fintons are responsible. There was also the hope you'd say something to prove me wrong.'

The woman's eyebrows arched, but instead of taking up the last point as he'd expected, she asked: 'And the person you say witnessed Oliphant's death. He . . . he or she can identify the so-called assailant?'

Treasure remembered well enough what Larkhole had said, but he still replied, 'I think you'd better count on that, yes.'

The silence that followed lasted for nearly a minute and was broken only by the drone of an aircraft passing high above the house. Maggie's face was almost void of emotional expression, particularly after she closed her eyes, so that when she opened them again, the decision in them was the more contrasting.

'Since I shan't be able to deny a few of the things you allege, I've decided to admit them,' she said, her tone determined, not resigned. 'But only to establish the circumstances were quite different from those you've imagined. Quite different,' she repeated, then paused. 'What happened wasn't premeditated. None of it. If it had been it would have been better organized,' she added with the ghost of a smile. 'And there were no murders,' she concluded distinctly and with authority.

The speaker's gaze now moved from Treasure to a narrower-eyed study of the burning logs. 'Understand, I had the difficult task of making that wretched girl agree to an abortion,' she went on. 'It was imperative to the future of the company. For Julius. We had reached impasse again with her lawyer. So I decided to approach her direct, with more money. It was my own initiative. Julius knew nothing about it. On Friday evening I telephoned her to say we must meet immediately. That was just before seven. I asked her to wait for me. Not to go to the meeting till she'd seen me.' She hesitated, breathing in deeply before continuing. 'It's true I got Oliphant to come with his gun to lend me, to frighten her, but later I decided the idea was ill judged. And since he was late arriving in the car park, I went in without seeing him.'

'But surely, having him there was evidence of premeditation?' Treasure put in.

'If having him provide a gun for a piece of playacting was that, then, yes, it was premeditation. But not of murder,' she answered brusquely. She leaned further back in the chair, her demeanour still carefully relaxed, her narration calm. 'And yes, I did go through the warehouse. It was drier that way. I have no idea how the front door came to be open. The girl was impossible again. Worse than ever. She even threw that wretched fish away. Out the window. To show her contempt. She said I'd bought it to kill her other fish. It wasn't true. It was a peace offering, exactly as you said. I didn't know what it would do to the other fish. Neither did Ted. He wasn't told.'

'The aquarist said he was.'

'Then the aquarist is a liar. Perhaps for an obvious reason. It must be quite difficult to sell lionfish, don't you think?' She gave a half smile, but didn't wait for an answer. 'Janice throwing out the fish may seem nothing now, but it made me very angry at the time,' she continued. 'She meant the car alarm to go off too. It was an act of noisy, vulgar defiance. To call attention to herself. I really thought she'd gone mad. You know she stuck her head out in the rain screaming obscenities about Julius? About my being his whore before her? About my being jealous? It was so malign, so bitter, so untrue, I just saw red. Something snapped in my head. Snapped,' she repeated the word with finality, as if it explained everything. 'I just had to stop her. Pulling the window down seemed the obvious way. I swear to God I never intended to hurt her. Not seriously. Not to kill her.' She had turned to look at Treasure now.

'I see. And Claude Oliphant?' he asked without emotion.

'I swear that was an accident. A terrible accident. As I got into his car, before I had a chance to explain I'd seen Janice already, to tell him what had happened, he was beside himself, insisting I must make her give up the letters. That I should threaten her with the gun. He was forcing the gun handle into my hand as he spoke when . . . when the thing went off.' She shook her head violently as she spoke. 'It was a terrible thing. The most terrible experience of my whole life.' She swallowed. 'He died instantly. Horribly. It was no use going for help. That was the first thing I thought of, I swear . . . and then . . . and then . . .'

'You saw you could have him look responsible for Janice's death? To get yourself off the hook?'

'That was it. Exactly it, I swear. You believe me, don't you?'

'The jury was only out for half an hour,' said Treasure to his wife.

'But you didn't wait?'

'No. I'd stayed for the judge's summing up. We heard the verdict on the car radio on the way home.'

It was late in the following March. Maggie Halliwell and her husband, Edmund Legion, had jointly been tried at Nottingham Crown Court for murdering and conspiring together to murder Janice Weggly. Both had pleaded not guilty, though Maggie had admitted to the lesser charge of manslaughter. The trial had lasted three days. Legion had been acquitted. Maggie, who it emerged had married Legion secretly, in Australia, more than a year before, had been convicted and sentenced to five years in gaol. Treasure had been a witness at the trial.

'She got off lightly, didn't she?' said Molly, sipping a pre-dinner glass of Chablis. The two were in the drawing-room of their Chelsea home. Treasure had just returned from Nottingham.

'Maggie's counsel insisted Janice had provoked her beyond endurance. In sentencing, the judge said he accepted there were grounds for mitigation.'

Molly sniffed. 'Well, I think Maggie was lucky. And do you really believe Major Oliphant's death was an accident?'

'Only Maggie knows the answer to that,' he observed, pouring himself a whisky. 'Just as only Maggie knew what really happened between her and Janice. In any case, Oliphant's death didn't come into the trial. The coroner and one assumes the Crown Prosecutor had accepted Maggie's word it was an accident. That's all that mattered. She could have been telling the truth.'

'Like Felicity Finton and the switched coffee cups?' Molly questioned.

'Exactly. The coroner certainly accepted that was an accident. A tragic one, of course. As for Janice Weggly's death, the expert medical witnesses said—'

'Those top psychologists Julius laid on with no expense spared?' Molly interrupted.

Treasure's forehead wrinkled. 'Julius pulled out every stop, certainly. Which is no more than one would expect in the circumstances. Maggie was clearly obsessed about protecting him. To the point where she really didn't know what she was doing. Julius's own defence of what Maggie did was very moving, too. Practically shifted all the blame for everything on himself.'

'But without getting himself accused of anything criminal,' commented Molly drily.

'Well, obviously he had nothing to do with the actual deaths. That was clear beyond any doubt.'

'Well, that's a blessing.'

'Yes.' He had been too preoccupied for the sarcasm to register. 'And the medical experts had made the case for provocation very convincing,' he completed.

'It seems they convinced the judge if not the jury,' said Molly. 'And had Maggie ever been Julius's mistress?'

'Almost certainly not. I don't believe he mixes business with pleasure. Not that kind of pleasure. Anyway, she's not the type he favours for extra-marital attention.'

'Which may be to her credit, judging by the sort that is the type. Judging by Mrs Task's description of her sister.'

'Maggie was just a totally dedicated executive,' he answered, without taking up Molly's comment.

'Dedicated to her boss?'

'Yes.'

'Could she have gone on brazening it out without admitting she was involved in either death? There were other suspects. That's why you got so involved, after all? Rescuing Bea Delgard from police clutches? Your Mr Larkhole didn't positively identify Maggie, did he?

'No, he didn't. I'm afraid I misled her slightly over Larkhole.'

'In the cause of justice, and Bea, and the Fintons, and even the wretched Mrs Task and husband,' said Molly brightly.

'Yes.' Treasure frowned as he walked across the room to an armchair. 'Anyway, I don't believe that was what tipped the scale for Maggie. When she decided to confess. There was the other evidence,' he added. 'And when she knew I'd worked out what happened without corroboration, she accepted the police would do the same with it. Prevarication isn't her style.'

'Because she'd prepared a convincing variation on what

happened? That threw a quite different light on the part she played. It could have got her off entirely.' Molly paused. 'Anyway, it may have saved her an extra twenty years in gaol.'

Treasure shook his head. 'I meant that her not prevaricating saved other people embarrassment. Kept some of the dirty linen out of sight.'

Molly beamed. 'Like the sheets from Janice's bed? The ones Maggie put in the washing machine? Was that an attempt to protect Julius's good character?'

'Yes. It failed, though. Not that it seems to have mattered. Julius was right about that. His affair with Janice doesn't seem to have hurt him publicly. He's survived, and so has Henfold. The golf plan has gone through. I understand Julius becoming Party Treasurer has been delayed, not abandoned. So really Maggie needn't have been so paranoid about protecting him.'

'Was it just to protect him?'

Treasure drank some whisky. 'No, I'm beginning to believe it wasn't just that. When you think about it, Janice Weggly's revelations were going to hurt Maggie just as much as Julius. Perhaps more.' He put his glass down and clasped his hands behind his head. 'Maggie had devoted herself to Julius and the job for fifteen years. She'd made a lot of money, shares in the company, acquired a lot of business status. But I suppose what she really wanted, what she was on the point of achieving, was a new sort of social status. Respectability of the kind that for her meant something as close to the ultimate as one could get.'

'She was going to be a viscountess?'

Treasure brought his hands down in front of him. 'Yes. As night follows day, she was going to be a viscountess. When Tug Delgard dies, Maggie's husband gets the title.'

'Which is why she married him?'

'Almost certainly. He's crazy about her, of course.'

'Only if Julius really had been discredited locally through a scandal over Janice?' Molly began.

'As Maggie was totally sure he could be.'

'Then down came the house of cards, including the golf course plan, and the happy ending Maggie had arranged for self and loving husband,' Molly continued. 'I suppose it was Maggie who'd fix it so the nice but not terribly bright Ted got the job managing Henfold in the Midlands?'

'Really as a wedding present for Maggie from Julius. Her bonus. Ted was to get a five-year contract, too. And an option on ten per cent of the golf club shares. That was why their marriage was kept such a secret. Even from Julius. Maggie wanted outsiders to think Ted had got everything on his own merit. Not through his wife's influence. Anyway, I'm not sure what happens now.'

'So Mrs Task was right? About those free shares?'

'Certainly not. The local politicians aren't getting options, and nobody's getting shares for nothing.'

'And what about houses on the golf courses? Was there anything in what she said about that?'

Treasure sniffed. 'Let's say that as part-owner of the course, Ted would have had a great incentive to get some houses built. Eventually.'

'Well, I think that's sneaky.'

He shrugged. 'His appointment made sense for the company, anyway. A local lord, or even prospective lord, would have made a good front man up there for Henfold. They have quite an ambitious development programme in the area, that's in addition to the golf courses. Maggie intended they should live in the Dower House eventually, too.'

'But not any more?'

'No. When Maggie's released they'll be leaving England.'

'For Australia?'

'I don't know. More likely a country where they're neither of them well known. Maggie has a plan, I gather. Made during the trial, actually.' He grinned. 'Ted probably won't be using the title either when Tug dies. They'll have plenty of money, of course. Her shares in Henfold will see to that. But it's a sad outcome.'

'Well I expect they'll make the best of it,' said Molly, fingering her glass. She looked up. 'For someone who's just been found not guilty of premeditating murder, Maggie certainly plans ahead,' she added drily.

Treasure made no comment.